Soul Money

CHUCK BOYER

ISBN 978-0-7414-7622-7 Paperback
ISBN 978-0-7414-7623-4 eBook

Printed in the United States of America

Published November 2012

INFINITY PUBLISHING

Toll-free (877) BUY BOOK
Local Phone (610) 941-9999
Fax (610) 941-9959
Info@buybooksontheweb.com
www.buybooksontheweb.com

This book is dedicated to my wife Rachael
who provides constant support, unfailing love
and delightful companionship.

FRIDAY, SEPTEMBER 23

one

Jon Farrell looked at the bite marks on his arm. Blood still oozed from the saw-toothed lacerations where Eddie, a hyperactive, autistic patient, had clamped down with strength driven by a mixture of fear and anger. The altercation occurred an hour earlier when Jon and another staff member had attempted to stop Eddie from chewing his wooden bed into small pieces. The "client house" had been hardened to prevent such behavior, but the plan had neglected to incorporate a metal bed and Eddie, possessing a need to taste his environment, had been checking out the palatability of his bunk.

Jon, director of Futures, Inc., propped his feet up on his office desk, stared at the wounds on his arm, and questioned the government mandate to close the institution that Eddie had previously called home. He agreed with the general premise, but the open wounds on his arm made the concept worth revisiting. He buzzed his secretary.

"Jackie, would you check my file and get me the date of my last tetanus shot?"

"Rough day at Union?" Jackie shot back. Union was the street where Eddie lived and therefore the name of his house.

"That's putting it mildly."

"I'm sure your last tetanus was when you came on board, but I'll double check for you."

"Thanks."

Jackie buzzed back in a matter of minutes. "You're okay as far as tetanus goes. How about Eddie?"

"No," came Jon's cynical retort. "I didn't bite him back."

"You know that's not what I meant. Any risk of AIDS?"

"Isn't that confidential information?"

"Right," Jackie replied, somewhat cynical herself. "We do, however, have his medical file and I don't think you'd cross any ethical boundaries if you took a look."

"Thanks, Jackie. I appreciate the concern and advice." Jackie's advice was always welcome and her concern appreciated, but he had already checked Eddie's file and saw no evidence of AIDS or any other communicable diseases. That knowledge lessened the concern in his mind but not the pain in his arm.

Jackie buzzed again with a message that he had a call. He picked up the phone expecting another emergency. Futures, Inc. had many emergencies. Their clients were explosive people, people John Q. Public did not want in their neighborhood.

Jon offered the caller a cordial and practiced greeting.

"This is Jon Farrell. How can I help you?"

"Jon, this is Neil."

It was Neil Danielski, Jon's friend and his link to a semi-blind date set up for later that day.

"Leslie wants to know if she can meet with you this afternoon."

"Can't wait to see me, huh?" The false bravado was transparent.

"Sure thing, Romeo," countered Neil with friendly sarcasm. "She sounds anxious all right, but I doubt it has anything to do with your renowned image. She'd like a call ASAP. Can you manage that?"

"I guess so. What's the rush?"

"I'm not sure but she definitely wants to bend your ear. Have you met her before?"

"I met her briefly at a Timbers' game in July, but it was a ten-minute encounter at best."

"Probably to your advantage," quipped Neil.

"Thanks, pal."

"Just kidding. Maybe she actually liked what she saw and wants to get an early start on the relationship."

"What's your guess?" Jon baited. "Is it my charm or my good looks?"

"I'd guess, neither," admonished Neil. "May I remind you of your last two attempts at a love life?"

Jon reflected on his last two attempts at gaining a social life. They had both failed miserably and he was certain the fault had been his. Dating was difficult enough given the demands of his job, but was further complicated by his natural uneasiness around women. They intimidated him, and what's more, he was certain most of them knew it and took full advantage. His insecurities multiplied when confronted with personal relationships.

"Your support is appreciated, Neil. What's her number?" Jon put his feet back on the floor and his head back into dubious reality. "I'll call and see what's going on. An old boyfriend has likely reappeared or maybe someone's pet lizard has suddenly passed away." Now past the stage of false bravado, Jon was moving toward the more familiar territory of creative yet acceptable rejections.

Jon got Leslie Covington's number and after a few moments of preparation for what he considered the inevitable, he pressed the seven digits.

"Hello," the voice said on the opposite end of the line.

"Hi! Is this Leslie…, Leslie Covington?"

"Yes. Who's this?"

"Jon Farrell," he replied, taken somewhat aback by Leslie's tone.

"Jon! Thanks for calling. I'd like to meet. Can you be at the Andromeda in thirty minutes?"

Jon was intrigued. "Could you tell me what we're meeting about?"

Leslie's voice retained the curtness. "I can't talk on the phone, but we need to talk. Please," she added softly, "save your questions until we meet."

Jon felt better with the tone change, but his insecurity had gained a foothold. This was supposed to be a simple blind date, if there was such a thing. If Leslie wanted out of the date, she could have done that over the phone. Or did she simply want to get a better look at him before deciding to share an evening? Jon swallowed hard and, as always, proceeded cautiously.

"It looks like I can get away. You said the Andromeda in thirty minutes?"

"Yes," Leslie replied. "I'll see you there." She hung up.

Jon returned the phone to its cradle and his feet to the top of his desk. He rehashed the conversation before heading to the Andromeda Café.

Jon walked to his rendezvous since it was only a few blocks away from Futures' office. The short jaunt took him through the town's university area and a landscape creeping into autumn colors. It was an old, sprawling campus nestled in the heart of town surrounded by the humdrum of Ashton's business world. Thick ivy hugged the red brick walls of turn-of-the-century buildings. Twisted and vibrant vine maples and patriarchal conifers lined the maze of walkways and cast cordial shadows on clusters of frenetic students. Stoic bronzed statues of Oregon's pioneers kept a steady and watchful eye on the comings and goings of wide-eyed freshmen. The campus was alive after a summer's slumber.

It wasn't that long ago that Jon was imbedded in the campus lifestyle. His college days were some of the best times of his life and were easily recalled with visits to the university. He couldn't help but wonder where all that energy had gone; at what point it had deserted him. The quest for knowledge, once a major force in his life, had somehow escaped and been replaced with indifference and the uncertainties of middle age.

Jon arrived early. The Andromeda was one of the more popular haunts on the university campus. It offered a cup of cappuccino that was actually filled to the top with liquid rather than foam. The scones, bagels and croissants were fresh. As was typical of most campus cafés, the customers supplied the entertainment. Colorfully clad students milled about engaged in conversations ranging from particle physics to the merits of true socialism. Opinions were as numerous as the fallen leaves beginning to gather on the sidewalk outside the café.

Jon walked through a web of young people and worked his way up to the counter. A sullen, dark-haired woman with a diamond stud protruding from her nostril and a tattoo on her right arm greeted him. The inked image resembled Jerry Garcia. Jon looked at her with wistful amusement and ordered a tall cappuccino. He got his change and a smile from the Deadhead and sat by a window to continue his musings of days gone by. His somewhat embellished reminiscences were halted when Leslie Covington walked through the door and altered the direction of his eyes and thoughts. She was even more attractive than he had remembered.

"Jon! Thank you so very much for coming," Leslie said as she seated herself in the chair closest to him. "I'm sure I have you somewhat confused."

Jon agreed with her assessment, but simply nodded and smiled. He executed a visual scan of his tablemate. She was dressed fashionably, the outfit color-coordinated with the show of colors beginning outside the café's doors. She had a charming and cheerful hat perched atop her head. Her multicolored dress accentuated her body and her skin had the remnants of a tan applied by the fast fading summer. Leslie's long blonde hair bounced about her shoulders and had a tendency to occasionally obscure her sky blue eyes. Her face was beautifully sculpted, her smile warm. More than a few men in the café paused to catch a glimpse of Leslie Covington.

"Well," he replied shyly after ending his inspection and blushing when caught, "I've always had a curious mind. And besides," he added more boldly, "any opportunity to get away from the office must be given serious consideration."

"Just the same, I appreciate your willingness to see me earlier than we had planned. Our date, by the way, is still on, assuming you still want to see me after I've shared my secret with you."

Jon offered controlled interest. "I've been known to enjoy a mystery. What is it exactly that requires my undivided attention?"

Leslie started somewhat hesitantly.

"I must admit that I'm not sure you're the one to talk to, but Neil told me of your involvement with the university and also spoke of your commitment to ethics."

"Bless his somewhat misguided little soul."

Leslie smiled and continued.

"You're probably not aware of what I do for a living so I'll begin with that. I work in the grant distribution office for the University's Education Department. I'm the department's business manager and there isn't much that I don't see or have access to. I review and push a lot of papers related to the dispersal of grant moneys. And, as any business manager would tell you, I have to make sense of what I see. Things literally have to add up."

Jon shifted his position closer to Leslie. "I'd imagine there would be a significant amount of money to account for in your area." In his position at Futures, Jon had become acquainted with grant money streams and the university's role in acquiring them. The relationship was not always positive, but it was necessary.

"Yes, a lot of money, and I fear I may have discovered that somebody is helping themselves to large amounts of it."

Leslie made a quick visual inventory of the café before she continued. "And I think you may be acquainted with the people involved."

Jon suddenly lost whatever amusing edge he may have had for this meeting. Within the field of human services, there were often accusations of mismanagement of dollars, abuse of clients, or falsification of documents. He had, up until now, remained free from involvement in any such scandals, and for that he was extremely grateful. He had worked very hard to build a reputation based on integrity. It had not always been easy, given the number of people he had to please and the variety of demands imposed on him. Ironically, the human services field seemed to attract more than its share of people who were themselves in need of some sort of human service. Sorting out the good people from the bad had become an integral part of Jon's job. He'd seen careers destroyed by accusations such as the one Leslie Covington was talking about, true or not. It could be very nasty business. He nervously turned the half-consumed glass of cappuccino in his hands and did his own inventory of Andromeda's patrons.

"And what, Ms. Covington, are you basing your suspicions on?" he asked coolly.

Leslie straightened her already erect posture and responded assertively.

"That's where I hope you get involved, Jon. I haven't been able to fully substantiate my suspicions, but I'm certain something illegal is occurring. What I need now is help in tracking some documents; documents that I believe have been altered for financial gain. I asked you here to see if you'd provide that help. Why? Because you have a horse in the race. Because if I'm right, then Futures, Inc. is involved in a major cover-up."

Jon's stomach churned. Red flags ran up his synaptic flagpole. He surveyed Andromeda's customers again for any familiarity among the crowd. To his relief, no familiar faces appeared. His instincts told him to walk away from the Andromeda Café and from Leslie Covington. Something held his feet to the floor.

"Leslie," he finally said, pushing away the cappuccino. "Cover-up is a highly inflammatory word and a serious allegation. And you're telling me that you really have no real proof of anything. What exactly do you want from me?" His tone showed an edge.

"I'd like you to help me, Jon," Leslie stated matter-of-factly. "As far as I can tell, no one else will."

"Why me?"

"I've already explained that. I believe your organization is involved."

Jon stared at the space between his feet. His pulse quickened. He raised his eyes to meet Leslie's.

"Leslie," Jon offered, "I don't really know you and I certainly don't have any knowledge of any cover-up related to Futures, Inc. And I damn sure won't risk my reputation or my agency's based on your suspicions. I can't do anything without proof." He was hoping to end the conversation and the meeting. To hell with the blind date.

Leslie opened the brief case she'd brought with her and extracted a folder, laying it in front of Jon.

"I didn't expect that you'd jump right into this without evidence of some sort. In this folder are a few of the documents that I think justify my concerns. I was hoping that you'd look at them." She paused, waiting for a response. It didn't come. "If you think my suspicions have some basis and choose to help me, then we can meet tonight and proceed to the next step, whatever that might be."

Jon stared at the folder but didn't pick it up. Leslie took it and offered it to him.

"I don't know where else to turn," she stated plaintively, "and I really believe something is very wrong here."

Jon reluctantly accepted the papers.

"One last thing," Leslie continued, "and please don't take this the wrong way. I'm afraid if you decide not to get involved, we probably shouldn't keep our date tonight. There's a possibility we might end up on opposing sides of a highly charged fence."

Another failed romance, Jon thought, but with a serious twist this time. He scanned the contents of the folder, figured he could review the material in a couple of hours and decided it would do no harm to take a look. He sensed he might be about to make a move he'd regret.

"I've got to tell you, Leslie," he said. "This isn't what I had in mind for a date. You have, however, piqued my curiosity and if Futures is involved, I should be concerned. I'll examine these as soon as I get back to my office and give you a call around four-o'clock to let you know what I think. We can decide where to go from there. Okay?"

Leslie smiled and nodded.

Jon rose to leave, his posture less confident than when he'd arrived. Leslie did another quick inspection of the café, stood up and gave Jon a warm hug.

"I hope you decide to help, Jon," she said and added a wink.

Jon was sure he was being mildly seduced but uncertain why. He wanted to believe that Leslie had liked him and not just his potential to assist her in her version of ethical duty. He offered no response. She turned and walked briskly out of the café and down the street. Jon watched her carefully as she walked away. He wasn't sure if he would see her again and, if he did, where it would lead him.

two

Jon got up, walked back to the tattooed lady and ordered another cappuccino, this one to go. He paid for his liquid caffeine and headed back to the office to review the documents Leslie had given him.

The short walk was filled with questions. Who was Leslie Covington ... really? What were those documents under his arm? If there were a problem, how would he handle it? Would he speak up? Would he have the courage? Jon was not a risk taker. Although he appreciated life with its stimulating uncertainties, he had to admit that he was most comfortable with quiet, organized routines. Being the Director of Futures meant making decisions but those decisions usually affected others, not Jon Farrell. This one might affect him. Leslie Covington and her suspicions would require serious thought.

Jon arrived back at his office and was given a list of messages by Jackie. Jackie was one of the more pleasant aspects of the job. She was easy to look at, her smile ever present and genuine. She was also extremely proficient at her work and seemed to have a knack of knowing just what Jon wanted and when he wanted it. She had become Jon's confidante and friend during their four-year relationship. They both seemed to know there would never be a romantic boss-secretary liaison between them and this allowed their relationship to be both comfortable and enjoyable.

"The call from County is one they'd like returned sometime soon," Jackie reported. "Other than that, the rest can wait awhile. How was lunch?"

"Interesting," Jon responded as he fingered his folder of papers. "The food for thought menu was high calorie. Do you suppose County can wait while I look over some material I just inherited? It'll take me an hour or two."

"I don't see why not," Jackie replied. "You know County always wants a quick response, and when they get it, they can't remember why they called in the first place."

Jon nodded and moved towards the hallway that led to his office. "If I get any important calls, go ahead and bother me, but if they can wait, let them."

"No problem," Jackie said, and Jon knew that unless the President of the United States called, he wouldn't be interrupted.

Back in his office, Jon put the folder and his feet up on the desk. He stared out the window at the gently flowing current of the Willamette River. This was the third office for Futures, Inc. since Jon took over as its director. The first one had been typical of many small agencies. It was a run-down old house in a lower class area of town. The carpeting, what there was of it, was frayed and smelled of cat urine. In the winter months the warped window frames allowed the heat to escape and the cold, damp Oregon air to distract work efforts. Mold crept in at every opportunity. Jon had moved Futures to a better situation only to outgrow that one within a year. Jackie had spearheaded the relocation to the present office and, although Jon's frugal tendencies told him the move wasn't fiscally prudent, he now more than appreciated her efforts.

Jon finally opened the folder and began to examine its contents. The strong odor of duplicating fluid told him that Leslie had retained her own copies of the documents. Jon immediately noticed the bold stamp of the university at the top of the first page. No surprise there since that's where

Leslie worked and the university exerted significant influence in the community. Ashton would not be much of a city without it. Futures, Inc., in fact, would probably not exist without university support and Jon was more than a tad edgy rummaging through what might legally be defined as their property. Nervous anticipation growled in Jon's belly and he considered destroying the papers and ignoring the entire affair. Throughout his life he had gone out of his way to avoid making difficult choices. Conflict, specifically personal conflict, was not something he coped well with and this had all the makings of a serious personal conflict. His eyes returned to the river and he allowed its calming effect to filter in. A few minutes later he decided to honor his commitment to Leslie. Despite the residual rumblings of his anxiety, he felt good about the decision.

The papers were organized into approximately six groupings separated by variously colored plastic paper clips. Jon assumed that, given the apparent attempt at systemization, the group of papers on top were what he should look at first. After reading a few lines, he recognized the first document as a form letter that the university had been sending him for years. Without finishing the page, he flipped it over and was confronted with a signature he recognized—his own. Jon had signed thousands of documents in his years as Futures' director and the sight of his signature should not have alarmed him. He was, however, reminded of the words "cover-up" in his conversation with Leslie and his signature delivered new meaning.

Jon continued reading. The first three documents were the same form letter with various alterations that constituted letters of appreciation and support for the university. Those letters were part of a packaged grant application for one of the many federal grants the university sought. The letter stipulated the monetary request, in this case $50,000, to be used for research with the clients that were served by

Futures. Futures had received that amount for the last three years and it was well spent, adding greatly to the quality of life of Futures' clients.

The other letters in the first group of papers were similar form letters signed by other directors from other agencies and for a variety of dollar amounts. All of the letters requested funds of $25,000 to $50,000. Jon's name, however, was the only one that appeared more than once and for more than one year.

So far so good, Jon thought. There's no problem with receiving grant funds as long as you keep accurate data on the expenditures of those funds, and he was a fanatic in that area. He had turned in his accounting to the university every year and had kept back-up reports in his own files. He couldn't speak for the other directors who had signed the other letters, but he was safe on his records.

The next set of papers was unfamiliar. The stamped letterhead was that of the United States Department of Education. The words directly beneath the letterhead read:

Application for Federal Funds

The form was similar to something the IRS generates, one that only professional accountants can decipher. It had been filled in and was dated June 10, 2009. The dollar amount requested on this particular form was $100,000.

Jon didn't read the entire document, but scanned it until he reached the signature line. The name appearing on that line was a familiar one, Steven Gant. Gant was President of the Board of Directors of Futures, Inc. He was one of the original founders of the organization and a professor at the university. Though Gant's name on an application for grant dollars was probably not a cause for alarm, it was unusual. He looked at the other papers in the bundle and discovered that they were all requests for funds from the Department of Education. He noticed that they were all from the same year,

2009, and that they all had the same amount of dollars requested, $100,000.

What Jon was hoping not to notice, but could not avoid, was his recognition of the signatures on all the forms. Steven Gant's name appeared twice more and the other names appearing on the remaining forms were also familiar. They were Futures' other two Board members.

Futures was not your run-of-the-mill not-for-profit corporation, and its Board of Directors were not typical people. When Jon began his career at Futures, twelve people made up the Board and they came from various areas of Oregon, representing a diversity of visions regarding the treatment of autism. Jon grew to respect these people and had looked forward to the monthly meetings. They were a time for enrichment and direction.

Eventually, the novelty of board membership had worn off and travel commitments had become such a burden that most of the original members had departed. The Board's Executive Committee took full control of Futures and made the decision to not recruit any additional Board members. This system had now been in place for several years and, despite Jon's initial apprehensions, was a system that appeared to be working. The Executive Committee was made up of the three founding members of Futures, Steven Gant, Terrance Walk and Allan Trenholm. Those three names were appearing as signatures on the papers on Jon's desk.

Gant, Walk and Trenholm were all professors at the university and all three had achieved significant status as either researchers or advocates for disabled people. Much of their time was spent traveling across state lines to assist other states in the operation known as deinstitutionalization. This was the process by which mental institutions, those great human holding tanks for people with mental deficiencies, were to be replaced with community-based programs. Relocating autistic, developmentally disabled, and schizophrenic people into quiet neighborhoods proved to be a difficult task. It was met with great resistance from communities and complicated by the fact that not too many people knew what they were doing. Gant, Walk and Trenholm were touted as the experts in this enterprise. Futures, Inc. was their model.

Steven Gant had been a supporter of Jon since his appointment to the position of Executive Director. He was the political animal of the trio and held close and long relationships with many of the state's political movers and shakers. He was, in Jon's eyes, the supreme glad-hander, but Jon usually felt they had a workable relationship.

Terrance Walk was the most enigmatic of the three men. His notoriety was the greatest, yet, at least in Jon's presence, he was the most quiet and least assuming. His boyish appearance contradicted the stories of tyrannical rule with which Jon had heard he ran his university program. When speaking, Walk was deliberate and articulate. Jon often found himself looking up words he used. He was usually aloof toward Jon, an attitude he attributed to the typical Ph.D. response to those less academically endowed. After years of feeling trivialized, Jon had learned to ignore the snub. It was what it was. He simply needed to make sure he understood what Walk wanted and to try his best to give it to him.

Allan Trenholm was the old man of the group. He was in his early sixties, whereas the other two were in Jon's age category, about mid-forties. It was initially the age difference that intimidated Jon. His good Catholic upbringing had taught him to respect, if not fear, his elders. Trenholm had been in the military prior to his return to school and his subsequent attainment of the Ph.D. plateau. His military mind-set and academic arrogance had made Jon's relationship with Trenholm a very difficult one to cultivate. After years of trying, he gave up. He considered Trenholm to be rude and abusive and someone who felt entitled to exhibit those qualities on a frequent basis. Jon had endured Trenholm's belligerent side on more than one occasion and he would have welcomed the old man's retirement. Unfortunately, Trenholm didn't appear interested in retirement. He was, however, still very interested in the prestige and power his university connection provided him.

The next set of papers Jon perused contained more letters of support addressed to the Department of Education. He scanned for signatures and, to his dismay, the first two letters he saw possessed his signature. He flipped over the document and discovered the letters were exactly the same as the previous ones that he had read minutes ago. They were identical in every respect except one. The amount requested was for $100,000 rather than the $50,000 on the first copy. Jon didn't remember having ever been involved in a request for $100,000. Since the first year he had produced letters of support for the university, he recalled only signing his name to requests for $50,000. A quick check of his records could confirm his memory and he shifted his focus to a file drawer in search of that validation. In minutes he located the files on grant applications. He arrived at the section where the copies should have been, but they were not there. He expanded his search but again came up empty. He finally dumped the entire stack of grant applications he had written during his tenure at Futures on the floor. It was a significant amount of paper and seeing the task in front of him, he decided he needed help. As always, help meant Jackie and she made the trek down the office hall moments after Jon's SOS. She was confronted with Jon sprawled on the floor amid a labyrinth of paper. His puzzled face illustrated his predicament.

"Need some help, Jon?" she asked.

"I'm having trouble locating some grant related papers."

Jon wasn't sure he wanted her aware of the entire story so he simply stated he needed copies of the university's letters of support.

"I don't think those are due for at least another three months," Jackie pointed out. She was correct, at least for the current applications.

"They're not, but you know how I like to get a head start on things."

Jackie nodded, instinctively knowing that something was wrong. Jon liked to get a head start on things, but three months was a stretch, even for him. She also knew not to push for answers.

"Just tell me what you need."

"Well," he said, relieved to have the help without explanations, "I'm sure I filed them in this folder with the rest of the grant stuff, but I can't find them at the moment."

"How about we split them in half and do a methodical search?" Jackie suggested.

"Sounds like a plan."

Jackie joined Jon on the floor accompanied by a few groans and moans prompted by unhappy muscles. "Can you tell me specifically what I'm looking for so I'll know it when I see it?"

Jon described the documents and the search began. The hunt came up empty.

"Shit!" said Jon, his face contorted to emphasize his frustration. "I need those papers."

"Can you get copies from the university and work off those?" asked Jackie.

"It's not quite that simple," responded Jon, not willing to share the whole truth. "I don't want anyone at the university, especially the Big Three, to think I'm disorganized. Any idea why the documents aren't here?"

Feeling a bit defensive, Jackie stood up, straightened her torso along with her dress and replied, "Not really. I haven't seen them on your desk and I don't go into your files unless you ask me to get something for you. And no one's ever in your office but the two of us."

Jon noted the defensive nature of Jackie's tone and posture. The last thing he wanted or needed right now was to alienate Jackie. She was too important to him.

"I'm not suggesting you lost or misplaced them, Jackie, and I'm sorry if you took it that way."

The smile returned to Jackie's face. "No offense taken."

"Thanks for the help," Jon offered out of appeasement. "I may need more of it later."

"Just ask. You know I'm always more than happy to help." Jackie left and headed back to her desk. Jon returned to his chair and his view of the river. It was getting close to four o'clock and he had a decision to make.

three

While Jon Farrell struggled with his choices, a group of mental patients on Ward C at the Gustaf Clinic had no such luxury as choice. Gustaf's, on the outskirts of the city of Kirkenes, Norway, was home to twenty-five people who long ago had been labeled undesirable by the normal world. They were the remnant population of a clinic initially built as a full-scale mental institution in the late 1800s and rebuilt on a smaller scale after the Germans demolished it in World War II.

The Nazis had invaded Norway on April 9, 1940, in violation of its declared neutrality. The Germans had used the city of Kirkenes, just miles from Russia's northwest border, as the supply center for their defense of its northern acquisitions. The Norwegian population of the city numbered around seven thousand—the occupying Germans, ten times that many. The allies, being keenly aware of Kirkenes' value to the Germans, launched three hundred and twenty-eight air attacks on the city. The result was a denuded landscape and an emotionally obliterated populace. What the Allies didn't destroy, the Germans demolished as they retreated from advancing Russian forces toward the end of the war.

At one time the Gustaf Clinic had a reputation as one of the finest psychiatric treatment centers in Europe with links to Freud and Jung. In its present state, however, it resembled a prison camp more than a hospital. The reputation that it once held had long since been replaced by one of indifference, an attitude manifested most vividly by the condition of the people it quartered. As with most mental institutions of its era, it had been constructed miles from any population center to facilitate the societal apathy held toward mental illness. It now served as a repository for those afflicted with diseases possessing no known cures and with stigmas families chose to avoid. The clinic still existed because of its geographic and political remoteness and the fact that it created jobs for a depressed community.

Ward C was pungent with the odors of physical and emotional decay. It was only September but Kirkenes, prematurely cooled by Arctic winds traveling down the Varangerfjorden, was well into the onset of winter. The building was cold and damp. Its cement floors bore the blemishes of stagnant abuse. Patchwork walls hadn't seen new paint in decades. Windows with obscured views were barred with rusty, flaked steel. The gaps between the bars left just enough room for one of the patients to extend his substantial penis toward the outside world. His would-be attendant, clad in a yellowed and ill-fitted uniform approached the patient.

"What the hell you doin', Charley?" he asked.

Charley Orr didn't bother to answer. He never did. Not much of anything got a response from Charley.

"Charley, I'm askin' you a question, and I want an answer."

Again, no reply came. Another attendant walked up.

"Charley," continued the first attendant. "I got a new recruit here for you. I'm supposed to let him in on all of the weird shit you assholes do. So you gotta help me out." He gave Charley Orr a hard slap on his back. Charley lost his balance but didn't make a sound.

"What's his problem?" asked the new employee.

"He's crazy as shit. They call it autism, but that's just one of those fuckin' labels the doctors use. In my book, he's just crazy. The story I heard was that when Charley used to talk, he'd say he was controlling the world with his dick. I guess that's what he's doin' right now. He'd claim if he was to stop wavin' that dick of his out the window, the goddamn earth would stop spinning. I figure maybe he's right, so I don't stop him from wavin' it. Nobody else does either. I don't know what happens to Mother Earth when Charley goes to sleep at night."

"Maybe he's got a co-dick."

"Could be. As long as the planet keeps moving, I don't give a shit. Let's move on."

The new attendant lingered behind for a few words with Charley Orr.

"Hello, Mr. Orr. My name is Wayne, Wayne Burgess."

Charley was clad in typical institutional garb. His cuffed pants were drab green. His khaki shirt was spattered with the remains of more than a few meals. Beneath the khaki shell was an old, yellowed T-shirt, ripped at the collar. His shoes, worn and frayed, were brown canvas with rubber soles. He wore no socks. His hair, stringy and oily, lay caked on his scalp in blotches. His gaunt body shivered in the cold dayroom.

"I'm new here and I'd like to get to know you," Wayne continued. "But I'm only here for six months so if we're going to be friends, we'd better get started."

There was no response from Charley. Wayne lifted a small calculator from his shirt pocket and quickly punched some numbers in Charley's view.

"My figures indicate the earth's rotational momentum could be sustained for thirty minutes without your participation. Maybe you could take a break and we could spend that time talking. Please check my calculations and get back to me."

Charley Orr momentarily stopped twirling his penis and made eye contact with the newcomer on Ward C. After ten seconds of interrupted rotations, he reclaimed his position as Controller of the World. Wayne caught up with his new partner who had taken a seat in front of a silent television.

"You speak English very well," Wayne offered.

"Have to," replied his coworker. "It's the only way to get a job in this joint. For some reason you have to be able to speak English to work here. It wasn't a problem for me since my mother was from England. A lot of the locals picked it up from the war's limey leftovers. Even crazy Charley used to speak English when he actually talked."

Wayne wasn't sure what the reasons might be for the English rule at the clinic but he knew it would make his job easier.

"Why's the sound turned off?" he asked and pointed to the television.

"The Head Nurse says it's over-stimulation."

"For who?"

"Good question."

Wayne looked around at the three patients seated in the front row next to them. None was watching the TV. Two were rhythmically rocking back and forth in their vinyl chairs. The other one was biting his own arm.

"Shouldn't we do something?" Wayne asked and nodded toward the young man with teeth embedded firmly in his flesh.

Wayne's partner emitted a long sigh, got up from his seat and walked slowly over to the patient. He looked into the nurse's office and then over his shoulder and throughout the dayroom. Apparently seeing what he wanted, he slapped the patient violently across the face.

Wayne was stunned. "Why'd you do that?" he asked forcefully.

"Is he still biting himself?"

Wayne looked at the patient. He had stopped his self-mutilation.

"There's no other way?"

"Maybe, but none that work as quickly. I get immediate results." He laughed and returned to his seat in front of the silent television.

Wayne left his would-be mentor and wandered alone around Ward C observing more of its occupants. Most of them ignored his presence. Many were rocking like the two he had been sitting next to moments ago. Some of them paced back and forth and mumbled incoherently to themselves or to someone Wayne couldn't see. At least half of them wore some kind of headgear, presumably, Wayne thought, to keep them from banging their heads on Ward C's hardened environment. All of Ward C's patients had two things in common. They all wore filthy, frayed clothing, and they all had bruised and scarred flesh.

four

It was four-o'clock and time to decide whether or not to meet again with Leslie Covington. Jon sensed a need to know more about Leslie's money questions but an inner voice kept telling him to leave well enough alone. The wrestling match was both personal and professional.

What if all this was simply a fiscal misunderstanding and he started asking questions that pissed people off? How would this sit with his high-powered bosses? Then again, what if he had knowledge of some accounting miscues and neglected to investigate? The Board might be pleased to have an oversight brought to their attention and would have a perfectly logical explanation for a $50,000 grant request turning into a $100,000 one. After all, what he had looked at thus far wasn't the sort of stuff to get too worked up over—just some numbers that needed an explanation. There was certainly no hard evidence of a cover-up.

There was, however, the remainder of Leslie's documents still to look through. Jon mentally scheduled that task for later and promised himself additional time digesting what he'd already seen. Leslie's papers and the disappearance of the ones from his files had provided enough mystery for one day. He rationalized a further probe because it was in Futures' best interest and a second encounter with Ms. Covington could assist his inquiry. The fact that she was very attractive was also notable. He dialed the number she had given him.

"Hello." The voice was barely audible.

"Hi," Jon offered tentatively. "I'm looking for Leslie Covington."

"Leslie's not here. She's, she's..." the voice tailed off into sobbing. Moments passed before another voice spoke through the telephone.

"Hello. Who is this?" It was more a demand than a question. The voice oozed testosterone.

"My name is Jon Farrell. I'm calling for Leslie Covington. Is there some problem there? Who am I speaking to?"

"I'm Detective Sergeant Stan Iverson of the Ashton Police Department. What was your relationship to Ms. Covington, Mr. Farrell?"

The word "was" fell uncomfortably on Jon's ears. "What do you mean *was*, Sergeant?"

"I'd like to ask the questions, Mr. Farrell."

Jon wanted to hang up, but realized he had just identified himself.

"Fine. What can I do for you officer?"

"It's Sergeant Iverson, Mr. Farrell."

Jon's courage slipped backwards. "Sorry, Sergeant."

"I asked you what your relationship was to Ms. Covington."

"I actually just met her today, Sergeant. We had a blind date set for tonight but decided to have lunch beforehand—just to get acquainted. You know how blind dates can be."

"I'm afraid I don't, Mr. Farrell," snapped the Sergeant. "So the first time you met Ms. Covington was today?"

"Yes, Sergeant. We had a short lunch and agreed to meet tonight as originally planned."

Jon was not aware of his reasons for not offering this Sergeant Iverson the entire content of his conversation with Leslie, but he didn't. Somehow, it didn't seem right. He wasn't even sure he was talking to a policeman, and he didn't have a clue as to what was going on.

"Who made the arrangements for your blind date with Ms. Covington?"

Why does that matter? Jon thought. The situation was becoming increasingly suspect.

"I don't want to sound like I'm being uncooperative, Sergeant, but I feel I need to know more about what's going on before I give you any more information." Jon took a deep breath. "Just what has happened to Leslie?"

"Okay, Mr. Farrell," responded the Sergeant. "Leslie Covington is dead. From all indications, she has been murdered. Is that sufficient information to elicit your cooperation?"

The words were cold and penetrating. Jon's face flushed. His body stiffened and shook. His thoughts sped back to the Andromeda Café and then to the papers still on the desk in front of him. He needed time to regroup.

"Sergeant, I…I'm shocked," he finally said. "I really don't know what to say or, for that matter, what I should or shouldn't say. I need some time to think."

The Sergeant responded gruffly. "Something to hide, Mr. Farrell?"

"No. I just need some time to think."

"Think about what? If you've got nothing to hide, then you've got nothing to worry about."

"I've got nothing to hide, Sergeant," Jon asserted, "but I don't want to end up in jail for being stupid."

"Okay, Farrell," postured the Sergeant. "You've got two hours to sort out your thoughts. But I want to see you at six-o'clock at the station. If you aren't there, I'll come find you…wherever you are."

Jon hung up the phone and exhaled a long, troubled sigh. He slouched back in his chair and gazed out at the Willamette River. It offered no relief. He looked at the papers scattered on his desk, nervously gathered them together and placed them back in their folder. A new chapter in his life had begun and it was a troubled one.

five

Stan Iverson had been on the Ashton Police force for longer than anyone could remember. He was considered by most in the department to be the cognoscente of crime. Those below him in rank revered him for his wealth of knowledge and his uncanny ability to see through people. Those above him disdained him for the same reasons. Iverson had not achieved the ultimate promotion, that of Captain, because he was considered to be too abrasive to assume that more political and syntactic role. He had sought a promotion to Lieutenant only once and the very thought of receiving it had frightened him to death.

Iverson's love was the street and its repugnant but earthy inhabitants. He had grown up on those streets as a delinquent kid who had made the rounds of the city's foster homes. He had not known his father, and his mother had died of an undiagnosed illness when he was six. After four months of life with his mother's parents, he was bounced through the social service system like a ping-pong ball. New homes and pseudo-parents every six months created major behavior problems and made him an undesirable candidate for adoption.

At age fourteen, Iverson was in the juvenile justice system for car theft and was on his way to long-term membership in the adult prison system. It was there that he entered an innovative program for youthful offenders. The program stationed him in the Oregon wilderness for six months and in a highly regimented school the other half of the year. Three years of building hand-hewn bridges across Oregon waterways and carving trails on jagged landscapes taught him responsibility and provided an outlet for his anger. He also found in nature something he hadn't been able to find in the human world: an understanding and an appreciation of survival. He grew to be tough, but respectful of other people. At the age of seventeen, he had a goal. He wanted to be a cop. A damn good cop.

Iverson had been married up until two years ago, and although his lasted longer than many cop marriages, its dissolution was difficult for him. His wife had grown tired of the infrequent and less than quality time they spent together and of the constant fear that is endemic to being a cop's wife. Their divorce was a typical consequence of the job. In the past two years he had faced the fact that his real life's companion was his work and that meaningful human relationships were probably better left to someone else. In his job, detachment was probably an advantage. The fact his ex-wife was now cavorting with a young lawyer certainly contributed to his escape from emotional connections.

The Sergeant put down the phone after his conversation with Jon Farrell and turned his attention to a young woman who was sobbing into an already soaked handkerchief.

"I hate to bother you again, miss, but I need to get as much information from you as possible. I'd like you to tell me again what you saw when you came home."

Sandra McKinney looked up at the tall, rugged Sergeant and spoke in halting, barely audible tones.

"I can't remember everything," she muttered. "It all happened so fast. I was knocked to the floor and..."

"Did you get any glimpse of the intruder?"

"I saw him briefly as he was running out the door. I didn't see very much of him."

"Tell me what you did see."

Sandra accepted a much-needed Kleenex from a sympathetic policewoman and continued.

"He was a white man, I'm sure. He looked pretty young, maybe twenty-five or so."

"Tall? Short? Fat? Skinny?" asked the policewoman, now seated next to Sandra and busily scribbling notes in a well-worn notebook.

"I'm not sure. It's hard to judge when you're lying on the floor. But if I had to guess, I would say he was about six feet tall...probably average build."

The policewoman, with Sergeant Iverson's visual prompt, continued the questioning.

"Sandra, had you ever seen this man before?"

"I don't think so," Sandra answered with obvious pain. "I don't understand why anyone would want to hurt Leslie. She's such a wonderful person. She was..."

Again the tears flowed. "Who's going to call her parents?" The anguish was palpable.

The policewoman gave Iverson a look he recognized as "enough for now," and he got up and left Sandra McKinney in the capable hands of Officer Brenneman. He wanted answers, but he'd been at this long enough to know when to back off.

Iverson stepped outside the small house and lifted a Camel filter from its cellophane-encased package. Cigarettes were one of the many vices he possessed, and one, despite the growing social pressure to stop, he knew he'd retain until death did him part. He'd been told by the division's psychiatrist that the tiny white cylinders could be a replacement for his languid sex life. Had Iverson been more sensitive regarding the size or frequency of use of his most private part, he probably would have decked the meticulously dressed and arrogant shrink. In lieu of that particular avenue of expression, he had simply lit up in the good doctor's office amidst vehement protestations. When it was suggested that he leave and take his cancerous habit with him, he was more than happy to oblige but not without first extricating a thunderous and aromatic bit of gastronomic vapor. By such actions was the reputation of Stan Iverson made and sustained.

The Sergeant took a slow walk around Leslie Covington's house hoping to find something that would aid his evidentiary quest. The house and yard were crawling with blue-clad cops looking for clues, but none of them had the trained eye of an investigator with twenty-seven years of experience. Many of the younger men and women on the force made a habit of following Iverson around at crime scenes in hope of absorbing some of his wisdom. The attention both bothered and flattered him. It often got in his way but he understood the need to be a teacher. It was, after all, teachers that got him here.

As the Sergeant continued his walk around the house, his eyes searched for any possible shard of evidence that could lead to a piece of his new puzzle. Leslie Covington had met her death by the use of violent force. She had been beaten to death with the blood-stained baseball bat that now lay next to her lifeless body.

It had been a brutal yet probably quick end to her existence. A couple of heavy blows to her head had sufficiently cracked open her skull and allowed her life to escape. The murder weapon could easily have belonged to the victim as Iverson had noted baseball gear scattered about Ms. Covington's home. She had been a fan of America's game.

The house itself was not the most secure of buildings and was located in one of Ashton's lower class neighborhoods. Though the streets were blessed with Ashton's oldest and most charismatic trees, the Eastside also was home to the city's oldest and most ramshackle houses. These dwellings often housed Ashton's most transient and criminally involved population. A tour of the neighborhood parks would reveal plenty of broken Muscatel bottles and overused syringes. The area had its share of police calls for drug use and domestic violence. Ashton's homeless population lived in the Eastside parks because the city's upper echelons didn't want them in theirs.

Aside from cheap rent, the appeal of Leslie Covington's house was in its old Victorian architecture and the huge front porch that encircled it. Well-used, overstuffed chairs were scattered along the porch's scuffed and warped floor. Perched on its weathered railings, with green, multi-shaped tentacles stretching in all directions were myriad plants that someone had tended to good health. Iverson would have been comfortable drinking a beer on that porch.

What the Sergeant was looking for was evidence of forced entry and he was not able to find it. There were no pried-open doors or broken windows. There was no evidence of tampered locks. Maybe the house was unlocked, or maybe the assailant was allowed in because Leslie Covington knew him. As usual, questions outnumbered answers at this stage of the game.

Iverson finished his inspection and completed his notes. He would allow the uniformed officers to question the neighbors. The forensics team would undoubtedly work better and faster without him hovering over them and questioning their every move. After conferring with Officer Brenneman regarding Sandra McKinney and any more usable information, the Sergeant left the murder scene and headed back to the station. He would focus on Jon Farrell, Sandra McKinney, and ten names on a phone list he'd taken from the victim's refrigerator door. He would call the first name from the phone list, someone named Neil Danielski, and await Jon Farrell's six-o'clock visit.

six

Jon immediately left his office for home. He departed via the back entrance in order to avoid Jackie and her need for an explanation. He chose to keep the entire affair to himself, at least for the time being. He could count on a few people at Futures to help him, but not yet. He didn't have much to tell anybody. Hell, he wasn't sure about anything right now.

Jon settled behind the wheel of his Ford pickup and steered out of Futures' parking lot and onto the road home. Much of Ashton's workforce accompanied him hoping for an early start to a cool autumn weekend of barbecues and steelhead fishing. His truck was quickly enveloped by a variety of vehicles that paraded Ashton's cultural diversity.

Professors in Volvos and BMWs maneuvered in traffic accompanied by beat-up old pickups and multicolored Volkswagen buses driven by faithful but now prosperous hippies. Loggers roared across River Bridge on the last run of the day hauling thirty-foot long Douglas Firs stripped to their jagged and now lifeless bark. The vehicles merged as smoothly as did the unique collection of people. Ashton was an interesting city.

Jon's thoughts vacillated between Leslie Covington and his own destiny. Why would anyone want to murder a beautiful, young woman? What and how much should he tell this Sergeant Iverson? Was he going to be arrested for murder? Was his Board of Directors somehow involved in all this? Where were the answers to these questions? Where was his courage?

Jon arrived home in the usual fifteen minutes and settled onto the old, tattered couch that transported him into sleep more nights than his bed. The sagging mass of stained fabric was the Jon Farrell comfort zone. Jon's entire house was more of a statement than a home. Being single for so many years had birthed some interesting habits regarding personal housekeeping. The ubiquitous clutter of clothes, dishes, books and generalized jumble confronting him was a distinct contrast to the manner with which he managed his professional life. It was a more accurate indicator of Jon Farrell than was the organized ambiance at Futures.

On this day, the couch was unable to perform its usual magic. Jon found himself incapable of focusing his thoughts and they invariably wandered back to his afternoon meeting with Leslie Covington. He was shocked by her death and frightened that he was somehow attached to it. More questions surfaced. Were those damn documents the reason Leslie was dead? Could he be targeted next? Just what the hell was really going on? Leslie was so alive and so beautiful. Imagining her dead was difficult. "Murdered," he said aloud, more than once. His thoughts shifted to his conversation with Sergeant Iverson and the turmoil intensified.

Jon's experiences with the law had been mostly vicarious ones lived through the small screen in his living room or in the pages of books. He had experienced no real dealings with the police except for the occasional traffic stop. He knew he had nothing to hide and that he wasn't responsible for Leslie Covington's death but he couldn't help imagining a corrupt fate that would land him in prison, maybe for a long time. Jon Farrell was scared and he didn't like the feeling.

Jon got up from the couch and paced about the clutter. He had to talk to someone and he chose Neil Danielski. It was Neil, after all, who had gotten him into this mess. The blind date had been his idea. Neil had been in the University Law School for two years before tossing in the towel to the rigors of academic expectations. He could talk to Neil, tell him what had happened and maybe get some advice. His background regarding both Leslie and the law might be helpful. Jon dialed the number and the phone was answered by a hurried, feminine voice.

"Hello. Oh shit!" The phone echoed a loud thud. "God damn it, I'm sorry. This is Deb."

Deb was Neil's live-in companion. "Hi, Deb, this is Jon. I'm looking for Neil."

"He just left." She sounded edgy.

"Do you know where I can find him, Deb? This is kind of important. I need to speak to him right away."

"You might want to head down to the police station."

"The police station! Why the hell is he at the police station?" It was more reaction than question. He knew the answer. Deb's voice trailed off into tears and Jon grasped that Deb knew Leslie Covington and was aware of her death.

"I really can't talk now," Deb managed. "The police told me not to talk to anyone until they questioned me."

Jon did not accept the put-off.

"This is about Leslie, isn't it?" Deb didn't answer.

"Deb, are you okay?"

Still no response.

"Deb?"

"What?" she replied weakly.

"I'm sorry about Leslie."

"You knew Leslie?"

"I was beginning to," Jon replied. "We had lunch earlier today."

"I can't believe she's dead, Jon. Murdered! I've known her since high school. We were best friends."

The crying became more audible.

"What can I do to help, Deb?"

"Nothing."

"Are you sure there's not something I..."

"No, Jon!" Deb said angrily. "Nobody can help. She's dead."

Jon thought about it for a moment and decided he really wouldn't know what to do anyway. He was never good in these situations. He did, however, press for more information. It was callous but he was desperate.

"Deb," he began slowly, "the police already questioned me and plan on doing so again very soon. It would help if I knew more about Leslie."

"Like what?"

"What was she involved in that could have gotten her murdered?"

"I don't know," Deb replied feebly. "She was a sweet, simple person just trying to get by like the rest of us. I don't know why anyone would want to kill her." Deb paused, then offered her own question. "You sound like you know something, Jon. What is it?"

"I'm not sure," Jon returned. "As I said, I saw Leslie this afternoon and she shared some concerns she had regarding her job."

"What concerns?"

"Something about some missing money. She used the word cover-up in the same sentence with government funds. She shared her concerns with me because she thought it involved Futures."

"And, what did you tell her?" It was Deb's turn to request answers.

"I agreed to look into a few things and get back to her. But I don't think Leslie had shared her cover-up concerns with anyone else and I don't know that what she shared with me has anything to do with her murder."

"You don't know that, Jon," Deb asserted. "What are you going to do with the information Leslie gave you?"

"I'm not sure, Deb. I haven't even finished looking at all the documents she gave me. I have a date with a Sergeant Iverson in a few minutes and maybe I'll have a better idea after meeting with him. If Neil and I don't end up in jail, I'd like the three of us to get together and talk."

"Jail," Deb gasped. "Why would Neil end up in jail?"

"He probably won't," Jon hastily assured her, acutely aware that his own insecurities were affecting others. "Can we meet after Neil and I are done with the police?"

"I guess so," replied Deb. "I could use some company…and some answers."

"I'm not sure anybody will have answers for a while, Deb."

"Somebody better get them, and damned fast too!" Deb's anguish had switched to anger. Jon was uncomfortable with both.

Jon and Deb said goodbye and he was left to his own thoughts. Things were becoming increasingly more complicated. The fact that the police were talking to other people besides him offered some relief, but it was small consolation. Sergeant Iverson still awaited. His anxiety continued its upward spiral.

Jon got back into his pickup and began the short drive to the police station. He didn't want to be late for fear of creating even more suspicion than he imagined himself under already. He looked at the duffel bag on the seat. It was filled with fishing equipment and he dearly wished he were headed to his favorite fishing hole.

Jon arrived at Ashton's only police station with about five minutes to spare. He approached the front desk guarded by a bushy-browed cop in a crumpled blue uniform. He was overweight and balding, and methodically working his way through a mound of papers stacked on his desk. A cup of coffee and a half-eaten donut acted as paperweights. The nameplate on the counter said "Desk Sergeant, Thomas Crupa." Jon opened the conversation in halting tones.

"Is…is Sergeant Iverson in?"

The Desk Sergeant's gaze didn't leave his heap of paper.

"Who wants to know?"

The tone was gruff and distinctly lacking in interest. Jon was unsettled but responded ably despite his trepidation.

"My name is Jon Farrell. I'm supposed to meet Sergeant Iverson here." He stood as erect as possible. "Our meeting was scheduled for six-o'clock."

Sergeant Crupa took a bite from the crusty donut and gulped some of the tepid coffee. Powdered sugar now tipped his scruffy mustache. He still didn't look at Jon.

"And the nature of your business, Mr. Farrell?"

Jon's armpits gained moisture.

"I assume he wants to discuss the Leslie Covington murder."

"Oh, that," huffed the Desk Sergeant finally making eye contact. "Iverson told me to expect you. Park your tail over there."

He pointed and Jon followed the meaty finger to a large seating area occupied by what Jon quickly presumed were drug addicts and prostitutes. Jon balked at joining the station regulars in their acrid corner and chose instead a small unpopulated area of the station room. Within minutes a voice came booming down the station's main hallway.

"Farrell?"

Jon did not respond.

"If your name is Farrell, I want you over here."

Jon looked down the hall and saw a man staring directly at him and pointing to a spot two feet in front of his scuffed shoes. Jon didn't move.

The Desk Sergeant looked up and spoke with noticeable amusement.

"That's your date, son."

Sergeant Iverson was in his late fifties. His six-foot four-inch frame was encased in a rumpled shirt, baggy pants and socks that fell to the tops of his shoes. He wore many years on a weathered face. His expression showed no emotion, but conveyed steadfast determination. Compared to the Desk Sergeant, his weight was well distributed. His arms were those of a lumberjack, muscular and tan. His eyes moved with purpose.

Seeing Jon immobile, Iverson approached with a pale Neil Danielski following meekly behind him. He got within ten feet of Jon, stopped, said something in hushed tones to Neil, and pointed his piercing gaze at Jon.

"Right this way, Mr. Farrell," he said, and with a wave of his hand indicated a room at the end of the hall.

Jon desperately wanted to have a few moments with Neil, but Iverson insisted that he accompany him down the faded, dimly lit hallway without any side conversations. Neil gave him a puzzled look and a shrug of his shoulders. Jon managed to convey his desire to meet later as they passed, and Neil nodded his agreement. The interrogation room door closed and ended any further opportunity for communication.

"Now then, Mr. Farrell," began the Sergeant, "I want some information. You sit there."

Iverson pointed to a chair in the room. Jon looked around half-expecting to see the hot, bright interrogation lights he'd witnessed in late night movies. He was relieved not to find them.

The first set of questions was relatively easy. Jon simply had to recount his personal history. Thus far, all the Sergeant was asking for was information his doctor's nurse might request. No threats. No torture. At least not yet. He began to relax.

"Now, Mr. Farrell, tell me why you killed Leslie Covington?"

So much for relaxing. Jon's body tightened. His eyes grew large.

"I…I didn't kill her," he blurted. "What makes you think I killed her?"

"Why not?" Iverson asked rhetorically. "You told me yourself you met with her this afternoon. Leslie Covington died this afternoon, Mr. Farrell. That's a definite coincidence, don't you agree? The way I've got it figured, you two had some sort of relationship, and when it soured, you killed her. She probably told you to get lost and you got your revenge a little later."

"Fuck you and what you think," shouted Jon so instinctively that he shocked himself. He was shaking. The sweat was now rolling down his arms. "I told you the truth regarding my relationship with Leslie Covington. We met this afternoon at the Andromeda Café and then I returned to my office. That's the whole goddamned story, Sergeant."

Iverson smiled. He sat back in his chair, crossed his arms behind his head and fired off another question.

"And at what time did you see Ms. Covington today, Mr. Farrell?"

"I guess it was about 1:30 or 1:45."

"And how much time did you spend with her?"

"About half an hour, I guess."

"And why is it that you met with Ms. Covington?" Iverson was almost whispering now.

Jon's adrenaline was slowing but he was still on a state of alert. His hands stayed sticky-wet, his face crimson and taut. He did, however, hedge on giving Iverson the whole truth and nothing but the truth. His day so far consisted of a claim of a cover-up that could be tied to him, the mysterious disappearance of documents from his office, and a murder of someone he'd just met. He didn't know how deeply involved he was and he wasn't educated enough in the intricacies of law to figure out how to get himself out of it. He decided to play it safe, though he guessed it would piss off the Sergeant.

"I want an attorney before I answer any more questions," Jon asserted.

Iverson's face reflected tempered anger. It was as though he expected Jon's response sooner or later. He did, however, try one last tactic before abandoning his efforts.

"You know," he stated matter-of-factly, "people with something to hide usually hire lawyers to help them hide it. That couldn't be what's going on here, could it, Mr. Farrell?"

"No," replied Jon. "I told you Sergeant, I have nothing to hide. But contrary to what you might think or hope, I'm not stupid. This is murder we're talking about and I'm taking it very seriously."

"Well, it damn sure is murder, Mr. Farrell," snarled the Sergeant, jumping back from the table that separated them. "And you can be right, fucking sure that I'll also be taking it seriously. You can leave, but don't wander too far from Ashton." Iverson hunched over the table and glared at Jon. "And if you really are smart, Mr. Farrell, smart and have nothing to hide, you'll be as cooperative as a whore in war."

Jon left the police station shaken, angry and confused. He knew he needed some answers, answers that would be difficult to get, because he wasn't sure what the questions were. He did know, however, that he would start looking for the person who got him into this mess in the first place, Neil Danielski.

******

Jon drove directly to Neil's home, a comfortable house in the middle-class section of Ashton. Neil had purchased it a few years back with the help of his parents. Deb answered the door. He looked at her but wasn't able to come up with anything comforting to say. The awkwardness was apparent.

"He's outside," Deb said, and solemnly walked into the kitchen.

Jon walked out to Neil's favorite lounging spot and wasn't surprised to find him sitting on his back deck with a half-consumed beer in his hand. His eyes were red and blank, his posture slumped. Jon knew his friend probably didn't want conversation but he also knew they had to talk.

"Neil," Jon demanded, "just what the hell is going on?"

It was the wrong approach. Neil, like Jon, had just been through the Iverson gristmill and he'd also lost a friend.

"It's been a bad enough day without you coming over here and railing at me about how your life is all fucked up. If you think I'm to blame for your involvement in this, fine. I'm sorry. I just don't need your shit right now."

Jon realized his remarks were out of place. He'd forgotten the pain that people were feeling with the loss of Leslie Covington.

"I'm sorry, Neil," he offered genuinely. "I guess I'd forgotten you were close friends with Leslie. I'm truly sorry for your loss."

Deb stepped onto the deck holding a cup of hot coffee. She took a seat and announced that the Bailey's bottle was empty.

"I just have a hard time believing it's true," Neil continued. "I was talking to her a few hours ago and now she's dead. I've never had anybody die who I was remotely close to. And it's really devastated Deb. They were pretty close."

"It feels pretty shitty, doesn't it?" Jon responded with sincere empathy. His brother had died in an auto crash a few years back and both of his parents had died within the past five years. Death was familiar.

"Shitty is putting it mildly," Neil said, staring blankly at the warped wood decking between his shoes. "She was so young. So vital. And to die the way she did. It's really difficult not knowing what happened and why."

Neil emptied his beer can and tossed it onto the uncut lawn. He stumbled slowly into the house and returned with another for himself and one for Jon. He gave Deb a quick hug and sat down next to her. She was trying very hard to keep it together.

"What did the police ask you, Neil?" she asked.

They obviously hadn't yet discussed the visit to the police station. Her puffy eyes were testimony to how she'd been spending her time.

Neil took a long look at the beer can, gulped down half of it and replied.

"I didn't give Iverson a chance to ask me much of anything. I told him I wanted legal advice before I answered any questions."

Jon was pleased at the similarity with which they'd handled Sergeant Iverson, but was sure Neil's reaction was a more polished one than his had been.

"Same here," offered Jon.

"Well, I'm sure he's real pleased with both of you," said Deb. "He'll undoubtedly be calling again real soon."

Jon took a long drink of his beer. "How'd Iverson connect you two to Leslie anyway?"

"He found a phone list and Deb and I were apparently at the top of it. But it doesn't matter how. He'd have gotten to us sooner or later so it's just as well that it's sooner."

Jon nodded. "So where do we go from here?"

"We?" Deb asked. Neil reached over and squeezed her hand tightly.

"Jon's involved in this, honey. It might be best if we shared thoughts."

Deb gave Neil a cold look but said nothing. She was still looking for someone to be angry at. Neil broke the chill.

"I don't suppose you have a good lawyer at Futures who might be able to give us some free advice, do you?"

Jon recalled the lawyer retained by Futures, Inc. She was young, attractive, and very bright. She was also a friend of Steven Gant and did her work pro-bono for Futures as a favor to him. But given the circumstances and his concern over the folder of papers still sitting on his desk, he wasn't sure that she'd be a good choice. He conveyed his concerns to Neil.

"What about your law school connections?"

"Those folks are into corporate law and well-heeled clients. And besides, I didn't make any great connections in law school. It's a fast paced, cutthroat competition and friendships are rarely sought or offered."

Jon got up and paced around the backyard. He kicked the empty beer can a few times and wandered back to the deck. He had another question for Neil.

"If you were my lawyer, what would you be telling me?"

"That depends on the crime and your relationship to it. From what I heard at the station, the crime is murder. We know you had a relationship with Leslie."

"A very brief relationship," Jon pointed out…half in defense, half with regret.

"I don't think that matters to our Sergeant Iverson," Neil continued. "We're connected to Leslie Covington whether we like it or not. My advice to you would be to get a lawyer and, in the meantime, keep your mouth shut. Guilty or not, keep your mouth shut. A mistake could land you in jail."

Neil's assessment brought on a few moments of silence.

"What are you worried about anyway, Jon?" asked Deb. "Did Leslie tell you she was in trouble? Were you involved?"

Jon decided to get the burden off his chest.

"I might as well tell you," he began. "Leslie and I had lunch together at the Andromeda Café. What I hoped would be a prelude to romance morphed into a request to expose a cover-up."

Neil and Deb both moved to the edge of their chairs. "And Leslie made this request to you?" Deb demanded.

"She did," Jon answered. "She brought me a pile of documents that she claimed offered proof that large amounts of money were being mismanaged at the university. I've only had time to review a portion of the documents but, from what I've seen so far, Leslie may have had cause to be suspicious. She believed Futures was involved and that's why she sought me out through you, Neil. Now she's dead. Murdered. I can't help but think there's connection."

It was Neil's turn to get up and pace around the yard. He slowly walked to the madrone tree he'd planted as a sapling and nurtured to stable adolescence. He stroked its smooth surface, his eyes drifting toward the fading sun.

"Where are these documents now?"

"I left them at my office."

"Are they safe there?" asked Deb.

The look on Jon's face acknowledged the uncertainty of his answer. He excused himself from Neil and Deb's company and headed immediately for Futures.

seven

Stan Iverson sat in his dilapidated old chair, wedged in among the chaos of his area of the squad room. It was late and he was busy in thought, reflecting on the day's events. He tossed crumpled pieces of paper in the direction of a trashcan too full to hold them had his aim been accurate. He was not happy with the results of his interrogations of Jon Farrell and Neil Danielski although he pretty much got what he expected.

Most people involved in a murder can be expected to do one of two things when confronted by the police. They either pour their guts out or clam up. This rule applied to both the innocent and the guilty. The investigator sorted out which label fit and made certain that a case existed before filing formal charges.

The legal system had changed tremendously since Iverson's early years on the force and he had been forced to change with it. Computers and form filing had replaced walking a beat and bantering with those who dwelled there. Like many of their era, this change created frustration for old-school street cops who had been authority figures and problem solvers. Iverson grudgingly learned to adjust but his attitude now was to simply do his job … no more, no less. Right now, that job involved Jon Farrell and Neil Danielski and he wanted answers from both of them.

A uniformed policeman interrupted Iverson's thoughts and informed him that the Captain wanted a report on the Covington case and he wanted it now. The Sergeant was never eager to see Captain Denny. He was chronologically Iverson's peer but the similarity ended there. From Iverson's viewpoint, Denny had climbed the ranks of the police force in less than ethical ways. Denny's connections, not his skill, had facilitated his promotion to Captain a little more than a year ago. Iverson considered Denny a lowlife, a poltroon, and despite his rank, a person not to be trusted. He had spent very little time on the streets and thus had little respect within the department. Iverson was not alone in his contempt for Captain Denny. He was, however, alone in voicing it.

The Sergeant walked slowly into the Captain's office. It was a dramatic contrast to his chaotic cubicle in the squad room. Pictures of Denny posing with high ranking city officials festooned the walls and provided Iverson more fuel for his conspiracy theory. The papers on Denny's desk were arranged in neat stacks, and his pencils and pens stood at attention in a shiny brass cup on a high polished desk. A large wooden owl standing on a well-endowed but seldom-used bookshelf fixed its cold gaze at the chair opposite Denny's. The room was organized and sterile. The trashcan was empty. It made Iverson sick.

"Captain," Iverson announced, "Jensen said you wanted to see me."

Denny looked across his desk and stared at the unkempt Sergeant. "You know, Sergeant," he stated disdainfully, "it would be much better for the department's image if you wore some decent clothes while you represented the force."

"I get paid for how I think, not how I look," replied Iverson as he measured the tailored and pressed uniform of the Captain.

"That may be true, Sergeant, but it wouldn't hurt to pay attention to that aspect of your job."

Stan Iverson was not intimidated by the self-inflated Captain. On the contrary, what little enjoyment he extracted from this forced relationship was from their shared knowledge that Denny would be hard-pressed to get rid of him despite his obvious contempt. Iverson had too much support within the department, something Denny could only quietly envy.

"Is there a reason other than my wardrobe that you asked to see me about, Captain?"

"Yes, Sergeant, there is something else," replied Denny bluntly. "I need to know what you've turned up in the murder of that young girl. What's her name, Corcoran?"

"Covington, Captain. Leslie Covington."

"Whatever," responded Denny with customary indifference. "Tell me what you know."

"She was murdered by a yet to be identified perp, allegedly a white male, at approximately 3:30 p.m. today. She was bludgeoned to death in her home, most likely with a baseball bat. The bat was bloodied and was found lying next to the body. The alleged weapon and other preliminary evidence should all be at forensics."

"Any witnesses?" Denny intruded.

"We have a roommate who apparently interrupted the assailant after the girl had been killed. But she was also attacked and at this time is unable to make a positive identification."

"Her name?" Denny was taking notes.

"Sandra McKinney."

"And you say she's unable to make an ID?"

"That's what I said."

"Was she injured by the assailant?"

"Yes." Iverson was intentionally brief. He sighed heavily.

"Badly?" Denny demanded.

"No." Iverson was fidgeting. He wanted out of the conversation and out of that office.

"So she might be able to ID the guy?"

"I don't think so."

"You're certain? Why not?"

"She simply didn't get a good look at the guy."

"Are you sure, Sergeant?" Denny persisted on this point.

Iverson looked inquisitively at the Captain. He wasn't sure why he was getting grilled. He twisted in his chair.

"I'm never sure, Captain. But I'm not going to count on her ability to help us on this."

"Who else have you talked to in connection with this case?"

Iverson shifted his position again and produced another sigh, this one more audible than the last. Why was he going to write a goddamn report if this asshole was giving him the third degree now?

"I've talked to two other people so far. They appear to be either friends or acquaintances of the victim."

Denny pressed on. "Their names?"

"Jon Farrell and Neil Danielski."

Denny continued taking notes. "Neil what?"

"Danielski. D-a-n-i-e-l-s-k-i."

"What's their role in this?"

Iverson rose from his chair. He made no effort to hide the disgust on his face.

"I've already told you that they were friends of the victim. I've interviewed them and I'll be talking to them again. In the meantime, I'll be running their names through our glorious computer. I'm sure you're familiar with the routine, Captain."

"Well, Sergeant, that's the reason you're here. I'm about to change the routine."

Iverson's eyes widened.

"Just what does that mean, Captain?"

Denny looked out his office window as he spoke. "I've got a lot of hungry young cops who need a case to cut some teeth on. They want and need some experience. Most of them resent you always getting the meaty cases."

Iverson knew this was bullshit. A few in his squad may not have cared much for Iverson's sometimes belligerent personality, but there had always been a case assignment pecking order in the squad that was time tested and honored. Iverson, in fact, had mentored many of the homicide squad's current pool of cops. He had the respect of his peers because he had earned it.

"What are you getting at, Captain?"

Denny turned from the window and glared hard at Iverson, his arms folded over his chest.

"I'm giving this case to Sergeant Firnett. He deserves a chance to get involved in something other than chasing hookers down Lincoln Avenue."

Iverson was furious. Firnett was an incompetent and he was neither hungry nor young. He'd been on the Ashton Police Force for a number of non-illustrious years and had been given the not-so-kind nickname of Barney Fife. Something was not right here.

"Firnett is an idiot and you know it," Iverson snarled. "He can't find his asshole to shit with and he's probably been fucking any hookers he was lucky enough to catch. This is a murder case, Captain, and if you want it solved you'd better assign your top cop to it, and that's me. It's damn sure not an idiot like Firnett."

"I've already given this issue enough consideration. My decision is final, Sergeant. I'm assigning Firnett the case and you're off it, immediately. Get a copy of your report to me and one to Firnett, then stay the hell away from this case. Understood, Sergeant?" Denny's glare intensified.

"I hear you, Captain, but I damn sure don't understand. This is a mistake!"

"You're not in a position to question my decisions, Sergeant," Denny snapped. "This conversation is over."

Iverson scowled for a moment before leaving Denny's office. He had no argument that would make Denny change his mind, because Denny wouldn't hear it. The Captain held the power to assign cases as he saw fit. This one, however, had a bad smell to it. He was angry and puzzled over Denny's decision, a decision he was not ready to accept.

eight

Jon left Neil's house and arrived back at Futures around eight- o'clock. He turned off the alarm system and hurried to his office in the back of the building. He unlocked the door and immediately looked at his desk. The folder of documents was gone.

The shock passed in moments and Jon considered the possibilities. Jackie may have come in and looked for the missing papers they had tried unsuccessfully to locate earlier. In the process she may have put the folder somewhere other than where he had left it. He quickly located Jackie's phone number in the Rolodex and punched the numbers.

"Hello," said the familiar and friendly voice at the other end of the line.

"Hi, Jackie. It's Jon. I hate to bother you at home but I have a question that needs an answer."

"Sure, what do you need?"

"Remember the folder of papers I was looking through when you came into my office this afternoon?"

"Sure."

"Well, I'm in my office right now and I can't locate it. I'm wondering if you might have stashed it somewhere."

Jackie reflected for a moment then answered with certainty. "I didn't go back into your office after you left."

Jon's heart plummeted and his stomach churned again.

"Was anybody else in my office?" he asked hopefully.

"Not that I know of, Jon. I take it these papers are pretty important?"

"Their importance is growing." Jon was speaking more to himself than to Jackie. He shifted his weight in the chair and slouched backwards.

"What time did you leave today?"

"Right around five-o'clock, and I was the last one out. I locked the doors, turned on the alarm system and left. My usual routine." There was a moment of silence before Jackie asked the next question.

"Do you think someone got into your office and took them, Jon?"

"I can't, at this point, imagine another reason for their disappearance. The alarm system allows us to see what time the system is turned on and off, right?"

"Yes, I believe it does. We get a printout every month as to the activity on the system. Why?"

Jon's brain had shifted into a higher gear.

"Then the system should let us know if someone entered the office after you left this evening. If someone did, and the alarm didn't go off, then it was someone who had an access code. How many people know that code?"

There was a pause as Jackie recalled a complete list.

"Eight people have an access code. Six others besides you and me."

The next question was obvious, and Jon didn't have to ask it. Jackie listed the other six people as Futures' five-person management team and one member of Futures' Board of Directors, Steven Gant. It was Gant's name that fixed in Jon's brain.

"Would I be correct in assuming that when you locked the office tonight you also locked my office?"

"As always," Jackie responded confidently.

Jon had arrived at a critical question.

"How many of those other six people have a key to my office?"

Again, Jackie paused before answering.

"None," she finally said. "The managers only have access to the main entrance and their own offices. The only two keys to your office are yours and mine. Wait...," Jackie continued. "That's not currently true."

"Please explain," Jon prompted, his slouch giving way to an erect, tense posture.

"When you were on vacation last month, Steven Gant asked me to make him a copy of your office key so that he could come and go as he pleased and not disturb me. Since he was acting Director in your absence, I figured it was okay. He never returned that key to my knowledge."

"So Gant has complete access to our offices including mine?"

"It would seem so."

Jon now had some possible answers but he wasn't sure he wanted them.

"Jackie, I have to ask you not to breathe a word of this to anyone."

The request was more out of concern for Jackie than for her ability to maintain confidentiality. Jackie was devoted to both him and Futures and she never had a problem keeping things to herself. Jon simply didn't want her getting caught up in a situation that was getting worse by the minute.

"I won't, Jon, but I must admit you have me worried."

"I have to confess to being worried myself. Something's going on here. I'm not sure what, but I need to figure it out soon. When I do, I promise I'll share it with you...as always. I'll see you Monday morning. Have a good weekend."

Jon flipped through the Rolodex again, this time in search of the number for the alarm company that serviced Futures. He found it and called the after-hours service number. After a lengthy and somewhat testy discussion regarding who he was and what he wanted, he gained some information. Someone had shut the alarm system off at 6:18 p.m. that evening and had reengaged it at 6:32. There were some reasonable explanations for this, but none that encompassed the simultaneous disappearance of the folder from his office. His suspicions grew with his anxiety.

Jon wilted into his chair and contemplated the simple act of staying uninvolved. His thoughts raced from Leslie Covington to Sergeant Iverson and to the missing folder of papers. He reflected uncomfortably on the many occasions he'd chosen to avoid conflict, to avoid making decisions and to play it safe. As a result, he had a trail of failed relationships and a pretty damn lonely existence. There was also his relationship with his family. His brother, a distant relationship at best, had suddenly and tragically died in a car wreck. They had just begun to connect when he was killed and the emotional aftermath was still taking its toll. Jon always felt that they would have time to become real brothers but the accident changed that plan. He had waited too long to make that connection and it had cost him. It was an opportunity lost due to his inability to take action and he had not yet forgiven himself for that failing.

Jon's father had died shortly after his brother from incurable cancer. They had never understood each other. They rarely spoke. Jon still had not figured out how to feel about his death.

His mother died only last year and the anguish remained visceral. She was his strength, his support and his single source of unconditional love. She seemed to know him better than he knew himself and possessed an unspoken understanding of his sadness. The void created by her death was enormous and the psychic wound he suffered remained raw. He had not attended her funeral, fearing his uncontrollable sorrow. He now held deep regret at the lost opportunity to offer a final goodbye in her presence.

Thinking of his mother's inner strength and his lack of it, he decided Leslie Covington's death could not and would not be ignored.

nine

Jon arrived home with internal resolve. Having made the decision to get involved in this affair, the next step was to acquire answers. He called Neil.

"Neil, we have to talk."

"I agree," replied Neil. "But it'll have to wait until tomorrow. Leslie's parents are on their way down, and I just promised Sandra McKinney that I'd go with her to the airport to meet them."

"I don't envy you that task."

"I don't relish it either, but somebody has to be there to take them down to the police station and help them get settled. It's not going to be easy for anybody and Sandra really can't handle this by herself."

Jon didn't want to be insensitive, but he pushed for more information.

"What can you tell me about Sandra?"

"She's been a friend of Leslie's forever," Neil explained. "Leslie, Sandra and Deb were pals in high school back in Deb's hometown. Deb sort of drifted away from the group when she moved in with me but Sandra and Leslie have been on and off roommates since they arrived in Ashton. She's really broken up about all this. She was attacked, too, you know."

Jon didn't know. It offered some hope.

"You mean she can identify Leslie's killer?"

"Apparently not. She said she didn't get a good enough look at the guy to identify him. He clobbered her pretty good before he took off. All she remembers at this point is seeing Leslie lying in a pool of blood on the floor."

"I need to talk to her, Neil. I know the timing is all fucked up, but do you suppose she'd be willing to talk tomorrow?"

Neil was getting irritated.

"You're damn right it's fucked up, Jon! Who pinned a badge on you all of a sudden?"

"It's callous, I know. But you'll understand my reasons after we've had a chance to sit down and talk."

"Fine," Neil relented. "I have to go. We can meet at my place at ten in the morning. I'll ask Sandra to join us but I wouldn't count on her being there."

"Thanks, Neil," replied Jon. He hung up the phone and let his body fall into his chair. His bloodshot eyes stared at the bookcase across the room. The books residing there had provided most of the adventure in his life. He wondered how this very real mystery would compare to all those he had experienced vicariously. What role would he play? Was his character up to the task? His lapse into protective apathy was countered by new reflections of his mother and his courage resurfaced at the thought of her. He got up, retrieved a beer from the refrigerator and returned to the secure embrace of his chair. After three repeat trips along the same path, he was asleep.

SATURDAY, SEPTEMBER 24

one

Detective Sergeant Stan Iverson staggered out of bed at six-o'clock having decided to ignore his Captain's orders. The Leslie Covington murder case was his and he would not let some idiot like Bill Firnett mess it up. He knew Captain Denny wouldn't formally reassign him back to the case but he wasn't about to let Denny's questionable decision screw it up.

Iverson opened his front door and surveyed the cool autumn morning. He took a couple of deep breaths into his tarred lungs and lit up one of the tightly rolled barrels of tobacco responsible for the cough that followed. Oregon was beautiful this time of year and he enjoyed autumn more than the other seasonal offerings of the Pacific Northwest. Winter was too wet, and summer too hot. Spring was for the young and restless and Iverson didn't own either of those characteristics.

He bent over, stretching tired muscles and the worn fabric of his robe, picked up the morning paper and began the routine of his day. He poured himself a cup of strong, hot coffee and sat down to read the sports page.

The first few minutes of each of Iverson's days were spent checking on the progress, or lack of it, of his favorite sports teams. He viewed sports as a microcosm of society … people constantly seeking to be on top and many using illegal means to get there. Within this context, Iverson perceived his role in the game of life as that of referee. His function was to watchdog the players and to keep them as honest as possible. He didn't have perfect success at his job, but he was satisfied with his contribution. The Covington case was an opportunity to make a significant dent in the bad guys' game plan.

After a shower, shave and a breakfast consisting of a black-jacketed banana washed down by a second cup of now lukewarm coffee, the Sergeant was out the door and on his way to Jon Farrell's house. His instincts told him Farrell knew something and he wanted to know what that was. He knew Farrell would be exhausted after yesterday's ordeal and he wanted to hit him with another round of questions before his mind awakened enough to defend itself.

two

Jon had been up since his dreams had jerked him out of bed at 4:00 a.m. Dreams he couldn't remember, but didn't need to. He was sure their content reflected the conflict his conscious mind was waging.

Six-o'clock arrived and Jon grew tired of the dilemma confronting him. He drove to his favorite fishing hole on the river, a place where his thoughts usually flowed with the same ease as the rippled current of the water. Minutes after Jon's arrival, the sun emerged over the ridge that paralleled the river and began to dust the painted leaves of the vine maples. Forest residents hidden by thick underbrush heralded in the new day. Rainbow trout, many that Jon had taken out of this hole and returned to it, were rising to a breakfast of freshly hatched callibaetis flies. Amid these morning rituals, Jon wedged his body between two boulders, closed his eyes and gained the sound sleep that had eluded him at home. He awoke from his riparian respite two hours later feeling refreshed and ready for human contact.

It was close to nine-o'clock. Jon knew Neil would be close to consciousness and would tolerate an early visit as long as he brought a bottle of Bailey's to mingle with the morning coffee. He left the river bank and trudged up the path to his truck. Within twenty feet of the old, beat up Ford, his senses, always heightened by a trip to the river, detected a feeling of being watched. The feeling was different from the ever vigilant critters observing him. This felt intense and personal. He stopped and surveyed the multi-colored hills around him but saw nothing to validate his intuition. He chalked it up to paranoia but quickened his pace nonetheless. He was relieved when he reached the truck.

Jon arrived at Neil's house at 9:30 and banged on the front door. Neil, with facial evidence of his own insomnia, answered the door.

"Little early, aren't you, Jon?" he grumbled.

"Yeah, but I come bearing gifts."

Neil glanced at the brown bag with a bottle neck jutting out the top. He assumed the contents and produced a tired grin across his puffy face. He widened the door's opening.

"In that case, I guess I can let you in," Neil managed. "A quick shower and I might be ready for intelligent conversation. Coffee should be ready, though," he said while walking toward the bathroom. "Help yourself."

Jon stepped through the hallway and watched his friend amble toward a date with streaming, hot water. He surveyed the disarray that was Neil's living room and moved to the kitchen in search of the coffee. He mumbled something out loud about the absence of clean cups. Neil, now out of earshot, didn't respond, but Deb Sutter did.

Deb had been Neil's roommate and lover for about four years. She had seen him through two-thirds of law school and had not hidden her disappointment when Neil opted to cease that vocational chase. Jon had always held the notion that Deb's interest in Neil was related to the long-term financial security that a practicing attorney could provide. He never felt she was attached to Neil as a person. It was a perception he kept to himself.

Deb was mildly attractive and kept her body in superb shape with extreme weightlifting. She was, in fact, a competitive body builder with more than a few trophies to show for her many hours of pumping iron. Jon had to admit to a secret desire to view her sculpted body in the unclad state, but he managed to keep that to himself as well. Their relationship vacillated between good and bad and had, for the most part, reached a point of mutual tolerance.

"Clean cups," she hollered from the bedroom, "if there are any, are in the cupboard above the stove."

Jon shouted a thank you and searched for a receptacle suitable for his liquid breakfast. He found nothing resembling clean so mined one from the pile of dirty dishes in the sink. He washed away the remains of what appeared to be chicken soup and replaced it with equal parts coffee and Bailey's.

Deb had emerged from the bedroom and was now stretched out on the couch. Her eyes were red and surrounded by puffy flesh. She had made no attempt to brush the medium length brown hair that jutted out in assorted directions. Her robe, loose and haphazardly tied, barely covered her muscular torso. Jon found himself staring and embarrassed for doing so.

"Little early, aren't you?" she asked with poorly hidden irritation.

Jon's attention shifted from biceps to conversation.

"Couldn't sleep so I took a drive and then found myself in need of human companionship," he managed. He hoped Neil's shower would be a quick one.

"It's been a rough twenty-four hours, Jon," Deb said with a piercing glare. "Neil didn't get home until after two a.m." Her tone merged anger and fatigue. She was also protecting Neil. This was something Jon hadn't seen before.

"I'm sorry for the intrusion, Deb," he stated genuinely. "But we decided yesterday to get our heads together on this. Right now we're all confused."

"Confused?" Deb asked rhetorically and cynically. "I'm not confused. Upset? Pissed off? Definitely! And I think the last thing we need right now is somebody making it worse." Her words were obviously pointed at Jon.

Deb got up and hurried into the kitchen and Jon was happy for the momentary reprieve. She returned all too soon.

"Look, Jon," Deb said, apologetically. "I don't mean to bark at you. I know that you and Neil are friends and I respect your relationship. But right now I don't think we know who we can trust and…"

"Neither do I, Deb," Jon interrupted. "But we have to start trusting somebody, and we might as well start with people we have some history with. I'm trying to find some answers, okay? If you guys don't want me around, tell me to leave. But I think there are a few things you both might want to know before you do that."

"Like what?"

"I'd rather wait for Neil," then offering an olive branch, "but I want your input as well."

"I'm not going anywhere," Deb replied. Jon knew this was as obliging as Deb could be.

They sat in silence with their coffee cups until Neil reemerged, still looking tired but better. He walked over to Deb, gave her a warm squeeze on the shoulder and stroked her frenzied hair. He then headed into the kitchen in search of his own liquid meal. He returned in minutes to join the solemn twosome in the living room.

"So, Jon, what brings you and Mr. Bailey to our home this early? What did you find when you returned to Futures last night?"

"That's the problem, Neil. I found nothing. The documents Leslie gave me are gone."

Neil's slumped posture expressed his mental exhaustion. He'd been bravely trying to manage the grief of Deb, Sandra McKinney and Leslie's parents who were all leaning on him for support. He wasn't eager to start his new day with bad news. Jon ignored the body language and pressed ahead.

"As I told you yesterday, when Leslie and I met she requested my help in proving what she thought was a cover-up at the university. It involved a lot of money and she asked for my help because she thought Futures was involved."

Neil showed no visible interest in Jon's report. Deb, however, was glued to his words.

"We talked briefly at the Andromeda Café," Jon continued, "and that's where she gave me the parcel of papers … the ones now missing. We agreed to meet again if I thought her theory had legitimacy."

Deb took the next step.

"And now you think she was right?"

"I don't know, Deb. But someone killed her for a reason and there may be a connection. But now, with no documents to back up Leslie's claims, I'm at a dead end."

There was a long pause before Neil got up from his seat and paced the wooden slats.

"You're sure there's some kind of cover-up?" he finally asked.

"I'm not sure about anything, Neil. But it is a hell of a coincidence."

"Where did Leslie get the documents?" asked Deb.

"She told me she obtained the originals from her office at the university. She gave me copies."

"Then she probably made copies for herself as well. Right?"

Neil interrupted with what he knew was a rhetorical question.

"Why would someone kill her over some damn papers?"

Jon offered an answer.

"From what I saw of those papers, they showed a lot of federal money being diverted somewhere other than where the government was told it was going. If that's correct, then a crime has been committed. Criminals don't like being caught. Some criminals kill to avoid it."

Another round of silence followed and Jon started toward the kitchen for another cup of coffee. Deb was already on her way and offered to get him a refill. Jon slipped back into his chair and posed another question.

"Neil, did Leslie share any of this with you?"

"No," he replied softly. "She told me that she was getting into some trouble at work, but didn't specify what it was about. Maybe Sandra will be able to help you there."

"Sandra!" Jon had forgotten her until now. "Is she coming today?"

"She told me she would if she could. She was going to spend most of her day with Leslie's family. I'm sure they could use each other's support right now."

"Did you tell her that I'd be here?"

"I did. But that doesn't mean she'll be joining us."

Deb reentered the room with a fresh round of liquid caffeine mixed with creamy alcohol. She returned to the conversation she'd been following from the kitchen.

"What do you expect Sandra to know?"

"Roommates share things that other friends don't. I'm hoping that she and Leslie discussed her situation at work."

"And if she did?" asked Deb.

"Then maybe she can point me in a direction."

"To where? To what?" demanded Neil. "What the hell are you going to do, Jon? Last time I looked, your name wasn't Sherlock Holmes. What's gotten into you, anyway? You've never been the type to get involved in anything."

Jon was shaken by Neil's comments. The biting analysis left him wounded and searching for words. He wasn't prepared to discuss the reasons for his new found courage. He wasn't totally sure himself.

"I don't really know," he finally replied. "I guess partly because Futures is involved, and partly because I may not have any choice."

Deb threw in her opinion.

"I think you ought to let the police handle it. It's their job. Let them figure it out."

Jon allowed a long swallow of breakfast to fill the time gap between his thoughts. Their combined silence signaled the conversation's conclusion. The sound of the doorbell finally interrupted the void. Deb answered its request and returned with Detective Sergeant Stan Iverson.

three

Wayne Burgess had studied behavior as long as he could remember. It started with a childhood fascination for the comings and goings of ants and gradually morphed into an interest in the behavior of his fellow humans. He possessed a natural affinity towards people and an insatiable curiosity about what made them tick. His college courses focused on research psychology rather than the clinical variety because he wanted to examine the link between human physiology and human behavior. He was more than willing to allow the therapists to indulge in conjecture. He wanted science.

When working on his Master's Degree, Wayne found himself in need of a place to research the work necessary for his thesis, a comparative study of past and present treatment modalities for the mentally ill. His favorite professor suggested the Gustaf Clinic as a suitable site to gather materials for his paper. The professor had spent time at the clinic after the war and had found it to his liking, particularly since most of the area's population spoke English. He also recalled Norway to be a country of tolerant people who respected the quest for education. Wayne completed the myriad Norwegian government requirements and was granted a six-month educational visa. They would pay his living costs if he would publish and share his finished work.

It was a deal he couldn't pass up and he graciously accepted the offer.

Wayne started his second day of work at the clinic in hopes of perusing the records of some of the clients he had met the day before. He was disappointed when the head nurse informed him that it would be quite some time before he was allowed access to client records. Nurse Lai explained that the clinic had an obligation to protect the client's privacy rights. All new employees, especially those who were only on temporary assignment such as Wayne, were held under close scrutiny until the clinic's administrators determined that they would adhere to that standard.

Wayne didn't understand the need for such a rigid edict, particularly since he had already received clearance from Norway's government to do his research. Being a natural skeptic, he wondered if he was being denied access to records because they might reveal the reasons for all those scars on Ward C's patients. But Wayne also realized he was not in a position to argue. He was the newbie and an outsider and he needed this position to complete his thesis. A cooperative, low profile was probably his best option. His present could be spent becoming more familiar with Ward C's confined cast of characters. He could wait for an opportunity to review their past.

Time passed rapidly as Wayne immersed himself in the observation of behaviors labeled autistic, schizophrenic, and "just plain crazy." Gustaf's clients occasionally talked to themselves or invented others, paced the cold concrete floor or displayed behaviors Wayne found intriguing but couldn't explain. However, for the most part, they appeared to spend the vast majority of their time nestled in chairs in a state of semi-conscious catatonia.

On one occasion, Wayne noticed an oddly morphed gentleman busying himself with the construction of an imaginary device. The man had limbs disproportionate to his body, looking much like the Popeye of old Saturday morning cartoons. He carried invisible components with his oversized arms and placed them in an organized pile in the corner of the dayroom. Once the parts were sufficiently assembled, he would contort his body into elasticized shapes in an attempt to see something imperceptible to Wayne's eyes.

Wayne slowly and cautiously approached the patient. His bulbous forearms were caked with old, filmy grime mixed with what appeared to be dried blood. His T-shirt was frayed and yellowed, particularly around the pits of his massive arms. He smelled dreadful. Wayne stepped back a few steps, took a deep breath and initiated a conversation.

"May I ask what you have there, sir?" he asked politely.

The contorted man stopped his harried activity, gave Wayne a thorough looking over and responded.

"It's a goddamn telescope, stupid," he fired back. "Why? You gonna steal it?"

His English was halting but unencumbered by an accent. He was obviously not Norwegian. Wayne assured the man he was not going to steal his telescope and then asked the patient why he had it.

"I see friends better with it."

"You have many friends?"

"Plenty, but none here." He looked quickly about the room.

"What do you mean?"

"Can't say no more. You go away now. Please, now!"

Wayne sensed urgency in the man's voice and honored his request. The hairs on the back of his neck tingled. The telescope man might be crazy, but he was frightened too.

Wayne left the telescope builder and continued his observations of other Ward C patients. The range of behaviors was fascinating. The occasional outbursts of physical or verbal aggression were contrasted by an overlay of lethargic malaise. A sense of sadness permeated the diverse realities on Ward C.

As Wayne wended his way through the roster of patients, he found himself most fascinated with those he was told were autistic. These individuals presented a unique set of behaviors. They seemed to possess a greater need to control their physical environment, often to the exclusion of all else on Ward C.

J.J., as one of the autistic patients was called, always spoke in the third person. Lars, a patient with headgear covering most of his face, including a plastic visor, kept the fingers of his right hand constantly fluttering over his eyes. "Stereotypy," Nurse Lai called it. Lars had a need for continual stimulation and finger fluttering apparently provided it.

Autism was a magnet for Wayne because its etiology was highly debated in the field of human psychology. It was right up Wayne's research alley and he quickly decided that the patients on Ward C with autistic labels would fit nicely into his thesis. He began collecting information with the one he'd met first, Charley Orr.

Wayne surveyed the milieu of mental maladies in hope of locating Charley. He found him in his customary spot and, as usual, controlling the earth's pirouetting motion with his not so invisible axis.

"Hi, Charley," he initiated. "How's the world of applied science going today?"

As usual, no reply was forthcoming from Charley Orr.

"If you'll recall," Wayne continued, undaunted by the rejection, "I mentioned wanting to spend some time with you. How's today sound?"

Again, there was no reply. Wayne persisted.

"Since I appear to be the only one in a talkative mood, I'll start the discussion. I'll choose a topic you might find interesting."

Wayne paused, hoping for a hint of response. None was tendered.

"I think I've got it, Charley!" exclaimed Wayne in an attempt to arouse interest. "Let's talk astronomy. I can see you're involved in the subject and I have an interest myself."

Charley continued to twirl his penis, but the rate of rotation diminished ever so slightly.

"Let me just review what I know and you can jump in when you want, okay?"

Wayne looked deeply into Charley's eyes searching for a flicker of acknowledgment. None was detected.

"If I remember correctly," Wayne continued, "one hypothesis is that the universe is the result of a massive explosion some eighteen billion years ago. The 'Big Bang,' I believe they call it."

Wayne paused for a moment and thought about the futility of his endeavor but decided to press on.

"From that explosion came the first raw elements: hydrogen, helium, carbon, lithium and a few others that now escape me. Those materials would forge the beginnings of our solar system many years down the road. As time progressed, these elements developed, through either addition or subtraction of their atomic components, into the elements that now make up the periodic table."

Charley Orr still offered no measurable response. Wayne raised his decibel level a bit and proceeded with the lecture, now accompanied with expressive inflections and gesticulations.

"Ah, but what happened between then and now, you ask?"

As Wayne was about to orate about coalescing atoms and stellar formation, he glanced toward Ward C's office. Nurse Lai was glaring at him with a wrinkled but firm frown on her face. She motioned to him with a command gesture and Wayne followed the direction of her furrowed finger into the office.

"Mr. Burgess," she began theatrically, "do you intend to spend your time here at the Gustaf Clinic in meaningless conversation with our patients? We do have other things to do around here, you know."

"I'm sorry if you think my discussion with Charley is meaningless, Ms. Lai," Wayne defended. "I was hoping to develop some rapport with him."

"These people are beyond rapport," she replied with obvious disdain. "And they are most certainly beyond rapport with you. They are here because they have no place else to go. Nobody wants these people, Mr. Burgess. They don't need rapport. What they need is to be fed, medicated and put to bed on time. That's your job. They are who they are and Ward C is where they will be until they die."

Her bluntness was offensive.

"I'm aware you're here only for a short time, Mr. Burgess," she continued and moved closer, her breath hot, her face flushed. "And I also understand much of your time will be spent working on some goddamned piece of paper that will undoubtedly criticize what we do. Let me make it perfectly clear that I have little use for either you or your opinions. The sooner you understand that while you're here your job is to follow the rules, the better. And I, Mr. Burgess, make the rules on Ward C. Is that clear?"

"Yes, Ma'am," Wayne managed. "Very clear."

Wayne was stunned by Nurse Lai's verbal assault. He understood he'd be viewed with a certain amount of skepticism and probably labeled as a typically intrusive American, but he was not prepared for the overt hostility he'd just encountered. Maybe he was just naïve, or maybe he'd misunderstood the Norwegian government's explanation of his role at the Gustaf Clinic. Whatever the case, his six months stay at the clinic was not off to a good start and, given his waning relationship with the head nurse, the future didn't look all that promising.

While awaiting the next salvo, Wayne stared out the office's Plexiglas window and caught a glimpse of Charley Orr. He measured the many scars covering Charley's body and wondered if there was a connection between the mysterious wounds and Nurse Lai's attitude. His thoughts were quickly interrupted.

Nurse Nemesis, as Wayne mentally christened her, gave him a hastily scribbled piece of paper and a short, curt order to escort seven of Ward C's patients to the medical clinic. They apparently needed some tests. Wayne gratefully left the office and went in search of the clients whose names appeared on his list. With assistance from other staff, he gathered up the seven patients, including Charley Orr, and hurried out of Ward C. The brisk Scandinavian air offered a welcome reprieve from Nurse Nemesis.

Wayne found the clinic with little difficulty, herded his charges through a metal entry door and stepped into a vacuous, musty waiting room. Paint-chipped and rusted pipes hung from the ceiling suspended by thin metal straps. Brownish-red water droplets migrated down their slightly pitched slopes. A large stained and pockmarked wooden door hulked opposite their entrance. There were no windows. Three chairs with ruptured vinyl covers and a clapboard couch offered the visitors a place to sit. All seven of Wayne's companions chose a seat on the clammy, cement floor. Two patients fell into fetal positions and Charley Orr began to rock and emit high-pitched tones. Wayne eased onto the decrepit couch and took stock of his entourage. Their faces reflected fear; their postures passive resignation. An inventory exposed that his group comprised the total identified autistic population of Ward C.

After an uncomfortable five-minute wait, a large, disheveled woman strode through the wooden door and approached Wayne. She rattled off seven names in a monotone voice and then glared at Wayne. Interpreting her scowl as a solicitation for a response, Wayne took his best guess at what she wanted. He compared her names to those appearing on Nurse Nemesis' list. They matched and he shared his findings with the pear-shaped woman standing over him. She nodded her approval and replaced her glare with a forced half smile.

"I'll be back in a minute," she announced and exited through the wooden door. She returned in less than the promised time carrying a plastic tray holding seven small cups filled with a rosy colored liquid.

"What's in the shot glasses?" asked Wayne tentatively.

The large lady shot him a glance of disapproval. "Chloral hydrate, if you need to know. It helps settle them down."

Wayne was briefly intimidated but reminded himself that research involves asking questions.

"What do they need to be settled down for...if you don't mind my asking?"

"You're the new guy from the States, aren't you?" asked the woman, a more genuine smile forming and her tone mellowing.

"Yes," answered Wayne, somewhat amazed that he'd already achieved notoriety in the Norwegian hinterland. "I started yesterday."

"Why?"

Wayne was puzzled by the question's simplicity.

"Why what?" he returned.

"Why did you come to Gustaf's?"

"I'm working on a Master's project in psychology. A professor suggested the Gustaf Clinic as a good place to research the data to complete my thesis. He lived in Norway after World War II."

"Research, huh?" she replied, the sarcasm seeping back in. "I'm sure you'll find Gustaf's will provide you some interesting material."

Though curious about her remark, Wayne chose to return his focus back to his patients.

"What are these folks here for?"

"They're here for some tests. I would have thought you would have been told that."

"Nurse Nem ..., uh, Nurse Lai didn't get too specific," Wayne replied. "Maybe you can educate me. What kind of tests are we talking about?"

"Just routine tests," the nurse offered. "You just sit there and entertain yourself until we're finished. Then you can deliver these folks back to the ward."

"But it would help if..."

"They're just tests!" she shot back, the scowl returning to her face. "I'll be back with them shortly. You just sit tight and wait." She turned toward the patients and barked a command. All seven dutifully arose and followed her through the door.

Wayne slumped back into the old couch. He was unhappy with the results of his inquiries but a bit more knowledgeable about the workings of the Gustaf Clinic. Every little bit would help. He waited until he was alone in the waiting room and retrieved the book he carried in the pack that was semi-permanently attached to his body. His current readings dealt with the chemical treatment of mental illness. The book revealed that pharmaceutical therapy had been the treatment of choice for many years in an industry that pretty much had no clue as to what it was dealing with.

Despite centuries of probing, prodding, dissecting and studying, the human brain has remained largely a mystery. Treatment of humans whose brains fostered socially unacceptable behavior has been basically an experimental approach. The advent of chemicals in the mid-20th century, specifically psychotropic ones, had ushered in new hope for both the mentally ill and the societies that spurned them. Unfortunately, as with most new discoveries, chemicals were not fully understood and their abuse overshadowed their benefit.

Wayne lay the book in his lap and thought about those cups of rosy liquid. What drugs were flowing through the veins of Charley Orr and the other patients on Ward C? He brought the pages back to his eyes and continued his education.

A balding attendant returned the seven patients to Wayne about an hour after they had been herded away. They possessed dazed and vacant eyes. They shuffled slowly toward the outer door and waited silently for it to be unbolted. Wayne followed the human cluster, looked back to ask the attendant a question, but found he had already disappeared. He opened the door to the outside world and escorted his solemn, stoic charges back to Ward C. Back on the ward, the patients dropped onto empty spaces of floor, curled into tight human balls and plunged into deep sleep. Charley Orr lay still on the cold, hard concrete next to his barred porthole to the universe.

four

Jon was not expecting to see Sergeant Iverson at Neil's house. He knew he'd confront the detective again, but this would not have been his chosen venue. He tensed measurably as the old man strode towards him with tousled hair and clothes that followed suit. The Sergeant initiated the conversation.

"Good morning, ladies and gentlemen," he stated confidently. "How convenient that I've found you all in one place."

Neil responded. "What do you want, Sergeant?"

"I'm looking for answers, my good man," Iverson replied abruptly. He raised his eyebrows and fashioned a wry smile. "A lot of answers for a lot of questions."

Deb offered the Sergeant a cup of coffee and enhanced the offer with a Bailey's additive. To everyone's surprise, Iverson accepted both, and Deb went in search of one more cup. Iverson dropped his coat to the floor and found an empty chair.

"So what are the questions, Sergeant?" asked Neil impatiently.

"I like a man who gets to the point," Iverson countered. "I'll start with your connections to Ms. Covington. I realize I've asked this question before, but I'm getting old and forgetful. Indulge me."

Jon figured Iverson was looking for inconsistencies. He deflected the conversation.

"Are we suspects, Sergeant?" he asked.

"I suspect everyone, Mr. Farrell. That's my job."

Jon realized his question carried an obvious answer.

"However," continued the Sergeant, "I'd like to pare down the suspect list and maybe you can help me with that."

The statement failed to ease Jon's skepticism. "Right," he whispered, mainly to himself but heard by Iverson.

"Yes, Mr. Farrell. That is right. May I start with my questions?"

Deb returned with the Sergeant's coffee and submitted the answer.

"Yes, Sergeant. Please do. Let's get this over with."

In the next two hours Sergeant Stan Iverson got acquainted with the small world of the group seated around him. He listened intently, took copious notes and asked questions that at times were difficult to ask and more difficult to answer. Jon Farrell grew more comfortable.

At least two more pots of coffee were brewed and the bottle of Bailey's now stood empty. Most of the Sergeant's questions were directed at Neil and Deb since their history with Leslie was longer than Jon's. The Sergeant's interest in Jon grew when he shared his tale about Leslie, the university documents, and their subsequent disappearance from Futures' office.

"So," asked the Sergeant with heightened interest, "do you think there's a connection to Ms. Covington's death?"

"I don't know what to think," replied Jon. "I only had a brief glimpse of the documents and now Leslie can't shed any light on what they meant. But if the papers were really stolen from my office, I guess that would indicate that they were important to somebody. Maybe the university is involved. There are a lot of powerful people at the university, Sergeant."

"Any idea who might have invaded your office?" Iverson asked.

Jon hesitated. He didn't want to point a finger at Steven Gant. If he did, and he was wrong, his career was over. He answered cautiously.

"I ran a check on the security system at Futures," he began. "The company that provides us with overnight and weekend security has a log of all times the alarm is turned on or off. The information from the security logs, coupled with my knowledge of who has access codes and keys to my private office, leaves one suspect."

"And that would be?" probed the Sergeant. Neil and Deb sat attentively.

Jon paused, took a deep breath, and went all in.

"Steven Gant, the president of Futures' Board of Directors."

Once committed, Jon explained the details that led to his suspicions regarding Gant. Neil, Deb and Iverson absorbed his revelations. He felt he was cutting his professional throat, but also gained a sense of relief by sharing his burden. Jon's statement was interrupted by another ring of the doorbell. Neil responded this time and returned with a young woman. Jon's eyes immediately fixed on her striking appearance.

"Hello, Ms. McKinney!" greeted Sergeant Iverson. He rose and offered his chair.

Sandra McKinney slowly approached the group and took the chair vacated by Iverson. Her long auburn hair flowed past her shoulders and settled neatly on the curvature of her breasts. Hazel eyes were set back from soft skin puffed out from fitful sleep. She looked at Jon and conveyed a pained but sincere smile in his direction. He was immediately attracted to her physical and emotional presence.

As was his nature, Sergeant Iverson took control of the situation.

"What brings you here, Ms. McKinney?"

"I was invited," she replied with calm assertion.

Neil craned toward the kitchen, his eyes in search of coffee. Deb offered to brew a fourth pot.

"I asked Sandra to come by this morning," offered Neil. "She's had a rough day. Leslie's parents flew in last night and Sandra's been with them."

Iverson's voice softened. "That had to be tough for you. How are they taking it?"

"About as well as could be expected," answered the new member of the group. "They were a very close family. I hope you leave them alone for a while, Sergeant."

"How long are they in town?" asked Iverson, purposely ignoring Sandra's request.

"I suppose until after the funeral. They know where the police station is, Sergeant. They'll find you when they're ready to talk."

"Well," countered the Sergeant, "they might have a problem finding me there."

The remark brought inquisitive looks. "And just what does that mean?" inquired Neil.

"I'm not actually assigned to this case," Iverson stated somewhat meekly.

"Then what are you doing here?" demanded Jon.

"I should say I'm not *officially* assigned to this case. I am, however, pursuing it *unofficially*."

"And that means what, Sergeant?" Jon grilled. "And what makes you unofficial all of a sudden?"

"Let's just say I have my own set of suspicions regarding my own set of people in high places."

Jon pressed on, his intimidation fading.

"Sergeant," he asserted, "you asked us for answers and we provided them. I think we deserve the same courtesy. Tell us, why aren't you *officially* on this case?"

"My boss made that decision but provided no viable explanation," Iverson stated firmly. "He then assigned the case to the department's most noted dufus. Why? I don't yet know. Does it make me suspicious? Absolutely! I'm not sure what's going on but there's a certain stink to what my captain did and I want to know why. This was a heinous crime. It should not go unpunished. Like you, Mr. Farrell, I sense Leslie Covington may be dead because of something she knew. I don't yet know what it is that she knew, but I'm hoping that with your help I can find out.

Deb returned from the kitchen, once again with fresh coffee and a prepared question.

"So you're not really here?"

"That's correct," affirmed Iverson.

"I'm lost," Sandra interrupted.

"I'm sorry, Ms. McKinney," offered Iverson. "You've missed some conversation." He checked the watch on his wrist and bent over to retrieve his coat from the floor. "I'm afraid I need to go check on a few things. Maybe someone here can fill in the blanks for you."

Jon, ready for a change of scenery and seriously enamored with Sandra McKinney, offered to take her out for some food and fill her in on details of the discussion she had missed. Neil and Deb, still weary despite the caffeine, readily agreed to the plan.

Iverson obtained a few more tidbits of information from Jon on Futures, Inc. and after they all agreed to meet again the following day, the Sergeant, Jon and Sandra left Neil and Deb to their solitude.

five

Iverson drove back to the station and continued his unsanctioned investigation with a call to Futures' security company. They confirmed the information Jon Farrell had given him regarding Friday evening. He then turned his attention to the names on a list Jon provided. It was a catalog of Futures' employees who had access to the office and who could shut down the alarm system. He called each of the employees to ascertain their whereabouts on Friday night. He intentionally left the name of Steven Gant for last.

One by one the people Iverson called offered stories that, at least for now, satisfied his investigation. Steven Gant, however, had not yet been called. Jon Farrell's concern regarding Gant's possible connection to Leslie Covington's murder was shared by the Sergeant but not for the same reasons. Gant, if he was involved, would probably be but one major player among many. Alerting him now would warn anyone else involved. Iverson wanted everyone associated with this crime to pay for it.

Iverson also recognized that Jon's fear of losing his job was legitimate if he was right about Gant. What Iverson didn't need right now was his inside access to Futures cut off and the dismissal of its director would do just that. He decided on a more furtive approach to examine Steven Gant and Futures, Inc.'s other two board members.

As Iverson headed out the door, the one person he wished to avoid, Captain Denny, stopped him. He had hoped Denny would be out with his Saturday golfing partners discussing the latest in Armani suits and Gucci shoes.

"Sergeant," demanded the Captain, "where have you been all morning?"

Iverson had prepared for the inevitable confrontation.

"I've been checking some sources regarding the Langham kid. You remember him, don't you, Captain?"

Denny shot him a look of obvious contempt.

"That case is old news," he declared. "If you can't find an active case to work, I'll find one for you."

"I would imagine the Langham family would think my time is being well spent," Iverson responded calmly. "I'd be happy to call and ask them. I've got their number right here."

Christopher Langham had been missing for almost two years now and hopes of finding him alive had become remote. Christopher had celebrated his fifth birthday two days before he disappeared. Iverson could recall the mound of curly blond hair and the penetrating sky-blue eyes from the family photos. Tom and Muriel Langham had no other children, a circumstance attributed to their singular focus on the numerous and demanding behaviors their son possessed. Christopher had been diagnosed with Asperger's Syndrome and this malady apparently instilled in him a penchant for wandering away from the family home. For the neighborhood in which the Langham's lived, finding Christopher had become a fairly regular activity. Then, one day, he couldn't be found. The theory was that the boy simply had strayed too far. The Ashton community rallied behind the family and search parties combed the town and its surrounding areas for many weeks. The weeks turned into months and the months wore on but neither Christopher nor his body was ever found. Ashton police records formally listed him as missing and the case remained open.

The Langham case had thoroughly shaken the secure, moral fiber of the community and had received plenty of bold ink in the city's only newspaper. The case had even received brief national attention on CNN. Both the search for Christopher Langham and the subsequent investigation into his disappearance had been headed by Captain Denny and he took a great deal of heat for coming up empty. Iverson, working the case under Denny, had gotten close to the family and shared the pain at not being able to find their only child. He considered it a personal failure.

The Langham family eventually moved away but wrote a scathing letter to the newspaper before they left and their parting shot focused on Captain Denny's ineptitude—an opinion shared by Iverson. He felt Denny's efforts were focused more on his media image than on the case. Crucial time was wasted and Christopher Langham was lost—apparently forever. The case still lingered in hushed discussions between cops and in occasional editorials penned by Ashton's citizens. Denny loathed any reference to it and that was why Iverson chose it as his smoke screen.

"Just make sure you're not getting in Firnett's way," cautioned Denny.

"I wouldn't think of stepping on great minds," Iverson responded with unhidden sarcasm.

"Stay out of his way, Iverson!" Denny shouted, his face flushed with anger.

Iverson's blood pulsed as well but he said nothing. He'd achieved his goal. He took a few deep breaths, grinned slightly at his overheated boss and turned toward the door. The battle's just beginning, he thought.

******

The Sergeant arrived at the university, parked the car and strolled toward the Information Office to find his ex-wife's sister, the office's director. He knew she'd be there even though it was Saturday. She was a divorced workaholic like he was and found work a welcome diversion from failures.

The door to Kate's building was locked, so Iverson strode through heaps of lifeless leaves to the back of the building where her office was located. He peered inside the window and saw her busily thumping the keyboard of her computer. A few taps on the window got her attention and she motioned for him to meet her at the front door.

"Hi, Kate," he greeted with a smile she recognized as one involving a favor.

She looked too much like her sister, Beth, for Iverson's comfort, but her personality was overtly differently. She dressed meticulously and in a way that masked her fifty some years. Her career had given her a sense of importance that showed in the way she carried her still impressive frame.

Kate and he had gotten along rather well when they were in-laws and, during the infrequent times they socialized, they actually got along better than he and his ex-wife. For Iverson to actually enjoy socializing with anyone was a major accomplishment.

Unlike Beth, Kate understood what it meant to be committed to a job. She had worked for the university's Information Office before her divorce and had been its director for over five years. It was a demanding position and Kate was semi-important within the university's scheme of things. She enjoyed her role immensely. Iverson had been able to extract information from her and her enormous computer system in times past and he was hopeful she would be willing and able to assist him again.

"Hi, Stan," Kate said warmly. "How've you been?"

"Same as always, Kate," Iverson replied. "You know, all work, no play. I believe you know the routine. It keeps me busy but boring."

Kate gave him a genuine smile. "You may be many things, Stan Iverson, but boring isn't one of them."

Iverson enjoyed the compliment. "Tell your sister that. How is she by the way?"

"My personal assessment is that she's not well. Do you really care?"

Iverson reflected for a moment, then replied.

"Yeah, I actually do," he declared honestly. "But that's a conversation for another time. I'm here to see if you'll do me a favor."

"Now, why doesn't that surprise me?" asked Kate rhetorically. "Let's go back to my office and you can put your cards on the table."

Stan Iverson wanted the professional portfolios of Futures' three Board members. He wanted to know where they'd come from, what they'd accomplished and what they were presently involved with. Since the university employed them, much of what he sought should be available in the university's computer system.

Kate listened intently to the Sergeant's request, sat back in her leather-sheathed seat of power, and spoke after thoughtful digestion.

"Is this a formal police request, Stan?"

"Yes and no," answered Iverson tentatively.

"Do you mind explaining that?"

Iverson explained his predicament with Denny and his off-the-record relationship to the Covington case. It was more than he wanted to share but he needed information. He also knew Kate well enough to know that a full disclosure was necessary for her assistance. She again pondered his words before exacting a reply.

"I'll help you on one condition," she finally said.

Iverson knew the proviso.

"I'll call her tonight and see if she needs anything, okay? You cut a hard bargain, Kate."

"You'll get what you paid for, Stan. We both run a risk. Hopefully we'll both get what we want. I'll have your information by Monday morning. Is that soon enough?"

"Sooner would be better, but I'll take it when I can get it."

"If I get it sooner, I'll give you a call. Still got the same phone number?"

"Yeah, but I'd prefer you use my personal cell number." He wrote down the number on a pink sticky pad, gave Kate a warm hug and returned to his car. On the windshield was a parking ticket issued by the university's campus police. "An omen?" Iverson wondered.

six

Jon Farrell and Sandra McKinney headed out on River Road for a midday respite. The river was Jon's idea. He thought the gentle sounds of flowing currents might offer Sandra some comfort. At the very least he'd provide her with a change of scenery. They stopped at a sparsely stocked roadside deli and bought cellophane-wrapped sandwiches and a six-pack of Norwester beer. Jon pulled his truck into a small turnout and suggested they take their lunch down to the river. They spotted a path, walked to the water's edge and planted themselves in a pile of pine needles next to a large Sitka spruce. They sat in silence for a long time—Sandra obviously enjoying the reprieve from other people's emotions. Halfway through her sandwich she started a conversation.

"I'm afraid I'm not very good company," she said apologetically.

Jon gave her a long, sympathetic look.

"I have no expectations of you, Sandra," he reassured. "You're going through a very difficult time right now. I just want to offer whatever support I can. You don't have to talk if you don't want to."

"You obviously don't know me," Sandra replied with an attempt at a smile. "I normally have a hard time being quiet. But you're right. This is a difficult time. Coming to grips with Leslie's death is a tough task."

"You knew her for a long time?"

"Since high school," Sandra replied. She stared blankly at the river with teary eyes and exhaled a long, deep sigh. "We'd been pretty inseparable for the past five or six years. I wish you'd had a chance to know her. She was a special person."

"Sandra," Jon began hesitantly, "I'd like to ask some questions about Leslie, but I don't want to cause you any more pain than you're already going through. I just want to get some things clear in my head."

"It's about the documents she gave you, isn't it?"

Jon's surprise was written on his face.

"Yes, as a matter of fact it is. But my questions can wait. Really."

"It's okay, Jon. Ask away." She wiped her eyes with her shirtsleeve and straightened her posture.

"Okay. If you're sure.

"Jon, ask your questions. If Leslie was willing to trust you, I don't see why I shouldn't. What do you want to know?"

They sat by a large tree on the bank as dusk slowly crept upon them. They talked about documents, the university and Leslie Covington. Apparently Leslie and Sandra shared everything. Sandra, in fact, had convinced Leslie to ask Neil about Jon and it was Neil's portrayal of Jon that led to the afternoon meeting at the Andromeda Café. The blind date had obviously been a diversion but Jon Farrell could not have cared less. His attention now focused entirely on Sandra McKinney. The approaching twilight distributed fingers of shadows on her elegant features. She was a beautiful woman and Jon felt incredibly attracted to her.

The sudden and shrill sound interrupted Jon's wistful thoughts. Startled, they stood up to pinpoint its source. Their upright position offered an excellent target and the next bullet ripped into Sandra's left shoulder. She fell backward into the tree, her arm covered with warm blood and her beautiful hazel eyes filled with terror. Jon caught a glimpse of a man with a rifle moving toward them. Adrenaline surged through his body.

"Can you get up," he asked urgently.

"I don't know," Sandra replied and looked at her wound. "God, it hurts. I don't know if I can move." She had not yet panicked, but was on her way.

"We have to move," Jon countered. "If we don't, we die."

"Then I'll move," she said with grim determination, and stumbled to her feet.

Jon had seen only the one gunman and hoped he had no friends. He grabbed Sandra by her healthy arm and led her in the opposite direction of their would-be assassin. Another bullet whizzed by Jon's head and embedded itself in an old Douglas fir stump next to their hastily chosen escape route. Jon changed course and Sandra followed.

They crashed through branches of thick, prickly conifers and yellowing vine maples. Large, craggy boulders made course changes necessary every few feet. Jon looked back at Sandra and the urgency on her face mirrored his own. He recalled his earlier visit to the river and his sense of being watched. His instincts had been correct. Why hadn't he heeded them? Why had he brought Sandra back to the river? He'd led her into a trap. He cursed the man trying to kill them. He cursed himself.

Two more shots rang out, the last one slicing a branch from a tree a foot above Sandra's head. They leapt over fallen trees and plunged through blackberry thickets ripping flesh from their forearms. Jon tightened his grip on Sandra, fearing he'd lose her if he let go. Another shot pierced the air and ricocheted off a rock directly in front of him. They altered course again and kept moving.

Sandra suddenly jerked Jon's arm, "Over there," she gasped.

Jon followed her shaky gesture and saw a small two-person wooden canoe tethered to a tree at the river's edge. Turbid water surged violently just beyond it. The river was notoriously risky for those attempting to navigate its twisted, turbulent path. He glanced back in the direction of their pursuer and saw the gunman fifty yards away, poised to fire another shot at the now stationary targets. The decision was easy.

"Go!" Jon bellowed, and they slid down the slick rock embankment to where the canoe was fastened.

Jon wrestled the canoe's leash from its alder mooring as another bullet pierced the canoe just below the gunnel. Sandra got into the canoe and waited tensely as blood dripped down her arm and onto the wooden slats beneath her. Jon jumped in, pushed off into the swirling water and grabbed the boat's only paddle. The river's current caught them within seconds and ripped them away from the shore and their assailant. Their relief was short-lived. The river ahead was painted white with the froth of Widow Rapids. Jon was headed into class five water with one paddle and untested skills.

Only the rush of water could be heard as the canoe catapulted through a maze of jutting boulders. Rake-shaped branches from bent conifers leaned out from the river's flanks and threatened to scrape them from their boat. The sound was deafening, the relentless spray of cold water numbing. Sandra clutched a gunnel with a white-knuckled hand and looked hopefully at Jon. He glanced back and tried to present a confident face but fear betrayed his efforts. His flailing paddle made no purchase in the surging water and his efforts at guiding their route proved futile. He watched helplessly as the stream banks raced by. The river controlled their fate.

The canoe was suddenly airborne, launched from the water by a fallen tree concealed just below the foamed surface. It crashed back onto the water and instantly capsized, plunging its human contents into the swift water. The icy immersion stunned them and the relentless current pummeled their bodies as it drove them farther downstream. They gasped for air when possible. If they'd had time to think, they'd have thought of dying.

Suddenly, the water slackened into a pool of eddies. Jon popped his head above the surface, sucked in a mouthful of much needed air and searched for Sandra. He knew it would be a brief respite. They had to get to shore before the current yanked them back into the river's mainstream. He located her twenty feet away, flailing with her good arm in an attempt to reach the water's edge on the same side of the river where they'd left the gunman. He swam furiously to her, grabbed her by the waist and pointed to the opposite side of the river. She broke his grip and again struggled toward the potentially fatal shore. Jon grabbed her more forcefully and pointed again to the other side of the river.

"Sandra," he shouted above the river's roar. "Trust me."

Sandra stopped thrashing, looked directly into Jon's eyes and found conviction. With painful effort, she changed direction and together they swam to the south bank of the river and dragged themselves onto shore. Jon had no idea where they were or where their stalker might be. Sandra lay next to him, breathing noisily and rapidly. He briefly scanned the opposite shore before seeking greater security in the cover of bushes farther up the river's edge.

"Are you all right?" he asked a bedraggled Sandra.

"No," Sandra replied weakly. "Are we safe?"

"Safer than we were. I'm hoping the guy didn't have a boat."

"What...?"

"We're on opposite shores now. That should give us some time."

"So that's why…"

"Yeah, that's why I was insistent. Now please rest. I want to look at your arm."

He inspected her shoulder and found it still bleeding. The icy water had slowed the flow, but warm, red liquid continued to seep from the bullet's entry point. She had also been badly bruised from their journey down the river. He knew shock was imminent.

"We have to get help," Jon stated matter-of-factly. "You need a doctor."

Sandra responded with an anguished look and then closed her eyes. She was unconscious within seconds and Jon took the opportunity to inspect his own damage. Aside from numerous scrapes and bruises, he was intact and able to move. Within minutes, his instincts overcame his exhaustion. He surveyed the invading night sky and its near-full moon and decided they needed to move. They had no choice.

He probed the forest for sounds or sights of their pursuer. Finding none, he gently shook Sandra to wakefulness and announced it was time to go. Sandra, disoriented, weak and grimacing with pain, didn't argue. After thirty minutes of arduous walking with Sandra propped up alongside him, Jon spotted a primitive forest cabin nestled in a small clearing among old growth Douglas firs. Sepia-hued light emanated from its small, paned windows and circles of smoke trailed from its chimney. Jon sat Sandra down under one of the towering trees and took stock of their situation. He didn't know what or who was in that cabin. Their pursuer could very well be waiting with his feet up and his weapon ready. He looked at Sandra and his options shrank. She needed help and she needed it now.

Watchful and suspicious, Jon slowly approached the old log building. Its roof sagged under the weight of layers of moss cloaking the shingles. A cornucopia of river rocks offered a stable foundation to walls crafted from stands of Douglas firs. The place smelled like an old, wet dog. An old bamboo fly rod and a willow creel were propped up next to the front door. He began to feel better about the cabin.

Jon quietly stepped onto the pitched porch and craned his neck to gain a peek through a spider-webbed window. Standing out of the moon's light, he saw what he gauged to be a benign old man sitting by the fire. His attention was focused on the book cradled in his lap. A trace odor of freshly cooked fish drifted through a tiny crack in the window. Jon glanced back at Sandra and decided he had to take a chance on the old man in the ancient cabin. He motioned to Sandra to stay put, quietly strode to the door, and knocked on its weathered surface. The door didn't open, but the response was clear.

"Who the hell's out there?" the voice boomed.

Jon took a step back.

"My name is Jon Farrell," he answered boldly. "I need your help, sir. My friend's been shot."

The door opened a crack and the cabin's tenant could be seen standing back from the doorway with a shotgun pointed at the opening.

"Prove it," he demanded.

It was a chess match and it was Jon's move. He decided to play his queen. He motioned for Sandra to emerge from the shadows and to join him on the cabin's porch. She reached the first step before collapsing at Jon's feet. The old man opened the door fully, studied Sandra's crumpled body and put down the shotgun. Without words, they picked her up, and despite her audible pain, moved her into the cabin and onto a tattered couch.

"I'll call 9-1-1," the old man said, the gruffness gone. "You get her out of those wet clothes."

Jon removed as much of Sandra's clothing as his Christian upbringing would allow. He covered her with an old, musty blanket that had covered the holes in the couch. He made her as comfortable as possible then sank into a large chair by the fireplace. Their host returned and administered first aid to Sandra in what Jon perceived to be a knowledgeable fashion. He grinned a semi-toothless grin and whispered words of encouragement to a fully unconscious Sandra.

"She's going to be alright, isn't she?" Jon asked somewhat desperately.

"I think so," came the welcome if not certain reply. "She must be a tough cookie, though. That's a nasty gunshot wound."

She is tough, Jon thought. Really tough … and beautiful.

"We were attacked by …"

"Whoa!" interrupted the old man. "I don't have a need to know. Matter of fact, the less I know the better. I like my life simple. You can share all your details with the Mounties, okay?"

"Sure," Jon replied weakly. He happily slumped back into the chair.

The old man cleansed Sandra's wound and the myriad scrapes and bruises inflicted by their near fatal flight downriver. He sheathed her shoulder with strips of linen cut from an old sheet now dissected on the floor. He then replaced the musty blanket with a multicolored patchwork quilt he retrieved from his bedroom. Sandra didn't stir.

After tending to Sandra, the old man focused his large, round eyes on Jon. Jon was not seriously hurt but he was cold and exhausted. The old man retrieved a thick wool blanket from the back of the cabin and placed it around Jon's shoulders. He lifted Jon's legs and inserted an old army footlocker under them for support. He disappeared momentarily and returned with a large mug of hot cocoa. Jon thanked his host, downed two sips of the warm, creamy liquid and succumbed to sleep.

SUNDAY, SEPTEMBER 25

one

Wayne Burgess sat in his stark apartment and read from a book on contemporary treatment of autism. The text informed him that current philosophy recommended support for autistic people should incorporate highly structured environments to counteract what appeared to be their lack of social integration. Autism, the author explained, was a detached existence in which ritualistic behavior replaced normal growth and development. Traditional treatments, whatever they were, involved long-term commitments that usually provided short-term progress. Though the long-standing belief of laying blame on detached parenting patterns had been set aside, few workable theories had replaced it. Treatment remained guesswork at best and prevailing research appeared focused on the brain and those areas within it that dealt with perception.

Wayne set aside his book and appraised his situation. His college mentor had praised the Gustaf Clinic but had also cautioned him that it had been many years since he'd been there. "It could easily have fallen behind the treatment curve," he'd said, but also thought the clinic would offer contemporary ethics even if treatment modalities had fallen behind the times. Despite the chronological caveat, it seemed like the perfect fit for Wayne's research on contrasting treatment strategies for mental illness. But what Wayne was experiencing at the Norwegian clinic starkly contrasted to his pre-trip image of Gustaf's. Staff exhibited little if any respect for the patients and an uncomfortable aura of secrecy and distrust permeated Ward C. Nobody was giving him straight answers for simple questions and, most disturbing, there were all those mysterious scars marking the patients' bodies.

Wayne's suspicions would have been lessened had he been allowed access to client records. He'd certainly have been busily buried in patient histories and fully occupied fitting their stories into his research. The records might also have provided some insight regarding the behavior of Gustaf's staff. Access to those records, however, had been denied, and the attitudes and barriers he'd run into sounded an internal alarm. The records now became even more important. He wanted to find out what was really going on at the Gustaf Clinic.

******

Wayne arrived at work the next day with a smile on his face and furtive intentions in his heart. Sundays offered minimal client activity and, therefore, minimal staffing. Even Nurse Nemesis was off duty, a fact that would hopefully make Wayne's clandestine project that much easier to accomplish.

The morning went smoothly as Wayne followed the instructions of the weekend supervisor and helped deliver medications and meals to clients. Neither staff nor patients presented behaviors that would hinder Wayne's plan. If all went right, no one would be the wiser. If all went wrong, he would plead innocence by ignorance.

At one-o'clock, Wayne informed his supervisor that he wasn't feeling well and would appreciate a chance to rest quietly during his lunch break. He suggested a brief nap on the cot in the medical records room would soothe his aching head after which he'd capably complete his shift. The supervisor responded with a disapproving glare and a cutting remark about Americans with hangovers. Wayne responded with a sheepish grin that offered validation of her premise and, after he'd accepted the caveat that this would be a singular accommodation, the records vault was opened. The shift charge stood stone-faced as Wayne entered the windowless room, uttered a series of convincing moans and groans, and stretched out on the musty cot. The door closed behind him and the Burgess plan began.

The first targets were the records of Charley Orr and he located them with relative ease in the alphabetized drawers. As Wayne had hoped, the bulk of the chart's contents were in the English language. Tabs had been inserted in the faded folder to separate medical and social information as well as various other aspects of Charley's life. Wayne's eyes stopped at the tab marked "biography," and he fingered it. He read quickly.

Charley Orr arrived at the Gustaf Clinic in 1990. He had come from a facility in Austria but Wayne wasn't able to ascertain how long he'd been there. His family history notes were sketchy at best but appeared to indicate he had been diagnosed with autism at an early age and been given a prognosis with little hope. His German parents, with minimal monetary means and six other children to care for, had made a brief attempt to manage the disorder's difficult manifestations. But as Charley's behaviors escalated, his parent's energy waned and they put their son in a government-run mental hospital near Munich.

Autism was a relatively unknown illness in the mid-20th century and, as a rule, those afflicted were banished from society and merged into an institutional melting pot of outcasts. Wayne knew that the treatment of the mentally ill in the 1950s and ‘60s effectively consisted of warehousing the afflicted and controlling their behaviors with restraints, barbiturates, and electric shock. He had assumed that both social attitudes and therapeutic approaches had evolved since then but the wounds on Ward C's patients forced him to revisit this premise.

Charley's family apparently abandoned him shortly after his first hospitalization. His early years were spent at large, custodial facilities where therapeutic innovation was neither practiced nor considered. Charley undoubtedly had shared much of his life with the mentally ill and criminally insane, the typical residents of large, state-run institutions. In his subsequent years, his captive odyssey included at least three other institutions. His catalog of treatments included insulin shock, electro-convulsive therapy, cold water immersion, and a "minor" lobotomy. That he sought control of his world followed reasonably, Wayne thought.

On the last page of the biography section was a final, hand-written entry. "Please see autopsy report," it announced.

two

Jon woke up in the hospital. It took a few minutes to realize where he was and why. He then remembered Sandra. He was attempting to get out of bed when a portly nurse appeared and told him it was not a good idea.

"What's more," she said, "there're a few of Ashton's finest out in the lobby waiting to talk to you. I get the sense they'd be unhappy if denied the opportunity."

"I need to know what's happened to Sandra McKinney," Jon stated impatiently.

"She's doing fine," replied the nurse. "She'll be sore for a while, but she should make a full recovery."

"She's here in the hospital?"

The nurse stood tall and matronly, her presence hanging heavy in the room's condensed space.

"As a matter of fact, Mr. Farrell, she's in the next room. But don't even think about disturbing her. She's experienced significant trauma and needs her sleep. I doubt if she'll be awake for at least another four or five hours anyway. You can see her then."

Jon felt the wave of relief wash over his body. His thoughts drifted to their ordeal at the river. He was both astonished and gratified that they had survived. His manhood had been tested and he had passed the test. His personal epiphany was interrupted by the sudden appearance of Sergeant Stan Iverson at the door.

"Farrell," he said abruptly. "I've only got a minute before Firnett butts his pea brain in here, so I'll be brief."

"Who…?"

"Don't interrupt," admonished Iverson. "As you'll recall, this is not my case. It belongs to this asshole Firnett and if he sees me here, he'll report me to the Supreme Asshole back at the station. I don't want to be directing traffic on Main Street tomorrow morning so if you want out of the trouble you're in, you'll talk to me, not the idiot on his way in here. You're not hurt badly and should be out of here in a few hours. When you're released, call me and we'll meet. I gotta go."

Iverson opened the door, briefly surveyed the territory, then hurried off down the hallway. Jon was left more than slightly mystified by Iverson's behavior. He wasn't sure if Iverson was being truthful with him but he desperately needed someone to trust.

Minutes after Iverson left, someone Jon didn't recognize walked into his hospital room. He was an overweight, drab looking man, probably in his mid-forties. His hairline was receding and his budding dome reflected the room's fluorescent light. He wore a cheap suit and a lifeless tie. He smelled like English Leather.

"Jon Farrell, I presume?"

Jon was immediately protective.

"Who wants to know?"

"I'm Sergeant Bill Firnett from the Ashton Police Department. I'd like to ask you some questions about the incident involving you and Sandra McKinney."

Jon looked at Firnett for a long time before offering an answer. He was choosing his allegiance.

"I really don't feel like talking right now," he finally responded, his choice made.

"Come now, Mr. Farrell," placated Firnett. "You must realize that your life, for some reason, is in danger. Don't you want to help us find whoever tried to kill you and your lady friend?"

Again, Jon measured his answer.

I'm feeling tired, Sergeant," he feigned. "Come back in a couple of hours."

The nurse, who had entered the room with Firnett, stepped into the conversation and came to Jon's rescue.

"If Mr. Farrell says he needs rest, than rest he shall have. Everybody out please."

She looked at Jon and offered a furtive smile. Somehow he knew she was acquainted with Stan Iverson. He returned her smile.

Despite vehement protestations from Sergeant Firnett, he was obliged to leave. Jon thanked the nurse and asked again about Sandra. He was assured that she was doing fine but would be kept in the hospital for a few more days as a precautionary measure. The nurse left and Jon located his clothes and got dressed. He slipped out the door, took a brief glimpse at a sleeping Sandra McKinney in the adjacent room and, following the tactics of Stan Iverson, left the hospital undetected by people in uniforms.

Jon reached home and placed a call to Neil Danielski but got no answer. He then searched for the number Iverson had given him the previous day, dialed it and, after two rings, was greeted with a now familiar raspy voice.

"Iverson here."

"Sergeant, this is Jon Farrell."

"You made the right decision," Iverson replied confidently.

"Pretty sure of yourself, aren't you, Sergeant?"

"Part confidence, part luck, Mr. Farrell. But in my line of work you get a feel for people and I had an idea you'd be calling. I'm glad I was right."

"So you were right, Sergeant," Jon said, very businesslike. "Where do we go from here?"

"First things first. Tell me what happened to you and Ms. McKinney last night."

Jon relayed his harrowing story and Iverson listened attentively, interrupting only with an occasional request for more detail. At the story's conclusion, Iverson expressed his admiration for how Jon handled the situation. The words of praise pleased Jon. Iverson's approval was becoming important to him.

"So, what do we do next, Sergeant?"

"Ms. McKinney is safe in the hospital for now, but I'll ask a friend of mine to keep an eye on her just in case."

"In case what?" demanded Jon.

"Jon!" Iverson scolded, using Jon's given name for the first time. "Has it not occurred to you that whoever killed Leslie Covington also tried to kill you and Ms. McKinney? I want Ms. McKinney watched closely in case they try again. That work for you?"

Jon knew Iverson was right and offered only silent agreement. Surviving Widow Rapids was not the final, heroic chapter he'd have liked for this story and Iverson had just made it clear that the book wasn't fiction. The bad guys were real.

"Jon," Iverson continued, "I think you and Sandra are in real danger. For whatever reason, you two have become players in a high stakes game and I'd like to figure out what the game actually is and who the other players are. Mind if I swing by your place to discuss how you can help me with that?"

"Sure, come on by," Jon replied. "I'll brew some caffeine to clear my synapses."

"Great," Iverson confirmed. "See you in ten minutes."

three

Sergeant Iverson arrived at Jon Farrell's house exactly ten minutes after their phone conversation ended. He sauntered up to the front door, threw his still burning cigarette butt behind a half-dead azalea bush and gave the door a resounding, confident knock. The home's weary looking occupant answered the door.

"Synapses still asleep, Jon?" asked the Sergeant while surveying the chaos Jon called his living room.

"Sorry I don't meet your standards, Sergeant," Jon said cynically. "My normally radiant personality has taken the day off."

Iverson seated himself in Jon's favorite chair, wearing a subtle smile provoked by Jon's cynicism. It was a character trait he was familiar with.

"I could grow to like you, Farrell," the Sergeant disclosed."

"I'm not sure I take any comfort in that," replied Jon.

"I'm not here to offer comfort," Iverson stated matter-of-factly. "I'm here to prevent you from becoming a statistic."

Jon tempered his tone. "I appreciate that, Sergeant. How exactly do you propose to do that?"

"I'm hoping to leave here today with that plan in place but first I want to revisit the documents Ms. Covington gave you. I need as much detail as possible so, please, indulge my diminished memory and describe them to me again."

Jon again described the now famous documents and Iverson again took copious notes. When finished, they agreed that the papers were a key to their puzzle and, if copies existed, they needed to find them. The first logical place to look would be Leslie Covington's house. It might have police still milling around, which would pose a risk to Iverson's precarious position with Captain Denny. The risk was deemed worth it, however, if the evidence might exist.

******

They arrived at Leslie and Sandra's home and were not surprised to see bright yellow crime tape and a single, uniformed policeman securing the building. Iverson was undaunted. He marched directly and confidently up to the blue-clad cop and flashed his shield in the pubescent officer's face.

"Afternoon, officer," he greeted with authority. "I need to look inside."

"Sir," responded the young officer anxiously, "I … I've been given strict orders. No one's allowed inside unless they're accompanied by Sergeant Firnett."

Iverson exhaled audibly and gave the young cop an icy stare. He moved within inches of the cop's face.

"Officer," he stated calmly, "I don't have time to play games. This case is media hot and evidence cold and I'm the guy sent to change that. If you need your boss's permission to solve this crime, fine. Go ahead, call the portly prick and get your precious permission."

Iverson paused for effect, then coolly continued his verbal ambush.

"Time is of the essence here, son. If the killer gets away because the evidence got away, well, heads will roll."

Sweat trickled down the side of the officer's boyish face. His body slumped and his color grew ashen.

"I…, I still think I should call headquarters and get permission from Sergeant Firnett," he mumbled.

"Right," chastened Iverson. "And after that call your mommy and get her permission too. Make a decision, boy! I ain't got all fucking day."

Iverson hit the right button. The young officer straightened his posture and looked directly into the penetrating eyes of his superior.

"All right, goddamn it," he blurted. "Go ahead and do what you gotta do, Sergeant. But I'm coming with you. What we find, we share credit for. Got it?"

Iverson was pleased. He got what he wanted and, in the end, gained a morsel of respect for the young cop. They ducked under the security tape, entered the house and began their search … Jon and Iverson for the documents, the young cop for anything suspicious. Forty-five minutes later, Jon found what they'd come for. Leslie had taped copies of the papers into the jacket of a coffee table edition of Edward Curtis prints. Jon paused to admire her efforts and realized that what he now held had cost her her life. His visceral sadness was interrupted by Iverson's demand for a progress report. He gave the Sergeant a furtive thumbs up sign and Iverson nodded his acknowledgement.

Jon looked around for their blue-clad escort and, not seeing him, secured the papers under his coat. They thanked their unwitting accomplice and left Leslie Covington's home with a few of the puzzle pieces they were looking for. They'd been granted some of that luck Iverson had talked about.

******

Back at Jon's house, there were messages on the answering machine. One was from Neil. He wanted to know about the shootings at the river. The other message was from

Steven Gant. He wanted to discuss a recent Board of Directors' decision that concerned Jon. Jon and Iverson looked at each other as Gant's message ended. Nothing was spoken but they both instinctively knew the proverbial snowball was now headed uncontrollably downhill. Neither of them knew how large it would grow or what damage it would cause.

four

Neil and Deb spent Sunday at home, hoping to relax. Neil was an avid football fan and the season was just getting under way. Deb had learned that the one sure way to spend time with the man of her choice was to get involved in sports. Through the years she'd actually grown to like the emotional, competitive high that came with cheering for certain teams, particularly teams that Neil detested. The weekend diversion had become a standard for them between the months of September and January.

The knock on the door was loud enough to be audible over the cacophony emanating from the television. Deb answered the door and was greeted by two men in smartly tailored suits who presented badges recognizing them as agents with the FBI. Following Deb's inspection of their identification, they were allowed to interrupt the "game of the week." The men were interested in the death of Leslie Covington and in some papers that she had allegedly taken from the university.

"The FBI would like to have those papers," asserted the taller and broader of the two men.

"We don't know about any papers," responded Neil defensively.

The man persisted, a growing intensity appearing in his eyes and surfacing in his voice.

"We suspect that Ms. Covington stashed copies of these documents with a select group of friends prior to her death. We now also know that the two of you were among her best friends. We therefore believe you have what we're looking for."

The man's partner didn't speak. He moved slowly about the room and scanned its contents.

"Mister," Deb stated boldly, "we don't much care what you or the FBI thinks. We don't have whatever documents you're looking for and, if we did, there's a damn good chance we wouldn't give them to you."

The man grew visibly agitated. His chest puffed out and the veins on his neck and forehead bulged. He glared at Deb, then at his companion. The partner ended his household inventory and approached Deb Sutter. He glared at her with beady, blackish eyes.

"Lady," he said menacingly, "if you have what we're looking for, I'd suggest strongly that you find it and quickly."

Deb's heart sank. Her confidence vanished. Neil rose from his chair and quickly walked toward Deb and the alleged FBI agent. His accomplice grabbed Neil from behind and flung him back in his chair. Neil attempted to get up but a well-placed fist in the stomach halted his effort. Deb screamed and was slapped viciously across her face. She crumpled to the floor.

"You need to understand that our request is a serious one," the larger man stated impassively.

Deb was in tears. She crawled over to Neil and grasped his hand.

"We don't have what you want," she blurted. "Leslie didn't give us anything."

The smaller man bent over and pushed his face against hers. His hot, stale breath escaped through yellowed teeth.

"We don't believe you, missy," he said and slapped her again with an open hand. "Now you'd better find them for us, hadn't you?"

Neil tried again to stand but was beaten back with forceful blows. The two men stepped back from their terrified victims for a short, whispered conversation. Neil slithered down his chair and sat on the floor next to Deb. He surveyed the room for an escape route but found none. The men returned their attention to them.

"We've decided to believe you … for now," the larger man announced.

"Then you're leaving?" asked Neil hopefully.

"Of course," the man said, and motioned for his partner to follow him.

As they reached the door they turned in unison and pulled silenced revolvers from beneath their tailored suits. They showed no emotion as they emptied their weapons.

The two men stepped casually over the lifeless bodies and did their best to find the papers they had killed for. They left the house having gained nothing but the destruction of life. The televised and resonant cheers of faraway football fans fell silent on the motionless forms of Neil Danielski and Deb Sutter.

five

Jon returned Neil's call, but got no answer. He left a message on the machine and dialed the number of Steven Gant. Gant answered the phone with his customary greeting.

"Dr. Steven Gant speaking."

"Hi, Steve. This is Jon. I got your message."

"We need to talk, Jon. I know it's Sunday, but this really can't wait. Futures' office in thirty minutes work for you?"

Iverson sent Jon an inquisitive look from his seat on the couch. Jon shrugged his shoulders and looked at his watch.

"I guess I can make it. What's this about, Steve?"

"Just meet me at your office in half an hour," Gant stressed. "We can talk there."

"Okay, Steve," replied Jon, recognizing Gant was finished with phone talk. "I'll see you there."

Jon hung up the phone and returned to his chair wearing a look of confusion on his face.

"So, what's up?" inquired Iverson.

"I have a date with Gant at my office in thirty minutes."

"Interesting," speculated Iverson. "Any idea what he wants?"

"I'm pretty sure he doesn't want help with his Christmas list. Whatever it is, he wants to get it over with quickly."

"Hmmm," Iverson murmured. "Anything happen lately that you think might interest Mr. Gant?"

Jon looked intently at the Sergeant. To Iverson, Gant was a murder suspect. Though Jon didn't particularly like Gant, he couldn't imagine that he was involved in Leslie Covington's death.

"Thirty minutes, huh?" said Iverson. "We'd better hurry."

"We? Who invited you to this meeting?"

"Look, Jon," lectured Iverson, "There's a good possibility Gant's involved in Ms. Covington's murder. You've said as much yourself, although you may not realize you said it. At the very least, your office's alarm system's records indicate he's probably involved with the theft at your office. And let's not forget the attempt on your and Ms. McKinney's lives. I think the facts make a pretty good case for me going to your office ... if for no other reason than to offer you some protection."

Jon digested Iverson's words and decided he was right.

"Okay," he finally said. "You're invited. But we'd better hurry."

"We'd have been there already if you'd analyze less and act more."

Jon ignored the comment. He had neither the time nor the energy to debate Iverson's character evaluation and, besides, the Sergeant was probably right.

They arrived at Futures' office ten minutes after their departure from Jon's house. Iverson informed Jon that he would be a furtive observer rather than an active participant at the meeting. He suggested questions Jon should ask Gant if given the opportunity ... questions that could validate his suspicions.

Gant had not yet arrived so Jon gave the Sergeant a quick tour of the office and they chose an office directly across from Jon's for Iverson's clandestine presence. Jon left a crack opening in the door of Iverson's outpost and swung his office door fully open. Iverson wouldn't be able to see Gant but he should be able to clearly hear their conversation.

Futures' Executive Director sat in his office chair, stared out the window at the meandering river and nervously awaited the arrival of his Sunday guest. Steven Gant appeared exactly thirty minutes after the end of his phone conversation with Jon. Gant was habitually late and early to leave most meetings so this rare punctuality emphasized the peculiar tone of this encounter.

He entered Jon's office wearing his normal business demeanor.

"Hello, Jon. I appreciate you coming in on short notice."

"No problem, Steve. What's this all about?"

"It's difficult to say, Jon. I've had some recent conversations with Terrance and Allan. We're dissatisfied with the direction the agency is moving."

Jon was stunned even though he sensed it was coming. He tried unsuccessfully to hide his shock.

"Just what do you mean?" Jon asked respectfully, yet forcefully.

"I mean we're unhappy with you," Gant replied bluntly.

"Unhappy with what?" Jon appealed. "I think I have a right to know what you're talking about."

Gant's face showed the look of condescending intolerance Jon had seen many times before. His personality type didn't like being challenged.

"The Board of Directors," Gant continued impatiently, "has decided to change Futures' leadership. That's all I'm prepared to say at this time."

Iverson had tried to prepare him but Jon still felt emotionally bludgeoned. He was disappointed in Gant but more disappointed in himself. He had trusted Gant, Walk and Trenholm. He had tolerated their pompous attitudes and boorish behaviors because he thought they were trying to accomplish something that was morally right. Jon's new reality shocked him. His face flushed and anger swelled up inside him. The man sitting across from him may well have tried to have him killed.

Gant casually sat back in his chair and waited for a response. Jon desperately wanted to leap across the desk and beat the arrogant smirk off Gant's face. He wanted to tell him what an embarrassment he was to the human race. He held back, figuring there'd be a better time. He had his own game to play now. But he also now knew that when the time came, he'd do the right thing. It was a new feeling. A *great* new feeling.

"Fine, Steve," Jon stated confidently. "I'll be back tomorrow to close out my tenure as Futures' Director."

"I need you to do that today, Jon."

Jon was incensed.

"What the fuck do you mean, today?" Jon demanded. Iverson smiled his approval in the other room.

"I mean I need you to clean out everything that's yours today … before we leave."

Jon paused, took a deep breath and glared at Gant. He recalled Iverson's list of questions.

"Okay, Steven," he finally said calmly. "I'll take what's mine. We both know you've already taken what you wanted, haven't you?"

Gant shot him a look of surprise but composed himself quickly. He then smiled, folded his arms across his chest and sat back in his chair. He had a well-built facade.

"What could you possibly mean by that, Jon?

"I believe we both know an explanation is unnecessary."

"I'm afraid not, Jon."

"Bank your story safely, Steven," Jon said sarcastically. "You never know the costs down the road."

Gant chose not to reply but maintained the semi-smirk on his face. Jon knew nothing else meaningful would emerge from Gant so gave up the pursuit. He expected Gant to wait until he left before rifling the office for anything that might incriminate him.

Jon flashed on Iverson in the adjacent room. How was he going to get out of there if Gant lingered after Jon left. He quickly decided it was Iverson's problem to solve and began to gather his belongings. Gant sat quietly and stoically while awaiting Jon's departure. He wanted no further conversation. Neither did Jon.

Jon packed the few office items that he personally owned and headed to the door. Gant informed him he would receive his final paycheck in the mail. Jon nodded acknowledgement and left the office with the professor's eyes following him from an office window. He climbed into his truck and threw his box of belongings on the seat. Stan Iverson's rumpled frame was crunched on the floor.

"Let's move," the Sergeant stated forcefully. "It's damn uncomfortable down here."

six

The sound of a key turning in the door lock froze Wayne Burgess. He regained his composure, stuffed Charley Orr's file under his shirt and quickly lay back down on the cot. The supervisor's scowling face appeared in the doorway and announced his break had ended. He looked at her with fabricated weariness, managed a believable yawn, and said he'd be out in a minute. The supervisor sighed her disapproval and left. Wayne hurriedly gathered two more files and left the records room. He stashed the contraband in his daypack, deposited it in Ward C's unoccupied office, and returned to the dayroom and its schizophrenic banter.

One of Wayne's coworkers sat absorbed in the muted television. He and Holm had been introduced at the start of the shift. Holm stared at silent skiers cutting trails on slippery slopes, his interest in the magic tube competing with a catnap apparently sanctioned on the weekend shifts. Wayne interrupted both pursuits.

"What's on the television?"

"Nothing, unless you're a skier," Holm replied in perfect English, "and I'm not."

"I thought all Norwegians skied."

"Ninety-nine percent do," calculated Holm. "I help make up the other one percent."

"Since you're not absorbed in the snow folks," Wayne continued, "would you mind if I asked you a few questions?"

"Questions?" Holm asked suspiciously. "What kind of questions?"

"Medical questions, mainly," Wayne answered. "Treatment data is what I'm really after. I need all the data I can get to work into my Master's thesis."

"Questions can be risky, Wayne," stated Holm, squirming a bit in his chair.

"Risky? Why?" Wayne inquired.

"Because nobody questions anything around here," Holm answered cynically. "And if they did, they wouldn't be here very long."

"Why's that?"

Holm craned his head above his chair and carefully scanned Ward C before answering.

"Look," he stated bluntly after satisfying his search. "I come to work, do what I'm told, and pick up my paycheck at the end of the month. If I start having opinions, I'm out of a job and I can't afford that. Nobody around here can."

Wayne digested Holm's reasoning and concluded he was probably right. Jobs were undoubtedly hard to come by in Kirkenes and he didn't want to put Holm's livelihood in jeopardy. He needed information not enemies.

"So how long have you worked here?"

"Too long." Holm replied indifferently.

"How long is too long?" Wayne cautiously persisted.

"Going on five years, I guess."

"Five years!" Wayne lamented audibly. "Five years is a long time."

"I know what you're thinking," Holm responded defensively. "You think I don't care about what's happening here. Well it's not that simple, Mister Burgess. I don't need the judgment of some fucking American who's gonna be gone in six months. What the hell do you know anyway?"

"I wasn't judging you," Wayne quickly replied. "I apologize if it sounded that way. Your experience makes you incredibly valuable to these patients and to me."

Wayne's attempt at reparation was met with silence but Holm didn't walk away. He instead slumped back into his chair and stared blankly at the television screen. Wayne sat silently hoping the conversation hadn't ended.

"So," Holm finally offered quietly, "what do you want to know?"

"I'm most interested in patient histories," Wayne whispered back.

"Like I said, I've been here five years. What happened before that, I don't know."

"I understand that," Wayne pursued. "But you know five years' worth more than me, right?"

"It still ain't much."

Wayne's patience thinned but he forged ahead. "Please, Holm," he entreated. "Every little bit will help."

"Nobody, including me, does much of anything around here," Holm offered.

Wayne counted silently to ten, waiting for Holm to continue. He didn't, but Wayne sensed the dam had a hole in it.

"Let me be more specific," he finally said. "My research contrasts old and new mental health treatments and your experience at Gustaf's could give me critical information for that comparison. I just arrived here. You've had five years. You tell me who's better qualified to contribute to research on the treatment history of Gustaf's patients."

The idea of contributing to a research project apparently appealed to Holm.

"Will I be listed as a contributor on your research paper?" he asked sheepishly.

"Absolutely," Jon assured him. The flood gate opened wide.

Through strenuous and sometimes difficult dialogue, Wayne learned that Ward C's patients received what Gustaf's called "custodial care," a system involving very little of anything related to curative treatment. Their predictable days included a schedule of sleeping, eating, medications and regularly scheduled trips to the medical clinic. Holm's role in the clinic appointments appeared to be the same as Wayne's had been on his only assignment there. He escorted the patients to the clinic, patrolled them back and then watched them sleep for large amounts of time. Holm, however, saw nothing strange in this particular set of events and he had either failed to note or had grown hardened to the fear in the patient's faces when at the clinic.

Wayne asked more about the visits to the medical clinic. What were the patients being treated for? Why did they go so often? They certainly couldn't be sick every other day. Why did they sleep for twelve hours after clinic visits? What was the rosy liquid?

Holm provided few absolute answers but Wayne gleaned some useful tidbits of information and stored them for later use. He finished out his shift with mostly one-sided conversations with the inhabitants of Ward C. The time dragged and his mind drifted, much like those of his autistic acquaintances. But unlike the scattered and nebulous destinations of Ward C's residents, Wayne's thoughts traveled directly to the unseen pages of the records hidden in his daypack. He would see them soon.

seven

Sergeant Iverson unfolded his body in Jon's truck a block away from Futures' office. He surveyed Jon's mood and was pleasantly surprised. He'd expected depression. He saw determination.

"You're wearing your unemployment well, Mr. Farrell," Iverson quipped.

"That son-of-a-bitch. He's deceived a lot of people, including me. I was hoping it wasn't true, but it is."

"The truth does occasionally hurt, Jon," Iverson offered.

"Damn near killed me, didn't it, Sarge?"

Iverson smiled an appreciative smile. Jon Farrell was growing up.

"Jon," Iverson asked, "What do you think Gant will do now?"

Jon processed the question and its implication. The relationship with Iverson was now a partnership.

"If I were Gant, I'd try to find and destroy any copies of Leslie's documents. Those papers are the link to him, Walk and Trenholm." His voice trailed off and he looked blankly at the road ahead of them. "What makes people do something like this, Sarge?"

"There're a lot of reasons, Jon," Iverson replied. "I'm probably the wrong person to critique humans but I've seen enough of their behavior to have an opinion. When I was younger, I saw people in only black and white ... good and bad. As I've gotten older, I tend to fit humanity more into the gray end of the spectrum. There are good people and bad people but most fall into a simply-trying-to-survive category and that often means a life on the edge. Crimes can be committed out of necessity or circumstance. Starving people will steal food—threatened people will protect themselves. Some criminal behavior is inherited. Abused kids usually have parents who were abused and they, in turn, will probably abuse their children. Those behaviors probably aren't justified but, with close inspection, they are clarified.

"But the world is also populated with its share of evil and dangerous people. Our species has consistently been guilty of despicable behavior and today's headlines or Will Durant's' History of Civilization will validate that verdict. Your buddy Gant may be a high powered PhD, but my guess is, is that he's much more pedestrian. He's a common crook, and like most of them, he'll think he's smarter than he really is."

"He's a fucking idiot," Jon said emphatically.

"Well educated, though," embellished Iverson and they shared a laugh.

"Now," posed Iverson, once again serious, "who else might become targets?"

Jon pondered the question and replied. "Obviously Sandra and me, given what happened at the river."

Jon flashed on Gant again. The man tried to kill him. Would he try again? His palms moistened. His confidence leaked.

Iverson recognized the symptoms. "Jon," he chastised gently, "ambivalence can get you killed. You can't afford your apathy anymore."

Iverson was right. It was fight or flight time. Jon reflected on his life and it wasn't terribly pretty. Failed relationships, self-inflicted disappointments and a perpetual, unexplained emptiness that churned in his stomach. He thought of Leslie Covington. He thought of the bullets that sought him out at the river and the one that found Sandra McKinney. It was time to grow up … to fight.

"Sarge," he said confidently. "I'm in this thing."

"You sure?" asked Iverson firmly.

"Yeah, Sarge. I'm sure. Absolutely sure! Let's move on, okay?"

"Fine," replied Iverson. "So tell me what's next."

"The only other people with a connection are Neil and Deb."

"Then we need to see them," said Iverson. "The sooner the better."

******

They arrived at Neil and Deb's and found a maze of squad cars encircling their home. Bill Firnett was exiting the front doorway with a person Iverson identified as the County Coroner. Two stretchers with zipped body bags were being loaded onto an ambulance. Jon attempted to exit the truck but Iverson held him back.

"No need, Jon," he said quietly. "We both know what happened here. I'm truly sorry. They were good people."

Jon fought Iverson's clutch but the Sergeant's grip tightened.

"Now's not the time, Jon," he said firmly.

"I have to, Sarge," Jon pleaded.

"I know, but you can't help them now. No one can. There are other things we can and must do."

Jon stared into Iverson's eyes and saw both compassion and resolve. He sat back into the car seat and Iverson released his grip. For a brief, tortured time, they watched from a distance as Jon's best friend left his home for the last time accompanied by piercing sirens and bright, flashing lights. Pain etched his taut and drawn face. He couldn't speak.

"Let's get out of here," Iverson finally said.

They drove slowly away, unnoticed by the busy cadre of cops. Within minutes, a flood of imprisoned emotions erupted. The truck screeched to a halt. Jon got out, screamed a long streak of obscenities at Gant, Walk and Trenholm and beat fisted imprints onto the hood of his truck. Once past his rage, Jon settled onto the curb and buried his head in his lap. Iverson sat quietly next to him.

Twenty minutes later, Jon got up and climbed back into his pick-up. Iverson followed suit. They left Ashton's boundaries and silently traversed bumpy, backcountry roads lined with groping trees casting newborn hues. Jon finally broke the silence.

"Whoever did this, Sarge, they have to pay. They have to pay for what they've done."

Iverson smiled reassuringly and spoke from experience.

"I think we know who's responsible," he replied. "Proving their guilt is our task now."

"And how do we get that proof?"

"I'm working on that, Jon. What evidence we do dig up has got to be clean and convincing. I don't want any of these assholes getting off on a technicality."

"Sooo…?"

"Motive comes first," stated Iverson emphatically. "We've got to establish a motive for Gant, Walk and Trenholm to kill people."

"Wait a minute," interrupted Jon. "You're saying the PhDs killed Neil, Deb and Leslie?"

"Not personally," Iverson qualified. "I don't see the professors sullying their hands with the deed. But I think they have a role."

"What kind of role?"

"They could have paid someone to kill your friends," offered Iverson.

"If they did, how serious is their crime?"

"Very serious, Jon. In the eyes of the law, if you solicit murder, you commit murder."

"So who are we after?"

"I want the killers, but first I want the people who hired them. Stop them and we stop the killing."

"Okay, Sarge. I just want to make sure that the targets are Gant, Walk and Trenholm. If your investigation gets diverted from them, I can't help you."

"Understood," Iverson assured. "At this point, the professors are the best and only suspects and I'm betting that what we find in Ms. Covington's documents keeps them that way. By the way, where are the copies we found at her house?"

Jon shot a look of panic to the Sergeant. He punched the truck's accelerator and they took off toward Ashton at high speed. They arrived at Jon's house in thirty minutes, slowly approached the entry and searched for any sign of a break-in. The doors and windows appeared unmolested so Jon turned his key in the front door lock, opened the door and cautiously entered his home. The house looked as it had when they left it a few hours before. He went directly to where he'd stashed the documents, behind a large Oregon relief map hung on his bedroom wall, and anxiously peered behind the plastic-coated drawing. The copies were still there. Jon walked into the kitchen, returned with two semi-clean glasses and a large bottle of Korbel's brandy, Neil's birthday gift to him a few months back. They secured the doors, pulled the shades over the windows and got drunk. They talked of friendships, extra-terrestrial life, sports and the books of Michael Crichton. Then they fell into intoxicated sleep.

eight

Wayne Burgess sat down to a dinner of hard-boiled eggs, flinty cheese and three-day-old bread. He had found one last bottle of local beer in the fridge. The main course, however, was not food. It was the patient files he'd borrowed from the medical records room earlier that day. He was hoping for easily digestible material on both accounts. He initiated the written repast with a further inspection of Charley Orr's history, starting with examination of an autopsy report buried in the last few pages of the folder. Charley Orr had been declared dead on September 8, 1996. His autopsy report indicated a death due to pneumonia. Even in his present condition, Wayne thought, Charley looked pretty good for having been dead so long.

Wayne nibbled his rations and reviewed the contents of the other records he'd pilfered. They all held similar medical history accounts and all contained autopsy reports that indicated the patient died in 1996. The questions were obvious; the answers obscure. And if his encounter with Nurse Nemesis was any indication, they'd be hard to come by.

Wayne finished the poached files and dreary dinner, then contemplated his next move. His coworkers obviously didn't share his concerns and would offer no help. The Gustaf Clinic, even in its diminished and vestigial state, was a major employer in Kirkenes. A scandal would cost jobs and an American whistleblower would be unpopular at best. Wayne imagined himself in the pink-liquid line at the medical clinic but quickly washed away that discomfiting thought with the last slosh of beer. He was probably on his own and he kind of liked the idea. Contrary to Gustaf's records, the patients on Ward C weren't deceased. Many, however, looked like walking dead, but their scars and muted melancholy seemed to indicate that it wasn't a natural path they were taking. Indifference wasn't an option for Wayne. He would dig deeper into the Gustaf Clinic.

Wayne developed his strategy in the next few hours and would begin with a stealthy visit to the medical clinic under cover of night in search of additional records. He needed more evidence to prove his hypothesis that Gustaf's patients were being used as guinea pigs. Wayne suspected that Nurse Nemesis had already spoken to Gustaf's overseers about him and, if true, his days on Ward C might already be numbered. He needed to act quickly and decided there was no time like the present.

******

Nightfall brought a moonless sky, the sleuthing milieu Wayne had hoped for. He scoured his limited wardrobe for warm but dark clothing, dressed quickly, grabbed a flashlight and left his apartment to walk the mile to the Gustaf Clinic.

Wayne silently approached the gate that marked the clinic's entrance, sat down behind the concrete stanchions that anchored slatted steel and did a gut check. His legs trembled and his heart pounded audibly in his chest. He took long, slow sips of the crisp Nordic air and searched for the courage to move forward past his fear and the cast iron barrier in front of him. He found his inspiration in a vision of Charley Orr and the scarred landscape that was his body. Wayne scaled the gate and proceeded onto Gustaf's grounds. He reached the medical clinic ten, tortuous minutes later.

Shafts of yellow light emanated from several of the clinic's barred windows. Too many, Wayne thought. Why are there so many people here? He moved along the clinic's perimeter, concealed behind thick hedgerows that encircled the old building. No security guards were seen. Odd, Wayne thought. Odd, but fortunate. More well-lit rooms were counted as Wayne worked his way around the clinic looking for a safe entry. He wondered if people were actually working or if some security policy required that the lights be on. He got his answer when voices seeped from the illuminated chambers.

Wayne crept closer. He spotted a potential viewing platform below a window, a Hobbit-like hollow partially concealed by a thicket of thorny bushes. He probed the spikey shrubs for an opening, balanced and craned his body upward and peered into the room. Five men, clad in soiled, red-blotched uniforms, loomed over two patients from Ward C. Each patient's torso was confined to a vinyl chair with a wide, cloth strap tied over the chest. Leather manacles secured their arms and legs to cold, steel frames. Four of the attendants stood expressionless next to their captives while the fifth busied himself at a counter littered with small containers and syringes. Wayne watched as he measured and mixed liquids from the containers, filled the syringes with the concoction and laid them in neat rows on a metal cart. After a dozen or so were made ready, he rolled the cart to the harnessed patients and returned to the counter. He then opened and hastily scribbled something in a tattered notebook. Wayne watched intently as the attendant blandly approached each patient and injected the hybridized serums into their restrained arms.

The patients winced as the alien fluid painfully merged with their already swollen tissue. After a series of five injections each, the patients were freed from their bondage and led away by their keepers to a point beyond Wayne's vision. The attendants returned a few minutes later with two new patients. One of them was Charley Orr.

Wayne's heart pumped furiously and he desperately wanted to halt the pain rapidly on its way through Charley's veins. But he quickly reasoned that it would be but a brief respite for Charley and probably the last thing he would ever do at the Gustaf Clinic. He needed more information. More evidence. More time.

Wayne turned away as drugs were being injected into Charley Orr and decided to try and locate the two victims who had been led away. He left the security of the thicket and walked quietly around the medical clinic in search of a way in. He found it, to his surprise, at the first door he tested. He entered a long hallway with doors scattered every ten feet or so. Only one was open and loud, raucous voices sprang from beyond.

Wayne's pulse quickened. What was his lie to be if someone came out of that door? Would he even have a chance to lie? His flight urge surfaced but he pushed forward. Ten tortuous steps later, he recognized the sound of a chair being moved back from a table. Someone was leaving the room of voices.

Wayne froze instantly and searched for an escape route. He saw none. He tried the door closest to him but it was locked. He tried two others, but they were also secured. He put his hand on the knob of a fourth door as a body half-emerged from the room down the hall. It opened.

Wayne leapt through the opening and closed the door quickly and quietly behind him. He slid down the door's frame to a cold, damp floor and sucked in a panicked breath. He heard his heart again and saw a few snippets of his short life flash by. Five minutes passed and he remained undiscovered. He rose silently in the darkness and listened to his still pounding heart. He abandoned his plan, grasped the flashlight with sweat-lacquered hands and pointed its unsteady beam of light around the chamber now encasing him.

The room was stacked with swollen mounds of paper and bulging file cabinets. Wayne approached the largest file cabinet and surveyed the labels attached on the outside of its drawers. Names were alphabetized on the cabinet; the top drawer, Abramowicz J., the bottom drawer, Mueller G. The filing system continued on adjacent cabinets until it ended with Wysocki J. at the bottom of the third cabinet. The names appeared to reflect an array of nationalities but none sounded Scandinavian. Wayne guessed that the individuals attached to the names made up the corps of research subjects for the Gustaf Clinic. And given what Wayne had just witnessed regarding Gustaf's brand of research, it would certainly benefit the clinic to recruit their subjects from faraway places.

Wayne quietly opened the top drawer of the large cabinet and plucked out the front file. It was an immense collection of paper that required two hands to excavate from its berth. The flashlight's beam located a place to sit, a small opening behind a stack of boxes in the corner of the room. Wayne crept quietly to the cubby hole, slid himself behind the cardboard barricade, and began reading the history of J. Abramowicz.

As with the medical records he'd lifted from Ward C, these files had thumb tabs for quick access to specific information. Wayne scanned the tabs, stopped at the one marked "medical history," and went to the very end of its text. Of no surprise, J. Abramowicz was listed as "deceased 1996."

Wayne's fingers tabbed further and stopped at the section labeled "treatments." He crouched down to a more comfortable position and began reading the history of medications that had traveled through J. Abramowicz's veins. He noted the dates associated with the treatments. The last recorded injections were two weeks ago, long after

Abramowicz's listed date of death. Apparently cross-checking data was not a strong point of Gustaf's record-keepers.

An hour into the files, voices interrupted Wayne's exploration. He put the file on his lap, turned off the flashlight and hoped the voices would disappear down the hallway. They didn't. The door opened and the light burst on. Wayne watched from a small opening in his hiding place as two men approached the row of file cabinets. They opened a cabinet drawer and searched for a file on someone they identified as Stayton Marks. From what Wayne could gather, Marks was one of the patients he'd seen through the window earlier.

"Marks is having a tough time digesting his evening meal," quipped one of the men.

"I'm surprised he's lasted this long," replied the other. "Hell, I'm amazed any of them last as long as they do. I've heard the early ones fared a lot worse."

"So I've heard. But that's not our problem."

"It will be if these guys start dying. Rumor has it the Big Doc gets serious money for our data and the dead provide no data. No data for Big Doc, no paychecks for us. Pretty simple equation."

"And this information comes from where?"

"I listen to the rumors and when they reappear often enough, I start believing them."

"How much money you think Big Doc's making?"

"Enough to keep himself in old cognac and young, busty women, from the looks of it."

"It'd damn sure be nice if he shared the wealth a bit more."

"We've got jobs, don't we? This place is a shithole, but it comes with a paycheck. You won't hear me complain."

"Still … ."

A scratching sound interrupted the conversation.

"What was that?" asked the man farthest from Wayne.

"Shhh!" commanded the other.

The pause in the conversation caught Wayne by surprise. He sucked in his breath, afraid his labored breathing would be heard. They waited an eternity. Wayne covered his face with his arms, tucked it into his chest and took short, rapid breaths that matched his heartbeat. Finally, the conversation continued.

"Must be one of those rats we're seeing all the time," one guard offered.

The other man maintained his vigilance for a few moments, then agreed with his colleague. "As if the human vermin aren't bad enough," he finally said.

"I'm not sure who the real vermin are," countered the other. "I don't think the Gustaf Clinic will be winning the Nobel Prize for ethics."

"You're climbing onto that ethical horse of yours again, Sam, and I really don't need another lecture. I'm here to do my job and get paid. That's all I'm interested in. Got it?"

"Sure," replied Sam without conviction. "Let's finish up and get the hell out of here. God, I hate this place."

The two men spent a few more minutes finishing their business and left. Wayne slumped against the wall and let out a huge sigh of relief. He sat quietly, regaining his composure and refocusing his task. He'd pushed his luck far enough for one evening and it was time to head home. All he had to do was get there. Struggling against unsteady legs, he got up and again scoped the room with his flashlight, searching for anything worthy of scrutiny. He discovered a folder that had apparently not yet been cataloged in the cabinets. It had the letters "USA" scribbled in pencil on the cover. He glanced at its contents and saw two files, one inscribed on a cover sheet with "C.L. DOD 7/8/02" and another, thicker file labeled "miscellaneous." He stuck the folder under his coat, stepped cautiously to the door and listened for human activity on the other side. He glanced back at the remaining stacks of folders and wondered what evidence he might be leaving behind. He kept his lament short and returned his attention to the door. He heard nothing, slowly cracked it open, and peered outside and down the hall. He saw no one and decided to chance it. Not too many options, he thought.

******

Wayne reached his apartment as the clock in his kitchen touched 3:00 a.m. Sleep was out of the question. He grabbed a cold soda from the refrigerator, flopped into a chair and opened the poached file. The documents inside were in several languages, but one cluster held together with a blue paperclip was in English. On the cover page in large, bold letters was written:

"United States Department of Education"
"Application for Federal Funds"

MONDAY, SEPTEMBER 26

one

Jon woke up to a throbbing head and blurred vision. Stan Iverson still slept, wrapped in the frayed wool blanket Jon had purchased a few months back at the local thrift store. Jon pushed himself up slowly, his body and brain seeking equilibrium. He worked his way upright, shuffled to the window and flipped up the shades. He stared at nothing in particular and considered the events of the last few days. The chaotic mosaic wasn't a pretty picture. Someone had killed his friends and they were trying kill him. His dream girl was in the hospital with a bullet hole in her shoulder. He'd lost his job and discovered that the people he'd trusted were most likely murderers. And now he had a swollen head on his shoulders and a snoring cop on his floor. If he'd had the time, he would've been depressed.

"Morning," Iverson suddenly said from the floor. He propped himself up on an unsteady elbow.

Jon looked at Iverson and offered a hung-over half-smile. "Morning, Sergeant," he replied and returned his gaze out the window.

Iverson crawled to his feet and walked to the kitchen in search of the makings for coffee. He was apparently more experienced at recovering from the sort of evening the two had shared. Having found what he was looking for, he primed the brew and returned to the living room.

"One cup of coffee and then it's time to get moving," Iverson stated bluntly. "We've got things to do today, not the least of which is keeping you alive."

Iverson's frankness jerked Jon out of his fog.

"I'm certainly in favor of the keeping me alive part. How do you propose doing that?"

"Sticking together would help, but that would cut our efficiency. We've got a lot of bases to cover."

"For instance?"

"The hospital, for one. We've got to get Sandra McKinney out of there. After what happened to your friends, I think she'll be safer with us."

Jon suspected Iverson's assessment was correct. The killers were still out there and actively hunting. They had tried to kill him and Sandra once and there was no reason to think they wouldn't try again.

Jon got up and threw on a less rumpled shirt despite Iverson's appraisal that he was "fine as is." They each sucked down a half-cup of coffee and headed out the door with Leslie Covington's precious papers in hand. They boarded the Sergeant's car and headed to the hospital. On the way they discussed the bases Iverson wanted to cover. He first wanted to track down his university contact to get any information she'd uncovered. After that, he absolutely had to check in at the station. He hadn't been there in a while and didn't need Captain Denny getting suspicious. He also wanted to pump Bill Firnett about the three murders. Denny had probably put an in-house gag order on these cases, but Firnett was prone to loose lips and Iverson was hoping for a lead.

They reached the hospital and decided Jon would go in alone. Jon's presence would be less risky than Iverson's even though he had left the hospital the day before without talking to the police. The only person Jon might have trouble with was the one who caught him at the elevator door, Sergeant Bill Firnett.

"Well, Mr. Farrell," he said pretentiously. "You're just who I've been looking for. Where the hell have you been?"

"What's it to you?" Jon asked defiantly.

"We have a lot to discuss, Mr. Farrell," Firnett huffed. "We can talk here and now or Officer Garrick over there can escort you downtown." Firnett nodded towards a hulking, sullen cop who Jon figured wouldn't be fun to know. "Either way, we're going to spend some time together. Your choice."

Jon wasn't in a position to win an argument with Firnett and agreed to a conversation. He, Firnett and the hulk moved down the hall and entered an unoccupied room. Stan Iverson, following Jon and a hunch, watched them as they walked toward what the Sergeant figured would be a lengthy inquisition. With Firnett occupied, Iverson approached Sandra McKinney's room. The guard posted at her door recognized the Sergeant and they spoke briefly before Iverson slipped into the room and the guard regained his vigilant posture. Sandra was awake.

"What are you doing here?" Sandra demanded.

"Hold the questions, please, Ms. McKinney. We'll have plenty of time to talk once we get you out of here."

"We?"

"Mr. Farrell and yours truly."

"Jon? He's here? Is he okay?"

"He's fine, Ms. McKinney," Iverson replied hastily. "He's presently keeping your keeper busy while I escort you to finer accommodations."

"What the hell does that mean?"

"It means, my dear lady, that if we don't hurry our asses out of here, I'll be in very deep shit and you'll be staring at that beautiful view for at least another week."

Sandra glanced out the window at smoking steam vents and soot-laden tarpaper. "I'm with you," she submitted and rolled out of bed.

"Then let's get moving," Iverson instructed with a narrow grin reflecting his anticipated coup over Firnett.

Sandra found her clothes and slipped them onto her impressive form while Iverson politely turned away. She uttered subdued moans as she stretched the newly sewn tissue in her shoulder. Iverson opened the door, received an affirmative nod from the guard and motioned for Sandra to follow. They scurried down the hall and took the elevator to the lobby. From there they walked briskly out of the hospital and hopped into Iverson's car. At that point, Sandra figured it was time for some answers.

"Okay, Sergeant," she demanded. "Where the hell's Jon?"

Iverson admired the swagger. "He's fine, Ms. McKinney," he assured and provided a convincing image of Jon Farrell holding his own against Bill Firnett. He promised her Jon would be joining them soon. She was satisfied … briefly.

"So what's happened while I've been in the hospital?"

"It's not been pretty, Ms. McKinney," he said tentatively. "I'm not sure you want to know."

"Sergeant," Sandra asserted, "I've been stalked, shot and damn near drowned in the last forty-eight hours. My best friend's been murdered. Don't you think I might like to know what the hell's going on? Stop treating me like a goddamned child and start telling me the truth."

"Ms. McKinney, I…"

"Sergeant," Sandra interrupted. "Give me some answers or I'll find someone who will."

"And that would be...?" Iverson queried calmly.

"Jon Farrell, for one," Sandra said confidently.

"I believe he's currently occupied, Ms. McKinney."

"Then take me to Neil Danielski's. At least he'll treat me like an adult."

Iverson paused, deciding how to soften the coming blow. "You can't talk to Neil Danielski," he finally said.

"Really? And why is that, Sergeant?" Sandra demanded. "Have you put him in jail?"

"No, Ms. McKinney, but I truly wish I had." Iverson's tone was heavy and Sandra felt the weight. It was her turn to take a moment. Iverson had been right. Maybe she didn't want to know.

"What's going on, Sergeant," she asked softly.

Iverson's voice filled with gravelly emotion. "I'm sorry to be the one to tell you this, Ms. McKinney, but both Neil Danielski and Deb Sutter were murdered yesterday."

The words cut like a knife. Sandra slumped into shock. She didn't speak. Her tears flowed slowly at first, then unabated. Iverson started the car, pulled away from the hospital and headed to the university.

******

The parking lot was crowded but Iverson spotted an open slot and angled into it. Sandra stared blankly out the window with puffy eyes. The Sergeant sat next to her and offered silent companionship. Sandra eventually found the strength to speak.

"Who's doing this, Sergeant?"

"I don't know yet, Ms. McKinney."

"Do you know why?"

"I'm working on that."

"Then there's a good chance they're not done killing?"

"I'm afraid you might be right."

"So what do we do?" she implored.

"That depends," Iverson replied.

"On what?"

"In part, on you, Ms. McKinney. I'm a cop. I get paid to risk my life. You might be able to help solve these murders but you could also get killed in the process. You almost did already."

Sandra digested Iverson's words carefully. He was telling her that her ordeal wasn't yet over, something she didn't want to hear. But if her life was still in danger, she had to do something.

"Looks like I could end up dead no matter what. Tell me what I need to do to change that ending, Sergeant?"

"I don't have that totally figured out yet but I think there's a better chance of you getting older if we work together."

"What's Jon think?"

"Jon Farrell is very fond of you. I think he wants to grow old with you."

Sandra smiled to herself, though unsure of the full intent of Iverson's assessment.

"So he's signed on with you?"

"Seems he is," Iverson replied. "Shall we make it a threesome, Ms. McKinney?"

Sandra made her decision quickly and the unofficial investigation team signed on a new member. Iverson got her fully up to speed in the next few minutes and explained his stop at the university. He set off to find Kate Howser with Sandra in tow. He wasn't about to leave her alone while hired predators still pursued her.

Iverson stepped into Kate's office and presented the most charming smile he could muster. He hadn't yet kept his part of their bargain and was sure that Kate had already checked in with her sister to inquire if he had.

"Hi, Kate," he began sheepishly, an unusual role for him and one that he vigorously detested. "I was wondering if you had the information we agreed on the other day."

"I do indeed," was the reply. "But we do need to discuss the definition of agreement."

"I'm sorry about that, Kate," Iverson apologized. He looked at Kate and winced at her resemblance to his ex-wife. "I've been real busy. Shit, I haven't been home to call anyone, much less Beth."

Kate looked at the beautiful, young girl at Iverson's side and looked her ex-brother-in-law directly in the eyes. "Yup, I can see you've been busy?" she stated with playful sarcasm.

"Shit, Kate," defended Iverson, "she's involved in the case."

"Sure, Stan." teased Kate Howser.

"It's not what you're thinking, Kate," he claimed, "and you know I can't talk about an active investigation."

Kate would not let up. She was enjoying herself too much.

"And how active has this one been, Stan?"

Iverson rolled his eyes and motioned for Kate to join him in a private discussion away from Sandra. They walked to a spot down the hallway and spoke quietly.

"Listen, Kate," said Iverson, "I know what you're thinking and there's no truth to it. This woman has had three friends killed in the last three days. She's been shot herself. The hole in her shoulder will attest to that. Damn it, Kate, I just got her out of the hospital an hour ago. Give me a break, will you?"

Kate rolled her eyes and smiled playfully. She knew Iverson was telling the truth … he always did, sometimes to his detriment.

"Honest, Kate," Iverson continued. "The only thing I share with that girl is a desire to find out who killed her friends. The information I asked you for might help."

"What about Beth?" Kate asked flatly.

"I promise I'll call her as soon as I get the time."

"Are you sure, Stan? She really does miss you, you know."

Iverson shot Kate a look of surprise but said nothing.

"Stan," Kate persisted. "She knows she made a mistake."

"The information, Kate. Please?"

"Did you hear what I said, Stan?"

"Yeah, I did, Kate," Iverson answered, "but I'm not sure what it meant."

Kate Howser finally relented and walked back to her office. A grateful Iverson followed her. She dug out two large manila envelopes from a locked desk drawer and handed them to Iverson. She insisted that he forget where he'd gotten them, turned to Sandra McKinney and gave her a warm hug. "You can trust him, honey," she whispered. "He's a good cop and a fine man."

two

Wayne awoke to a loud banging on his door. He jerked upright, unsure if the intrusion was real or the remnants of a dream. The thumping was repeated and Wayne stumbled out of bed, walked to the door and opened it. He was confronted by one of Gustaf's security guards.

"Wayne Burgess?" the guard inquired in halting English.

"Yes," replied Wayne hesitantly.

"Dr. Croft wants to see you. I drive you there."

Wayne was half listening, half thinking.

"Who?" he asked, trying to buy time.

"Dr. Croft, the boss at Gustaf Clinic."

"May I ask why?"

"Not my business," the guard replied pithily. "I'm told to find you and drive you."

Wayne looked at the guard. His ample girth stretched the purple sweater protruding from under his coat. His grim, unshaven face was bulbous and stretched tight from the cold. This man would offer little information.

"What time is it?"

"Nine-o'clock," the guard replied abruptly.

"It'll take me a few minutes to get ready. I suppose you've been told to wait?"

"I wait in car," the guard answered and nodded toward a black patrol car parked on the street.

Wayne lingered in the doorway and considered his options. There weren't any.

"Give me thirty minutes," Wayne said. The guard didn't respond but turned and walked toward his vehicle.

Wayne closed the door and poked an opening between the window blinds. He watched the guard settle into the driver's seat beside a mounted shotgun. Alarm bells began to sound inside Wayne's head. Had he been seen at the clinic last night? Did someone notice that records were missing? What did Gustaf's boss want? He considered bolting out the back door but where would he go? He had no friends in Kirkenes and the American Embassy was in Oslo, eight hundred problematic miles to the south. He had to fully play this hand.

Wayne took a long, hot shower, imagined questions Croft might ask and practiced answers he might offer. As he dressed, he noticed that his black spook outfit still hung on the kitchen chair and the stolen files remained scattered on his bed. He obviously wasn't a seasoned spy. He gathered the files and searched for a place to cache them in case the surly guard returned while he was being interrogated by Croft. He found no suitable hiding place and hurriedly stuffed the incriminating papers back into his daypack, slung it over his shoulder and joined the brooding chauffeur in the waiting black sedan.

The ride to the clinic was a silent one interrupted only by an occasional glare from the guard. Once through Gustaf's gates, the guard drove to a building whose weather-warped sign announced it as the "Administration Building." Wayne was escorted into a waiting room where the guard gestured silently to a row of blue vinyl chairs. Wayne took the cue, walked over to the chairs and nervously sat down. A buxom, oddly coiffed secretary occupied a desk at the other end of the room. She paid scant attention to the new arrival, focusing instead on the small computer screen directly in front of her. She tapped slowly on her keyboard while chewing gum with unbridled vigor.

Croft's entrance was late, a strategy, Wayne thought, designed to heighten his anxiety. Unfortunately for Wayne, it was working. His apprehension grew and the clammy feeling on his hands migrated to his armpits. Finally, at eleven-o'clock, the door labeled "Director" opened and a short, squat man stood in the doorway. His eyes were small and set deep into the frame of his skull. His color was pallid. His tonsured head was the perfect apex for his acorn-shaped frame. Wayne was immediately uncomfortable with the man. The fabricated smile on Croft's face did not extinguish the feeling.

"Come in, Mr. Burgess."

Wayne rose from his chair and followed the director into his office. It was a room of large dimensions and opulent furnishings. It was the antithesis of all else at the Gustaf Clinic.

"Can I get you some coffee?" he asked with counterfeit politeness.

Wayne returned the etiquette. "Thank you. That'd be great."

Croft picked up his phone and spoke to someone he called Birne about getting coffee. Wayne assumed Birne was the magic-fingered typist outside the door.

After replacing the phone in its cradle, Croft returned his attention to Wayne.

"Did the officer get you out of bed this morning? I understand it's your scheduled day off and I apologize for any inconvenience."

"No problem," managed Wayne. "I needed to get up anyway."

Birne brought in the coffee. Out from behind her desk, she proudly displayed her physical attributes. A short skirt tightly hugged her hips and revealed long, shapely legs. She bent slightly as she placed the tray of coffee and condiments on Croft's desk and her plunging neckline bared much of her substantial bosom. Her perfume was pungent. She was a multi-sensory distraction and fully aware of it. Wayne recalled the conversation he'd overheard the previous night regarding the "Big Doc's" alleged fondness for "busty women and old cognac." Birne fit half of the appraisal. She left, and Wayne's reality returned.

"I suppose you're wondering why I wanted to see you, Wayne. You don't mind if I call you Wayne, do you?"

Wayne poured himself some coffee and mixed in three spoons of sugar and a swirl of cream. He looked intently at Croft. He didn't look particularly Norwegian and his English was perfect—not a hint of an accent. The few real Norwegians he'd encountered spoke English but they did so haltingly and with a Nordic inflection. Not Croft. He wondered where he was from.

"No, I don't mind, and yes, I am curious as to why I'm here."

"You're the first student we've had here at the clinic in a long time and I wanted to both welcome you personally and make sure you understood how things work around here. In case you didn't know, I actually fought your assignment here. I don't see the value in short-term help. But as long you're here, we may as well get to know each other."

Wayne wondered who had ruled against Croft and if he was digging for a reason to overturn that ruling. But Croft hadn't made any accusations … yet, and he was feeling a little more comfortable. He played along.

"I'd like to state first off that I really appreciate the chance to complete my thesis here at Gustaf's. It's a unique opportunity to conduct research."

"And exactly what type of research do you wish to conduct..., Wayne?"

"My work's focus is a comparative analysis of contemporary and traditional treatments of the mentally ill."

Croft sat regally in his overstuffed, black leather chair. He appeared calm but Wayne sensed a growing tension in the room.

"And where do you think my clinic fits in that analysis?"

"I'm not sure yet, Dr. Croft. I pretty much just got here. But your clinic is the perfect place for my thesis work and I'm hoping that in six months I'll be able to answer that question."

"You're being too kind, Wayne," Croft interrupted. "I think you already know that this clinic is more warehouse than treatment facility. Gustaf's, in fact, is "clinic non grata" in the international mental health community."

"No shit," Wayne wanted to say, but held his tongue. He also wondered why Croft was dissing his own clinic.

"Can I be candid with you, Wayne?"

"Sure," Wayne answered tentatively. He wasn't sure what Croft's candor involved, but he was about to find out.

Croft got up from his chair and walked casually over to an antique oak filing cabinet. From its interior he retrieved a bottle of amber liquid and emptied some of it into his cup of coffee. He didn't offer to share.

"The Gustaf Clinic is basically a holding tank for outcasts. Our patients have been rejected by their families, their communities and, in some cases, their countries. They've been in institutions for the majority of their lives and they know no other existence." Croft's voice got louder … his eyes larger. "You must agree that it's unconscionable to force people like this to live in neighborhoods like they're doing in the United States? They don't belong there."

Wayne took a sip of coffee and thought about candor.

"I understand what you're saying, Dr. Croft, but I'm not sure I agree with you. But I don't totally agree with what's happening back in my country either." Wayne was being honest. He had serious misgivings about some of the practices currently in vogue back in the States. "I think the policy makers typically have very little real contact with those they set policy for and that always causes a disconnect. Like you stated, the mentally ill are social outcasts. Historically, they have been banished to places like the Gustaf Clinic where they too often have their rights trampled on. I think that should change, Dr. Croft. I believe they have a right to be treated with dignity … just like you and I do."

Croft looked at Wayne scornfully. "An altruistic point of view, Mr. Burgess. And how typically American."

"I'm not exactly sure what typically American is, Doctor, but if advocating for human rights is an American trait, then I guess I'm typical. I believe…"

"Let me come to the point," interrupted Croft harshly. "I've already told you you're here against my wishes. The Norwegian government needs American aid and apparently student exchange programs buy political good will. I have no choice but to accept your presence here, but I don't have to tolerate your arrogance."

Croft rose from his chair and pointed a plump finger at Wayne. "Be aware, Mr. Burgess, that we have certain ways of doing things around here and you will not change that. While you're here you will keep your opinions to yourself and you will do as you are told, no more, no less."

Croft, breathing heavily, glared at Wayne before returning to the chair behind his desk. Wayne was surprised that he didn't feel intimidated. Instead, he was angry. He had done nothing but defend the rights of people like Charley Orr and he wasn't going to back down from his belief in human dignity. There was no reason for Croft to react the way he did unless he was hiding something.

"Have I done something wrong, Dr. Croft?" Wayne baited.

Croft's deep-set eyes flashed. "I've been told you've been nosing around, trying to get information that you have no right to have. You will not be allowed to do that, Mr. Burgess. You're damn lucky to be here and you'll be even luckier to be here in six months. If it were up to me, you'd be on a fucking plane home today."

"Excuse me," Wayne started. "I..."

"There are no excuses, Mr. Burgess. You're to conduct your goddamned research strictly through empirical means and nothing more. Any attempt to access the records of my patients will result not only in your immediate dismissal from this clinic but criminal charges as well."

Croft sat back in his self-appointed throne, crossed his arms and refocused his glare. Wayne silently weighed his options. He glanced at the daypack stuffed with patient records at his feet and decided an honorable retreat was in his best interest. A retreat, he told himself, but not a surrender.

"I understand, Dr. Croft, and I'll honor the rules and regulations of your clinic. I certainly wouldn't wish to do anything to hurt the patients here. Is there anything else?"

Croft raised the bushes above his eyes. "No, Mr. Burgess," he replied tersely. "Unless you stick your nose where it doesn't belong."

"I don't presume that I will, Doctor."

"Then we're done here, Mr. Burgess."

"Far from it," Wayne thought.

three

The door to the conference room opened and three casually dressed men entered and closed the door behind them. They placed bulging briefcases on a long wooden table and sat down with ample room between them. Steven Gant spoke first.

"We haven't entirely solved our problem, gentlemen."

"Where do we stand, Steve?" asked Allan Trenholm.

"There's a chance copies of the grant docs are still floating around somewhere."

"Do we know who has them?" queried Terrance Walk.

"Pat thinks Farrell and the cop either have copies or know where they are."

"Speaking of Farrell …," began Trenholm.

"I fired him yesterday," interrupted Gant, anticipating Trenholm's inquiry. "It's what we decided to do, isn't it?"

Walk ran his hands through his boyish locks and leaned back in his chair. "Yes, it is. But I can't help wondering what signal that sent to the cop."

"It was our only option, Terrance," responded Trenholm with typical conviction. "We couldn't afford to have him around that office anymore. He'd become a meddler and we couldn't risk him finding a connection to Kirkenes."

"Futures is clean, gentlemen," reassured Gant. "I've been through that office twice now and I've removed anything that might remotely have tied us to the clinic. We're safe there."

"And the killings?" inquired Trenholm. "Are we protected there?"

"We won't be tied to any murders," Gant assured. "That's in Pat's hands and he'll take care of it."

Walk got up and paced the floor of the spacious room. He planted his hands in the pockets of his pleated pants and asked another question.

"What I want to know is how vulnerable we are."

"We're vulnerable until we eliminate those documents," responded Gant.

"No more killings, though, right?" Walk asked.

"Don't go getting soft, Terrance," chastised Gant. "We did what we had to do and what's done is done. We all agreed it was for the greater good. The Gustaf research will eventually provide us with our cure for autism and the world will have little concern for how we achieved it. Besides, nobody can tie us to any murders. We've been too smart for that. If we stick together now, we'll have fame and fortune later."

"I agree with Steve," responded Trenholm stoically. "We have to move forward. I'm not going to worry about Farrell and his pal...whatever his name is. They can't hurt us."

Gant got up and stood next to Walk. He towered over the diminutive professor and looked down at him.

"Allan is right," he stated confidently. "Moving forward is the key. Pat has things under control right now but he needs to know what direction we want to take. What's it going to be?"

"What are the options?" asked Walk.

"I think we have to assume Farrell and his friend have copies of the grant applications. Option number one is to presume they're ignorant and won't be able to connect the dots."

"Not likely," interrupted Trenholm. "Farrell I wouldn't worry about. What do we know about this cop?

"Pat tells me he's old school," answered Gant. "Irascible and hard-headed. That appraisal makes me agree the first option isn't a good one."

"And the other options?" prompted Walk.

"I think there's only one other legitimate option," replied Gant. "Continue on the present course."

"At what cost, Steve?" asked Walk, obviously not comfortable with the price thus far.

"At any cost!" answered Trenholm without hesitation.

Walk and Gant returned to their chairs, Walk balancing on the very edge of his. He fidgeted with a gold-plated pen and stared at the grain in the table. "I guess we're in this too deep to back out," he offered with resignation.

"You're right, we are," Gant fired back. "And don't forget, Terrance, your reputation depends on Norway's statistical contributions … like it or not."

"Our reputations," corrected Walk.

"True enough," countered Gant. "And all of our reputations have an opportunity to grow exponentially if we don't get rattled. We just need more time. Farrell has the potential to fuck everything up and I'm not about to let him or anyone else do that. If that means buying his silence, so be it."

"We really don't have a choice," added Trenholm. "I vote we tell Pat to continue … at any cost."

"And the money?" asked Walk.

"There's plenty of grant money left," answered Trenholm.

"Terrance?" pressed Gant. "Do you agree?"

"As Allan stated," Walk replied weakly, "we have no choice."

"Then it's settled," said Gant getting up to leave. "I'm meeting with Pat in the next hour and I'll tell him to move forward."

Steven Gant hurriedly left the conference room and set out for his next meeting. Trenholm and Walk remained seated at the long table.

"Have you heard from Norway, Allan?"

"I got a letter from Croft last week. He said the research is going slower than normal and the trickle of data in the past six months would seem to verify that. Either Croft has lost his edge, or maybe he just wants a bigger payoff. Regardless, my last visit there left me unimpressed and thinking we should move our research elsewhere, or at the very least, get rid of Croft. I think he's become a liability."

"What's he working with now?"

"The last report was from July. Croft was trying some combinations within the Prozac family. He'd lost a few patients."

"A few? How many is a few?"

"Does it matter?"

Walk stared at the floor. He wasn't sure what mattered anymore. He'd let himself be talked into the Norway idea by Gant and Trenholm. They'd assured him that the risks were low, the rewards high, and that their legacies would be secured. His ego eventually trumped his ethics and he decided the end would justify the means. No one ever discussed killing people. He hadn't recognized the scope of destruction until it was too late.

"I guess it matters if we're put at risk," Walk specified.

"We all knew there'd be some risk, Terrance. But we all agreed it was minimal and worth it to achieve what we want."

"Do you think Steve knows what he's doing with this guy, Pat?"

"Steve's not stupid, Terrance. He has just as much to lose as we do. The fact is, we need some unpleasant work done and he's willing to do the setup on it. I don't know about you, but I'm more than willing to let him do it."

Walk stood up to leave and slowly ambled toward the door. He stopped with his hand on the doorknob and turned to say something to Trenholm. The words didn't materialize so he turned again, walked out the door and headed down one of the many hallowed halls of the university.

four

Jon Farrell was peppered with questions from Sergeant Bill Firnett for two arduous hours. He did his best to avoid giving answers that would connect himself or Iverson to recent events. The most difficult questions had been focused on the deaths of Neil Danielski and Deb Sutter. Jon had not known the details until Firnett illustrated them in painful Technicolor. He held back his emotions, but not without great effort. Firnett eventually realized his efforts were wasted and grudgingly ended the interrogation.

Jon lingered briefly with hopes of checking on Sandra McKinney but left quickly when he heard Firnett engaged in a heated discussion outside her room. He instinctively knew what Iverson had done. He was beginning to understand Iverson, a thought he considered both amusing and worthy of concern. He hopped a bus outside the hospital's main entrance that ultimately dropped him a block away from his house. His walk home was interrupted when Iverson's unmarked police car pulled up to the curb next to him. Sandra leaped from car and embraced him warmly.

"Jon! I'm so happy to see you," she exclaimed.

He returned the hug with equal vigor.

"I don't mean to intrude," interrupted Iverson, "but I'd like to get the hell out of this neighborhood."

Jon and Sandra hopped into the back seat of the Sergeant's car. Iverson pulled a quick U-turn and sped off.

"You think someone's watching my house?" asked Jon.

"Maybe … maybe not. But I don't think we should be taking any chances."

"Great," Jon responded. "Now I can't even go home."

"Sorry about that," Iverson offered. "Things could be worse, you know."

"Yeah, Sarge, I do know." Jon paused and thought of Neil. "Anything good happen while I was bonding with Sergeant Firnett?"

"I've updated Ms. McKinney and collected some information on the PhDs."

"Jon," asked Sandra softly, "is it really true about Neil and Deb?"

Jon looked into her pained eyes and gave her the answer she didn't want. "It is, Sandra. I really wish this were all a bad dream, but it isn't. I'm sure Sarge has also told you that the killers are still out there … that this isn't over."

"He didn't have to tell me. I was with you at the river, remember?"

"It would be tough to forget, even if I wanted to."

"Enough reminiscing, folks," intruded Iverson. "I have to swing by the station for appearance purposes so I'm going to drop you folks at a safe place for a while." He crisscrossed his way through the city until he felt certain they weren't followed, then steered out of town. He drove down tree-lined roads and basalt-coated canyons before stopping at an isolated and weathered building. A buzzing neon sign proclaimed they'd arrived at The Old Country Inn. Sandra's frown was audible.

"Hope you guys don't mind a bit of the rustic," Iverson quipped. "The caretaker here owes me a few favors. He lives out back. Just tell him I sent you and he'll understand."

Jon and Sandra exited the car and inspected the surroundings. Rustic was an understatement, but Jon wasn't about to be fussy.

"Looks fine to me, Sarge," he appraised.

Sandra shot Jon a disapproving look. She wanted further inspection, but the Sergeant quickly accepted Jon's answer as joint approval. Iverson promised he'd return in a couple of hours and would stop off for some food on his way back. Food would be nice, Jon thought. He hadn't eaten in a long time.

"Still have the precious papers, Jon?" asked Iverson.

Jon tapped the briefcase slung over his shoulder, indicating an affirmative answer. Iverson lit a cigarette, checked the road for traffic and left.

The two visitors walked around the decaying front of the old roadhouse and located the structure in which Iverson's friend presumably lived. It was a windowless, box-formed shack with an old stovepipe jutting through a listing roof. The pipe spewed grayish-brown smoke carried lazily upward by the whims of an unsteady breeze. The yard was cluttered with old, rusty car parts and scattered bundles of twined newspapers.

"I do take you to the finest places," joked Jon.

Sandra presented a smile that migrated to laughter.

"What's so funny?" Jon asked.

"You are," she replied, and embraced him warmly. Her affection was welcome relief to a day filled with tension.

"Thank you," Jon offered.

Sandra broke the embrace and stared into Jon's eyes. "You don't need to thank me, Jon Farrell. You saved my life, if I recall. I owe you more than a hug."

Jon's face flushed. "I guess I'm not used to being hugged."

"Then you've been deprived."

"I guess there haven't been whole lot of opportunities."

"Maybe we should change that."

Jon looked at Sandra warmly. He didn't feel so alone right now.

"Shall we see if anybody's home?" he asked.

Sandra nodded approval and Jon knocked on the shack's loosely hinged door. They were greeted by a man with a weathered face and tousled gray hair. Craggy crow's feet crept from his eyes and untended stubble framed a semi-toothed mouth. He was an older man, but outwardly fit with a barrel chest and muscular arms. Thirty feet of split firewood stacked chaotically next to the weather worn building testified partially to the method behind his fitness. He drew back from the doorway and inspected his visitors with intense blue eyes and a guarded posture. Jon figured he didn't get too many visitors.

"Well, what do you want?" he demanded gruffly.

"We were, ah ... just dropped off here by Sergeant Iverson," Jon stammered. "He said you would put us up for a while."

"Iverson? Where is the old fart?" asked the man, craning his neck to see around Jon.

"He had business to take care of," Sandra answered. "He'll be back later."

"Business, my ass," the old man rasped. "*Business* is Iverson code for trouble and I'm bettin' you two are runnin' from somethin'. Go ahead, tell me I'm wrong."

Jon and Sandra looked at each other and then back at the old man.

"No," Sandra confirmed. "You aren't wrong. We'll be honest with you. Somebody seems intent on killing us and the Sergeant is trying to figure out who that somebody is before they succeed. Three people have already been murdered and..."

"Enough!" the caretaker interrupted. "The less I know the better. Follow me."

They were led on a two-minute walk down a narrow, overgrown trail to a small cabin hidden from the road. The caretaker extracted a key from the front pocket of his overalls, turned the key in the lock and opened the front door. He gave the key to Jon, mumbled something about

Iverson and walked back toward his shack. The guests stepped inside their new accommodations and surveyed its offerings. It wasn't what they'd expected. Hand-hewn beams stretched across a lofted ceiling and connected wine-colored walls. A Spanish tiled floor was bedecked with two overstuffed chairs facing a cavernous fireplace where a portion of the caretaker's woodpile provided the next fire's fixings. Slivers of light, filtering through tall trees and a paned bay window, gave the small room a warm glow.

"Wow," proclaimed Sandra.

"The Sarge's little secret?" Jon wondered out loud.

"Not any more," Sandra said. "It's really beautiful. Can we have a fire?"

"Sarge said to be comfortable," Jon assured.

"He absolutely did," agreed Sandra quickly. "If you'll get the fire going, I'll check out the rest of this place."

Jon beamed his approval of Sandra's idea and searched for matches around the ample hearth. He found them in a hammered copper canister, set the kindling ablaze and stared blankly at the crackling flames. The past few days had been a time of deep trauma but also a time of personal growth. Sandra McKinney was complicit in his metamorphosis ... her poise and confidence had proven contagious. But the choice of fight over flight had ultimately been his and he was genuinely proud of himself. It had been a while.

Jon's fire soon radiated its warmth about the old cabin. Sandra returned from her exploratory venture and snuggled up next to the fire. She gently stroked the hair on the back of Jon's head and stared into his weary eyes.

"I need a hug, Mr. Farrell," she said softly.

Jon embraced Sandra eagerly and completely and they allowed their passion to ease their pain.

five

Stan Iverson liked being a cop and loved working the streets. The station, however, had become his least favorite place. For most of his career, his role was well defined: Catch the bad guys. But things had changed and Iverson felt political correctness now governed departmental decisions and shackled his ability to do his job. He'd fought the changes that he believed protected predators and put honest people at risk but he won few battles, always lost the war and inevitably gave up the cause. His thoughts of an early retirement were quickly discarded after a brief but serious conversation with himself. He wasn't ready for daily doses of Sports Center and CNN. He ultimately chose to focus his energy solely on those things he could influence … his cases. As long as he produced results, he was fine, and he usually produced results. He was, however, growing weary of the game.

He walked in, strode directly to his cluttered desk and began sorting through messages that had piled up in his absence. He caught the sound of fast approaching footsteps.

"Iverson, I want to talk to you!" shouted a red-faced Bill Firnett.

"Sure, Mr. Bill," Iverson replied in low, contrasting decibels. "What can I do for you?"

"You can stop fucking up my case, that's what you can do," Firnett huffed. "That little prank you pulled at the hospital earlier today ought to be enough to get you suspended after Denny gets wind of it."

"What little prank would that be, Mr. Bill?" asked Iverson, innocently.

"You know exactly what I'm talking about, Iverson. And don't tell me you don't. You'll only find yourself in deeper shit if you deny it."

Iverson had sensed the inevitability of this scene when he'd laid the foundation for Sandra McKinney's exit from the hospital.

"Listen, Bill," he said with theatrical sincerity, "can we have this discussion somewhere else? How about a cup of coffee down at the cafeteria? Hell, I'll even throw in a doughnut and we can munch and chat, man to man." Iverson extended open palms.

"Fuck you, Iverson! I have no intention of going anywhere with you but to Captain Denny's office. We'll let him decide your fate." Firnett's arms were folded in righteous certainty.

"Fine, Mr. Bill," replied Iverson. "Let me get a few things together so we can have a nice chat with the Captain." He swung his chair around and opened a drawer.

Firnett had turned to leave, but Iverson's tone stopped him. He approached Iverson again.

"Is that supposed to mean something?"

"I still think coffee would be nice, Bill."

"You got something to say, say it here and now."

"I really don't think you want me to do that."

"Fuck you, Iverson! What the hell are you talking about?"

Iverson gestured toward the door. "Coffee?"

Firnett's face was bright red, the veins on his face bulging and pulsating.

"This had better be good, Iverson."

The cafeteria didn't provide complete privacy but it was significantly less crowded than the squad room. Iverson chose a table against the back wall and they sat down on opposing sides. Firnett took the offensive.

"All right, Iverson, what're you up to?"

"I just want you to be totally aware of what you're getting into, Bill. It's the least I can do for a fellow officer. I'd expect the same from you."

"I'm not the one in trouble here," Firnett asserted. "I didn't ignore orders." He got up and moved away from the table.

"Are Peaches and Veronica part of your ongoing investigation?" asked Iverson just loud enough for Firnett to hear. Peaches and Veronica were two of Ashton's better known strippers who moonlighted by selling more intimate encounters than those offered at the club. Both hookers were long-time street sources for Iverson and had kept him apprised of Firnett's sexual escapades in case he ever needed to leverage an angle. That time had arrived.

Firnett stopped in his tracks. He turned and walked slowly back to the table and took a seat next to Iverson.

"Should they be?" he asked timidly.

"I would think so," answered Iverson with a smile. "I happen to know that you've spent considerable time with them over the past six months. Now, I'm not one to pry into a man's personal life, but since you're hell bent on updating the Captain on my activities, I'm thinking it's only fair that I reciprocate by sharing what I know about yours. I'd be willing to bet he'd find your habit of spending on-duty time in the company of prostitutes pretty interesting. I'm sure he'd have a few questions, at least. And if your wife were to somehow find out..., well, I'd truly hate for that to happen to a solid family man such as yourself."

"You're bluffing, Iverson," Firnett said boldly. "You can't prove any of this!"

"Okay, Bill. Whatever you say."

"You don't know shit, Iverson. And if you did, you'd have played those cards before. Why wait till now?"

"I know when to hold 'em, Bill."

"I still think you're bluffing," Firnett stated with shaky confidence.

"Okay. Let's go see Denny," Iverson replied.

Firnett slumped back in his chair and it was over. He had caved quickly and easily with minimal effort and a little strategically applied pressure. Iverson never really doubted that he would. Firnett left without protest; beaten, angry and resigned to his defeat. Iverson loathed him. Firnett was a bad cop and a worse man.

Iverson returned to the squad room and discovered Firnett had retreated fully out of the station. He seized the opportunity to rifle his desk for any information that might help his furtive investigation. He found a folder marked "Covington," Xeroxed its contents, took the newly copied material and the folder from Kate Howser and set out for a quiet place to study.

six

Wayne was chaperoned back to his apartment by the same, sullen chauffeur who had woken him a few hours earlier. The wordless ride left him alone with his thoughts about his confrontation with Dr. Croft. He figured Croft didn't yet know about his clandestine trip to the medical clinic, but the director's tone certainly indicated that he suspected something. He entered his apartment and deposited his daypack and its valuable contents on the chair. The old afghan, usually draped over it to cover the worn spots, was folded and placed on the chair's back. Wayne had never folded the afghan. He cautiously examined the rest of the apartment and found other subtle evidence of an uninvited guest. A few books in his cinder block bookcase were stacked askew. The shirts in his closet were on the side where his pants normally hung and his old, scuffed suitcase lay flat rather than on its side. Wayne glanced at his daypack and its valued contents, and recalled the decision to take it with him to Croft's office instead of attempting to hide it in his apartment. Croft hadn't been the only one with suspicions.

Wayne slouched into his chair and measured his situation. His feeling of isolation had been magnified by the loss of privacy and the threat to his well-being. He recalled the conversation overheard the night before while hiding behind the cardboard wall. Something about an ethical horse and a guy named Sam. He'd like to talk to Sam.

Wayne brewed a fresh pot of coffee and made some creative phone calls to Gustaf's personnel department. A few hours later he had the address of Sam Henke. He knocked on his door at two-o'clock on a cloudy, brisk Norwegian afternoon.

"Sam Henke?" asked Wayne.

A rumpled and sleepy-eyed man replied, "Yes. What do you want?"

"I'd like some of your time, Mr. Henke, regarding a matter of importance to me and quite possibly to you as well."

"And what might that be, Mr. ...?"

"Burgess. My name is Wayne Burgess, Mr. Henke. I work at the Gustaf Clinic, same as you. It's about our mutual employer that I wish to speak to you."

Sam Henke's eyes widened and the sleepiness evaporated. "I'm not sure I want to talk to anyone about anything, let alone my employer."

"If you'd just give me a few moments of your time, Mr. Henke, I'm sure you'd consider it worth your while."

Henke looked around and behind his visitor until he seemed satisfied that Wayne had come alone. "I suppose," he relented, "but only for a few minutes. I'd like to get a few more hours of sleep before I go back to work."

Wayne entered the house and followed Henke into a small, cramped living area. It was obvious that Sam Henke, like Wayne, was not married. The house offered testimony to the law of entropy. Shed clothing mounds and yellowed newspaper stacks created webbed pathways between rooms. A cockeyed bookshelf clutched dust-covered novels, assorted videotapes and empty beer cans. Dishes holding the encrusted remains of more than a few meals were scattered about the living room. Wayne, accustomed to his own domestic chaos, found the home inviting. Henke pointed to a chair and Wayne lowered himself into it. Sam returned to the couch where he'd been sleeping.

"So, Mr.... Burgess, what is it?"

"Yes. Wayne Burgess. And if I may, Mr. Henke, I'd first like to explain my connection to Gustaf's."

"You can start wherever you want, Mr. Burgess. I'll let you know when you're finished."

"Fine, Mr. Henke. Let me begin by stating that I'm not actually an employee of the clinic. I'm an American student working on a Masters' with a focus on research. I'd heard about the Gustaf Clinic from a professor back home and he helped me get a six month position at the clinic to finish my thesis."

"Okay, so you're not an employee," said Henke impatiently. "What do you want with me?"

"As you have made clear, Mr. Henke, time is short, so I'll be blunt. I want your help."

"Help with what?" demanded Henke.

Wayne got up and paced around the clutter. "This is not easy for me, Mr. Henke," he said carefully. "If I've misjudged you, I'll be making a speedy exit from your beautiful country."

Sam Henke wasn't comfortable with the conversation's trajectory but allowed Wayne to continue.

"In my limited time at Gustaf's, I've experienced a few things that have aroused suspicions."

"Suspicions?" Henke queried. "Suspicions about what, Mr. Burgess?"

"It started when I asked to see patient records. I assumed, since your government reviewed and sanctioned my study, that they'd also authorized my access to patient information. But Nurse Lai, my ward's supervising nurse, apparently didn't get that memo and her hostile response to my request created my initial concern."

"An old, overworked and crotchety nurse," reasoned Henke. "There're plenty of those at Gustaf's."

"You may be right. But she's not alone in expressing hostility toward my curiosity."

"Meaning…?"

"Dr. Croft had a security guard escort me to his office today. His hostility reached an even higher level than Nurse Lai's. I have to think there's a reason for all this intimidation."

Sam Henke's eyes widened and his posture stiffened.

"Mr. Burgess," he stated coldly, "I've heard enough. You've picked the wrong person to share your troubles with. I have no desire to get involved in any problem you may be having with Dr. Croft."

Wayne knew he was seconds away from losing Sam Henke.

"On the contrary," Wayne bargained, "I think I'm talking to the only person who *can* help me. Please, Sam, a few more minutes of your time?"

Sam ignored his internal alarm, and Wayne accepted the reprieve.

"In the past few days I've acquired and read a select group of patient's records."

"How did…?"

"I'll get to that later, Sam," Wayne promised. "What I've read is confusing and disturbing. A large number of Ward C's residents have been declared dead; patients that are very much alive as far as I can see."

"What do you mean dead?" asked Henke, truly not understanding.

"I mean dead, deceased, passed on. Their autopsy reports are in their files."

Sam sat back in his sofa and visibly released the tension in his body. His calm misery indicated both a knowledge of and conflict with Croft's experimentation. Maybe he could be swayed, Wayne hoped. The two men sat quietly while Sam chose his path.

"So why me?" he finally asked.

"Because you're involved, Sam, and I don't believe you want to be."

Sam rose from the couch and walked to a window overlooking bent, brown grass and patches of dirt. When he moved again, he walked towards the kitchen.

"I need a beer, Mr. Burgess. How about you?" he asked.

"I'd love one," Wayne replied. "And please call me Wayne," he added, hoping the relationship was evolving. Sam Henke was still an unknown and he'd taken a huge risk trusting a man who could prove more than distrustful. But his burden had become unbearable and his isolation complete.

Sam returned with German beer, French cheese and Swedish crackers. He pushed aside a pile of dirty dishes on an old trunk table, placed the repast in the newly vacant space and sat back down across from Wayne. They had a lot to talk about, like raising people from the dead at the Gustaf Clinic.

seven

Stan Iverson drove to his favorite hideaway, The River House, found his favorite table and sat down. The waitress, accustomed to his patronage, brought him a cup of thick coffee and a pastry. Iverson offered an appreciative smile and explored the contents of Kate Howser's folder. Kate had organized the information by names: Steven Gant, Terrance Walk and Allan Trenholm. The reading was dry and tedious, but Iverson digested both the sugared pastry and the written material with equal vigor. The files consisted mainly of listings of the credentials and accomplishments of the three PhDs. How ironic, thought Iverson, that these men, who had earned reputations as great human advocates, actually had little regard for human life.

Trenholm was much older than the other two and possessed a larger dossier than either Gant or Walk. He had spent his early years in the military where he'd gained a reputation as a son-of-a-bitch. Upon retirement from the service, Trenholm chose the field of education for his next ladder to climb. He quickly attained the same standing within the field of academia as he had in the military. Gant and Walk had been college classmates and had emerged in the same field at the same time. Gant, it appeared, had a tendency to spread himself around and dabbled frequently in the political arena. Walk focused mainly on research. The university was their common playground.

In 1994, they began appearing together on governmental committees and private boards. In 1995, they banded together to create a group called the Special Education Committee. The SEC contracted with the State of Oregon to set up a network of agencies that operated community homes for disabled people who'd left the state's institution after its forced closure. Iverson assumed correctly that Futures, Inc. was one of those agencies. The professors contributed their expertise and reputations in the areas of behavioral research, political acumen and fund raising. Through the university, they published papers on the research conducted at the homes and provided consultation to other states attempting to close institutions.

The waitress returned to fill Iverson's cup. She was attractive for her age and, considering her occupation, perpetually cheerful. Since Iverson was a regular customer and a better than average tipper, they were on a first name basis. They exchanged a few remarks regarding their personal lives before Iverson continued his reading. He found the bulk of it uninteresting and most likely of minimal importance. Then, while reading a printout labeled "International Consultation," he made a connection regarding a series of trips the professors had made on behalf of the university.

Gant, Walk and Trenholm had all utilized a "research opportunity" to visit the same place. The records revealed that at least once a year, from 1995 until the present year, one of the three had spent at least a week in Kirkenes, Norway. Maybe that wasn't odd for university professors, thought Iverson, but he couldn't imagine why high profile researchers would concentrate their "research opportunities" in one place. He wasn't a Ph.D., but Iverson did conduct his own brand of research, and he knew a fundamental tenet of investigation was to gather information from as many different sources as possible. Sound conclusions are best drawn from multiple sources.

Iverson wasn't sure what it meant. Maybe nothing. But the documents from Kate hadn't given him much else to go on and he needed something to label a clue, even if it was a feeble one. He could easily check it out and he didn't have much else to follow up on. He decided he would run by the old roadhouse, check on Jon and Sandra, and then renew acquaintances with a couple of detectives he'd met on his one and only trip across the pond.

eight

Jon looked over at the woman cuddled next to him and stroked her thick, radiant hair with a gentle hand. He surveyed the bandages on her shoulder and knew she still suffered pain. He also was becoming increasingly aware of the inner strength that allowed her to ignore it. He was pleased and proud to have attracted such a woman.

"I sure hope you'll respect me in the morning," she said coyly.

"I imagine I will," answered Jon, administering a reassuring hug.

Sandra sat up and looked at Jon seriously. "What are you feeling right now, Jon?"

"I'm not really sure, Sandra," he replied. "I'm content and comfortable right here … right now. That's got a lot to do with you, I'm sure. But to be honest, I've not been in close touch with my feelings for a very long time and I'm not real sure what I should do with them."

"Sharing them would be nice."

"That's not something I'm accustomed to, Ms. McKinney."

"Well, maybe we'll have to change that, Mr. Farrell."

"I'm willing to give it my best shot."

"That's all I ask, Jon."

They shared another smile and were about to celebrate their relationship a second time when a knock on the door brought them back to reality. Jon jumped up, hastily threw on his clothes and peered anxiously through a slit in a shuttered window. He was relieved to see Stan Iverson's impatient face staring at him. He opened the door.

"Didn't disturb anything, did I, Jon?" asked Iverson wryly.

"No, Sergeant, not a thing," replied Jon unconvincingly.

Iverson walked through the door in time to see Sandra scurrying into the bathroom, not quite fully clothed.

"Not a thing, Jon?" Iverson quipped.

Jon's face flushed and his vocal cords ceased function. He was embarrassed but content with the cause.

"It's okay, Jon. I'm not your priest..., just your friendly, neighborhood detective. If anybody needs some positive emotions right now, I guess it's the two of you."

Jon's voice returned, and with it, a change of subject.

"And just what has the friendly neighborhood detective been up to?"

"He's been doing some reading and maybe, just maybe, he's found something interesting."

Iverson loosely deposited Kate Howser's papers on a table and combed through the pile for the ones he wanted to share.

"You haven't by chance seen a world map anywhere?" he asked hopefully.

"I really haven't spent too much time looking around," Jon answered shyly.

"Sorry, I forgot," replied Iverson. He was amused and pleased with Jon's demeanor. "Take a quick look around for one, would you?"

"Sure," replied Jon, and he busied himself in search of a map.

Sandra emerged from the bathroom and took up the conversation with the Sergeant.

"Any news?" she asked. "And where's that food you promised? I'm starved."

"Oh, shit! I forgot the food, Sandra. I'm sorry. We'll go find something after a brief pow-wow."

"Promise?"

"I promise." Iverson held up his hand and took a phantom oath. "I'm pretty hungry myself, come to think of it."

"I'll hold you to it, Sergeant," said Sandra, her stomach growling for emphasis. "So you have something interesting to share?"

"Maybe. Jon's looking for a map to help my navigational bearing."

"A map of what?"

"I need a map of Norway."

"Norway!" Sandra exclaimed. "Why on earth do you need a map of Norway?"

"I'll fill you in when we've got the map," Iverson insisted.

Jon's search didn't produce a map so Iverson sent him to the shack at the top of the hill to see if the old man had one. The caretaker directed him to a storage shed behind the house with vague instructions of where best to continue his search. He returned to the cabin ten minutes later with a Rand McNally Book of the World, vintage 1978. The antiquated atlas was yellowed and crumpled, but usable.

Iverson flipped to the section showing the Nordic neighborhood and shared his discovery of a possible PhD connection. Jon examined the map's details and found Kirkenes, Norway, the favored destination of Gant, Walk and Trenholm.

"There it is," he said blandly. "It doesn't look like much, Sarge."

"Look, Jon," said Iverson, somewhat irritated. "I'm trying to figure out why people are getting killed ... why someone tried to kill you and Sandra. That little dot may be a big deal or it may be just a little dot. I really don't know which at this point. What I do know is that I have very little else to go on right now and unless you've got something more compelling to do, I suggest we check out the fucking dot."

"Sarge is right," Sandra interrupted. "It is pretty odd that all three of those guys would be spending time in a place as out of the way as Kirkenes, Norway. At the very least, let's try and find out what's there that might attract their attention. What have we got to lose?"

"Our lives, Sandra," responded Jon. "Maybe we should just lay low."

Iverson glared at Jon. "And do what, Jon?" he demanded. "Please share your plan."

"I don't have a plan, Sarge," Jon countered. "But I think time away from here is probably time spent less safe."

Iverson paced the floor and measured his response. "Let's talk about that, Jon," he said impassively. "If all you want is safety, I can accommodate that. I can take you both down to the station right now and stash you in a ten by ten cell that, at least in theory, should be safe. You'll get three hots and a cot, learn some new words and meet lots of real interesting people. Of course, in that scenario, you'd have to leave your fate in the hands of Bill Firnett and hope for an outcome that you can live with.

"Sarge, I didn't..."

"Let me finish, Jon," Iverson said calmly. "On the other hand, if you want to find the bastards that killed your friends and are doing a pretty good job of fucking up your lives, then you're just going to have to take some chances, and you're going to have to trust me. I like you, Jon. I really do. But I'm getting a little tired of having to jump start you."

Jon looked at the Sergeant, then at Sandra. He was embarrassed and angry.

"I'm worried about Sandra, not myself," he said truthfully. His protective instincts had kicked in for the woman he was falling in love with.

"Wait just a minute," said Sandra sternly. "I appreciate the concern, Jon, but I'm not ready to release the responsibility for my well-being to either you or the Ashton Police Department. So if your motives are related to my protection, I decline the offer."

Jon looked at Sandra, then at Iverson. The laying low option was off the table.

"Well, I guess it's settled, Sarge," he announced. "Let's talk about Kirkenes." Sandra offered an approving smile. Iverson returned to business.

"Does that work?" asked Iverson, pointing to a touch-tone phone suspended from a wooden stud in the kitchen.

"I haven't tried it, Sarge," answered Jon.

"Oh yeah, I forgot. You guys were too busy to make any calls."

nine

Sam Henke popped open his can of beer, sat down and restarted his conversation with Wayne Burgess.

"So tell me, Wayne, what else do you know about the Gustaf Clinic?"

Wayne reported all he knew to his new confidant. He shared his tale of nocturnal snooping in the medical clinic and about the conversation he'd overheard between Sam and his coworker. He spoke eagerly and without hesitation. When he finished, Sam shook his head slowly, slumped farther into the rumpled sofa and downed a long gulp of his beer.

"You've uncovered things I've suspected but didn't want to acknowledge," he admitted. "What exactly do you plan to do now?"

"I was hoping to get part of that answer from you, Sam. Right now I'm alone in this…," he looked at Sam hopefully, "unless you decide to help me."

"And what could I possibly do to help?" Sam asked.

"First off, you could tell me who I can trust. I'm obviously under scrutiny and Croft made it very clear what would happen if I pursued my suspicions. One screw-up and I'm gone … or worse. That would help no one."

Sam gave the American a long, hard look.

"You can't trust anyone," he stated bluntly. "What makes you think you can trust me? What makes you think I won't call Croft as soon as you walk out that door?"

"I don't know, Sam. I guess I'm banking on my intuition. What I overheard the other night at the medical clinic made me think we had similar definitions of right and wrong. I think you know these experiments are contemptible and must stop. If I'm mistaken, I'll pay a price. Obviously, I hope I'm not wrong."

Sam Henke didn't reply. He took another walk to the window and stared blankly out at the crisp, Norwegian autumn. Wayne pressed on.

"Sam, you know treatment here is a joke. The Gustaf Clinic is conducting experiments. Hapless human beings are being physically and emotionally tortured and somebody's undoubtedly making a lot of money off their misery." Wayne paused and walked slowly over to Sam. "My guess is that you're losing some sleep over it. Am I right?"

Sam still said nothing. Wayne finished off his beer and waited for a response. It didn't come. He gently put his hand on Sam's shoulder and craned to look into his eyes.

"Is it worth it, Sam?"

"I don't know, Wayne," Sam whispered. "Opposing Croft means losing my job."

"What have you already lost, Sam?" Wayne queried back. "The guy I heard last night sounded like a man in conflict. Doing nothing will feed that conflict. Doing something might resolve it."

"Shit!" Sam exclaimed and stared at Wayne with wide eyes. "You don't really understand where you are, do you. This isn't the good old U.S. of A., Wayne. If we get caught, you get deported to a cozy beach condo and I end up buried in an ice field."

Wayne had no response to Sam's sobering and possibly very real outcome. The Gustaf Clinic was undoubtedly a moneymaking enterprise and people kill for money. Having met Croft, Wayne knew murder could well be in his protective arsenal. He returned slowly and somberly to his chair.

"Well, I still have to try and do something," he said finally and quietly. "I can't just run away from it. Let's leave it at this, Sam. If you decide you want to get involved, call me. Better still, come see me. I'll leave my address here on the table." He paused and wrote down his address. "I'll understand if you decide against it. Really, I will."

"Would you mind defining 'involved'?" asked Sam.

"Information, Sam," Wayne replied without hesitation. "I need more and better information about the clinic's patients. Your job in the clinic allows you access to information I can't get from inside Ward C."

"Shit," Sam said softly and to no one in particular.

"Somebody needs to tell the public that Dr. Frankenstein is alive," Wayne postured.

"What public?" demanded Sam. "Where do you plan to take this information?"

"I don't have that all figured out yet, Sam. I don't know anyone here, so I don't imagine I'd be going to the local authorities."

"Good decision. Kirkenes is concerned only with its own survival and justifiably so. Life is hard here. It's probably why Croft began his misguided enterprise here in the first place."

"Please think about it, Sam, and think about it seriously, okay? In the meantime, I'll try to stay out of jail." Wayne got up, walked to the door, and added one more thought. "I hope you decide to help me, because I need your help. More importantly, the patients at Gustaf's need your help."

Sam offered a hesitant nod of his head. Wayne left, his alliance uncertain, but his burden lessened.

ten

The shotgun blast blew away a large portion of the cabin's front door. Two men strode confidently through the jagged doorway and eyed their surprised prey.

"All of you, over there, against that wall," demanded one of the men. He pointed with a large revolver to the area he wanted them to go. He was well-dressed, clean-shaven and deadly serious.

Jon and Sandra shot a panicked look at Iverson. He responded with a nod indicating that they should follow the intruder's directions. If Iverson was surprised by the invasion, he hid it well. He immediately understood that these men were here to kill them. The only question was how long it would be before they attempted to accomplish their task.

"I think you know what we want," the man with the shotgun announced. "We get what we want and nobody gets hurt."

He stepped toward Sandra, rested the shotgun's two barrels on her shoulder just below the ear, and spoke directly to Jon. "The documents, mister. Understand? If I don't get what I want, this pretty little head gets separated from its body." He calculated Jon's reaction then turned his attention to Sandra.

"Looks like I just missed the other day," he said, inspecting the bandages on her shoulder. He tapped the wound with the gun. Sandra sucked a breath, but blocked the pain.

Iverson stepped forward with his hands clearly in front of him. He didn't want to provoke the man with the shotgun.

"And what documents might you be looking for?" he asked calmly.

The man turned to Iverson.

"Don't fuck with me," he cautioned. "I'm not in the mood for games."

The other man, with steely eyes matching the color of the gun in his hand, glanced at his partner and then walked over to the table. He quickly probed the papers that Iverson had been shuffling through before the door exploded. Iverson stepped forward again only to be forced into retreat by the shotgun now pointed directly at his heart.

"Don't be a hero, Sergeant," threatened the man. "And I'll take that gun of yours."

Iverson's eyes widened and he focused them directly on those of the man wielding the double-barreled weapon.

"You're smart enough to know who I am, so I'll assume you're also smart enough not to kill a cop." It was a line of logic Iverson knew would carry no weight, but he had to extend his think time.

"The gun, Sergeant," the man repeated. "Now!"

With his fingertips Iverson slowly removed a gun from its holster under his jacket. He carefully placed it on the chair next to the coffee table. The intruder motioned for the Sergeant to back away, grabbed the gun and tossed it on the couch behind him. Iverson watched its flight carefully. The shotgun was lowered and its owner laughed cynically.

"We've already negotiated our immunity, Sergeant," he said boldly. "We don't have to worry about who we kill."

The words struck Jon and Sandra hard, and they now understood what Iverson understood. These men were there to kill them.

Iverson used the killer's boast as leverage for more time and questioned his claim of immunity. He spoke calmly, his subtle movements barely noticeable. Jon watched with anxious eyes as the Sergeant inched himself to within a few feet of the table between them and their would-be assassins. He wasn't sure what Iverson was up to, but he was methodically getting himself closer to the couch where his gun now rested. He watched for some sign that he was to have a part in the plan and found himself surprisingly eager for the opportunity.

The man holding tightly to his revolver scooped up the papers from the table and stuffed them inside his shirt. His partner then directed him to the bedroom and he disappeared in search of more paper to line his clothing. A voice suddenly came from the newly ventilated front door.

"What the hell's going on in here?"

The old caretaker, apparently checking out the sound of gunshots, stepped into the room. His eyes split wide when he realized what he'd interrupted. He died instantly when the spray of shotgun pellets blew away much of his face and spattered it on the ground outside the door.

Iverson's actions were catlike as he leapt over the table and retrieved his gun from the couch. He fired two quick shots into the old man's killer as he fell to the floor. He turned quickly and fired another bullet into the killer's partner emerging wild-eyed from the bedroom. It was over in seconds. Iverson quietly checked the two men. One was dead, the other soon would be. He took a moment to stand over the old caretaker's remains and then slowly walked over to Jon and Sandra.

"You guys okay?" he asked quietly.

Sandra could not reply. Her mouth opened, but nothing came out. She was trying desperately to maintain control. Jon managed a nod.

"I'm going to take a look outside," Iverson said. "You guys stay here, okay?"

"Sure," Jon managed. He stroked Sandra's hair and tried to assure her that it was over.

Iverson returned in moments and announced that the two men were apparently alone.

"But let's get out of here, now!" he ordered.

"What about the bodies?" asked Jon. "What about him?" He pointed a shaky finger at the old caretaker.

Iverson paused and took a long, audible breath. He had known the old man for a long time and they had shared many stories over many beers. Iverson would miss him. His life as a cop had produced a long list of people he'd miss.

"I'll call it in from somewhere else," he finally said firmly. "We can't help him now and we need to get out of here. Get yourself and Sandra into the car and I'll take us somewhere safe."

"I thought this place was safe," muttered Jon, half to Iverson and half to himself.

"So did I," said Iverson, embarrassed but realistic. "Apparently, we were both wrong. We'll have to assume no place is safe until we get the bastards who hired these goons. At least now, they'll have to hire new help."

"I'm hoping there's a limit on applicants," said Jon, his emotions regaining balance.

"Unfortunately..." Iverson began, then stopped short. "Shit, never mind. Let's just get the hell out of here!"

Jon helped Sandra navigate around the splattered remains of the caretaker and they made it to the car. Iverson retrieved the papers stuffed inside the dead man's coat, grabbed Jon's briefcase and joined them. Though shaken, the Sergeant looked unruffled. It was a practiced and seasoned exterior. They had been lucky and he knew it, but three more lives had just been lost, one that mattered to Iverson. The total dead was now six, and he knew that if he didn't figure this case out soon, that number would grow.

Something one of the killers said kept floating through Iverson's head. It was the gunman's statement about immunity. It had not been an empty boast. The man truly believed his actions had impunity. Where could such arrogance come from?

******

Iverson drove deep into the country. He stopped at a moss-blotched market that had an anachronistic phone booth outside, wedged among a couple of rotting timbers. He took out his cell phone, turned it off and instructed his companions to do the same. He entered the doorless phone booth, dropped a quarter into the antiquated apparatus and called the Ashton Police Department to deliver an anonymous report about the killings at the cabin. He finished his call and detoured into the store before returning to the car. In the paper bag he set next to him were four large bottles of beer, two Budweisers from St. Louis, a Coors from Colorado and an unpronounceable brand from Brazil. The bag also contained two large bottles of coke, three crusty sandwiches and a bag of Doritos. He opened the Coors, placed it between his legs, and shoved the Budweisers toward the back seat. Jon snatched the two long necks, passed one to Sandra and took a prolonged drink of his brew.

"Thanks, Sarge," said Jon. "We really needed that."

Iverson turned and stared at his two companions. "I'm truly sorry about what just happened. I didn't anticipate anyone finding that place."

"That," replied Jon, "was the scariest ten minutes of my life. I'm still shaking. So is Sandra. But we're still alive thanks to you so no apologies are necessary. You never guaranteed that we'd stay out of harm's way. It was our choice to see this through, so let's do that. Let's move on."

Iverson smiled and turned toward the road. No jump start needed, he thought. Mr. Farrell is coming around.

They drove off in search of safe haven. Iverson was aware that he'd made a mistake, that he'd obviously been followed to the cabin by the two men he'd been forced to kill. He wouldn't make the same mistake again. He cautiously drove paved and graveled back roads, stopping occasionally to make certain they weren't shadowed. Twilight set in, and he continued to drive. There was little conversation. Two hours after they had left the cabin and its lifeless occupants, and satisfied that they were truly alone, he looked for a place to spend the night.

Iverson stopped at what appeared to be an old, abandoned schoolhouse. It sat at the back end of a field populated with sleepy-eyed sheep that huddled close to a grove of ancient apple trees. Iverson steered the car off the main road and drove on rutted, bumpy topsoil to the rear of the building. He parked the car behind the old orchard and left the vehicle to check the school. He returned with an invitation for Jon and Sandra to join him. Once inside, the three wayfarers settled onto old, dust-covered floors and allowed their tense bodies the time to recuperate. They devoured the stale sandwiches and guzzled the coke. Conversation was sporadic. No one spoke of the cabin. Sandra regained her composure but remained distant and Jon did his best to tend both her physical and emotional wounds. Stan Iverson considered what to do next.

The old building offered little in terms of comfort, but Sandra succumbed to fatigue soon after their meager meal was finished. She crumpled up her jacket and fashioned a suitable pillow for her weary head. Jon removed his coat and placed it over her as she drifted off to sleep. He opened the Brazilian beer.

"Now that you're unemployed, Mr. Farrell," Iverson said, "what do you suppose you'll do with the remainder of your life, assuming, of course, there is a remainder?"

Jon handed the bottle to Iverson and propped his tired frame against the remains of an old chalkboard.

"I'm thinking I'll become a cop and team up with you, Sarge. What do you think of that idea?"

"I think you're too late, Jon. My cop career is heading into its final chapter."

"Why's that?"

"Well, if my captain doesn't fire me first, I had sort of planned on retiring sometime soon. That face in the mirror ain't getting any younger."

"But you're fermenting well, Sarge...just like a fine merlot. And besides, you're too good at what you do. Who could replace you?"

Iverson enjoyed the compliment and gulped some more beer.

"Captain Denny would replace me with Ronald McDonald if given the opportunity. In case you haven't figured it out, my boss doesn't exactly consider me irreplaceable. Anybody with half a brain and no backbone would suit him fine."

Jon processed Iverson's words with dulled synapses.

"Well, if a partnership is out, I may have to consider going back to school."

"And be just like your buddies?"

"My buddies?"

"Gant, Walk and what's his name."

"Trenholm."

"Yeah, Trenholm. You could get a Ph.D. and join the academic elites."

"Fuck them!" Jon said angrily. "They killed my friends, Sarge, and they're trying real hard to kill me."

"And don't forget about sleeping beauty over there." Iverson paused and asked for reason through the alcohol. "Where do these intellectuals get the right to kill?"

Jon motioned for the return of the bottle. Iverson took a lengthy swallow before complying.

"A Ph.D. is a special breed, Sarge. Most of the ones I've met have it up to here with arrogance." Jon drew a line across the top of his forehead. "They get pampered because our culture rewards education, and that coddling gets them thinking they have more rights than the rest of us. Sooner or later they start thinking they can do whatever they want because they have that pedigree."

"Obviously, that includes killing people."

"It appears that way, at least with these guys."

"What do you think they're protecting?"

Jon took another swallow and offered a somewhat hazy hypothesis.

"By the looks of things, I'd say they're protecting themselves. If they did skim money from those grants, and the Feds found out, their high-powered careers would be over and their precious reputations ruined. People like Gant, Walk and Trenholm usually claim they're working for the benefit of mankind, and some, I suppose, really are. But not these three. They're interested in their status and their pocketbooks … probably in that order."

"So you think it's really just about greed?"

"That's my guess, Sarge. Greed and an overly developed sense of self-importance. These guys look for people to manipulate and I'm afraid they found easy pickings in me. I should have known better. I just wasn't smart enough."

"Oh, sure, Jon," countered the Sergeant. "You were supposed to know that these guys were going to end up hiring thugs to kill you?"

"No, but I should have seen something coming. There were signs."

"Signs?" Iverson's ears perked up and his fog cleared momentarily.

"Well, they were never really involved with Futures unless something was wrong…, something that could reflect upon them in a negative way. They never had time to help out with Futures' problems, but they sure managed to take credit for all of its accomplishments."

"But stealing credit isn't murder, Jon. Why take it to this extreme?"

Iverson, even in a semi-intoxicated state, was probing, trying to gain some measure of insight into the minds of the criminals he wanted desperately to catch. Jon's mind was dulled as well, but its numbing effect was allowing him to take the time to explore explanations he needed.

"It's got to be the fame and the money. What else can it be?"

"People kill other people for money, power or passion," Iverson stated with experienced insight. "It sounds like these guys have at least two of the three motives working for them."

"Money and…?" prodded Jon.

"Power. Power equals fame, Jon, and your theory has them seeking large amounts of fame. And power and money certainly breed the arrogance you spoke of. I only hope their arrogance causes them to make a mistake. It happens frequently."

"I share your hope, Sarge."

The two men exchanged gulps from the bottle one more time and stumbled out of the building to relieve saturated bladders. They were greeted by a clear sky filled with glistening points of light.

"Maybe I'll become a starship captain," contemplated Jon. "I've always wanted to meet extraterrestrials."

"I think we ought to work on surviving a select few of Earth's predators first, Jon."

They returned to the ostensible safety of the old schoolhouse and found all the beer bottles drained. Jon posed the question that had been swirling around in his head since the scene at the cabin.

"Were those men in the cabin the same ones that killed Leslie, Neil, and Deb?" he asked.

"No doubt," replied Iverson.

Jon digested the Sergeant's reply.

"May they rot in hell," he stated emphatically.

TUESDAY, SEPTEMBER 27

one

The knock at his door aroused Wayne Burgess from crumpled and restless sleep on his living room chair. He leapt to his feet and threw the old afghan from his shoulders. His last visitor had delivered him to Denton Croft and most likely rifled his home so he quickly scanned the room for anything incriminating. His eyes stopped at the makeshift table next to his chair which held the stack of folders he'd pilfered from the medical records building. He collected the files, stuffed them under his chair cushion and peeked through the blinds out the window. It was Sam Henke, wearing wrinkled clothes and a satisfied smirk. Wayne shook the cobwebs from his head and opened the door.

"I just quit my job," Sam said matter-of-factly. "How about a cup of coffee?"

Wayne stared at Sam with red, swollen eyes and waited for his words to reach receptive gray matter.

"Well, you gonna invite me in or not?" Sam demanded jokingly.

"S…sure," Wayne stuttered, and gestured toward his living room. Sam bent over, lifted a large box from the stoop, and walked into the apartment.

"Sorry if I woke you, Wayne, but I do recall your telling me to come see you if I made a decision."

"It's okay, Sam," replied Wayne. "I'm happy to see you. Did you just say you quit your job?"

"Yeah, I walked out tonight. I've been thinking about our conversation and concluded you were right. I don't know what I'm getting myself into but I do know you were right about my conflict and I want to change that."

"But you really quit?" asked Wayne in disbelief.

"Our talk forced me to take a serious look at myself and I didn't like what I saw. I've ignored Gustaf's atrocities at great cost to my soul and I can't do that anymore. You've given me an opportunity, Wayne. Hopefully, one that doesn't kill me."

Wayne digested the news but was unsure of its implications. "Don't trust anybody," was Sam Henke's advice. Was Sam including himself? He studied Sam intently and then refocused on the package he'd brought with him.

"What's in the box?"

"It's a surprise. You get to open it as soon as I get some coffee."

Wayne walked toward the kitchen and Sam followed.

"You know, Wayne," Sam continued, "I'm scared shitless, but I don't care. I've done the right thing for a change and I feel like a glacier has been lifted off my back."

"You just walked out…, in the middle of your shift?" asked Wayne. He glanced at the clock hanging askew from the kitchen wall.

"I know it might cause some suspicion, but I just couldn't spend another minute there. I was going to quit at the end of the shift, but I felt my courage wavering."

"Courage?" asked Wayne.

"The longer I waited, the greater the chance I'd talk myself out of it. And besides, leaving mid-shift provided a better opportunity to get away with my prize."

"Prize?" asked a puzzled Wayne.

"The box."

"That box?" Wayne asked, pointing to the one on the living room floor.

"One and the same," replied Sam. His face glowed.

Wayne's curiosity, if not the rest of him, was now fully awake and in high gear. He put down the half-filled pot of water he'd been emptying into the coffee machine. He stared at Sam.

"What's in the damn box, Sam?"

"Caffeine first, that's the deal."

Wayne set the coffee to brewing in record time and seated himself on the chair in front of the box. Sam sat on the floor. They looked like kids on Christmas Eve.

"I think you'll be pleased with your present."

"I have a feeling I will, but I also have a suspicion there's a good story behind this box. Mind sharing some details?"

"I was hoping you'd ask."

"Well I've asked, so tell me."

Sam straightened his posture and initiated the story behind the box.

"Your visit had its intended effect, Wayne. After you left, I spent quite a few hours analyzing my life and didn't find too many things that I liked. I'm not a bad person. I know that. I, like most of Kirkenes, have been in a long-term rut. Maybe it's the weather or maybe it's a residual, large-scale and long-term depression due to the war. I really don't know and I really don't care because, either way, it's no excuse for what we know exists at the Gustaf Clinic. What I'm sure of now is that I can't sanction it anymore … no matter the price. I made the decision."

"Decision?"

"For a very long time, my sense of right and wrong has been held hostage to financial and social survival. Life up here is hard and I guess maybe we get so caught up in survival that we forget about the values that make us human. I took a long, hard look at my life and decided I needed to seriously consider a change. I tallied up the pros, weighed them against the cons, and made a choice."

"The pros outweighed the cons?"

"Absolutely not. This has got to be one of the worst decisions I've ever made. But it's the right one."

Wayne offered an amused and approving smile and asked to hear more. Sam was eager to share.

"I went to work an hour early and told the supervisor I had some extra prep work to do for some experiments. It's not unusual, so I was allowed in. Once inside, I went to the records room, the one where you hid the other night, and searched for evidence against Croft. I think I found it. This box contains research records on clients from 1996 until now."

"How did you get them out of the medical clinic?"

"That's where it got interesting," chuckled Sam, obviously pleased with himself. "Being an inexperienced thief, I just planned on taking them. It's when I actually had them that I realized my problems had just begun. Somehow, I had to get them to my car. Then there I was, box in hand, when in walked a security guard. I was sure I was doomed to either life in prison or death under the tundra. Neither seemed a good option."

A hint of a smugness crept into Sam's face. His eyes showed growing excitement.

"Well, what the hell happened?" demanded Wayne.

"The guard saw me and, of course, asked what I was doing. I was about to wet my uniform when, somehow, my brain got creative. I mumbled a story about preparations for a new research project and told the guard to carry the box out to my car because I'd hurt my back wrestling with a patient the night before. He looked suspiciously at the box so I told him it contained papers I needed to write a report on the new project for Dr. Croft. He still wasn't convinced so I dropped the box at his feet and told him 'Fine, you write the fucking report,' and started to walk out."

"And then?"

"He hollers 'Wait,' picks up the box and asks directions to my car. I turn, look thoroughly disgusted, and give him the directions and keys to my car. He stomps off and ten minutes later returns with my keys. Unbelievable."

"That's an incredible story, Sam. I applaud your bravery."

Sam's face blushed red and flashed a self-satisfied smile.

"Thanks, Wayne. I feel better than I have in a long time."

"I have to wonder though," said Wayne somewhat cautiously, "about leaving early. Won't there be some suspicions."

"I told my supervisor I was fed up with Gustaf's and was quitting. She's seen my moods lately, and I think she half suspected something. I really don't think she'll be a problem. She knows nothing about the box."

"I hope you're right, Sam. But I can't help but think she'll snoop around some, especially if she's tied in with Croft. That's a suspicious group of people working there."

Sam's euphoria was deflated by Wayne's realism.

"There's not much we can do about it now, is there? What's done is done. You asked me to make a decision and I've made it. I'm ready to live with it.

"*We'll* live with it, Sam. But let's agree to make decisions of this magnitude a joint affair from now on, okay?"

"I guess I did get carried away. I guess once I knew what the right thing to do was, I wanted to do it quickly and remove the burden from my soul. But I agree, from now on, decisions are a joint effort."

Wayne accepted the new relationship eagerly. "Let's open Pandora's Box," he said.

"The coffee?" asked Sam with a grin.

Wayne leapt out of his chair, hurried to the kitchen, and returned with two cups of fresh coffee.

"A toast to the Grand Thief of Kirkenes," he proposed and handed a steaming cup to Sam. They clanged cups, took a celebratory swallow and turned their attention to the cardboard container in front of them. Sam opened the box's flaps and shuffled through its contents until he found what he wanted. He blew the dust off its cover and smiled.

"I remembered you said you liked this guy," he said and offered Charley Orr's file to Wayne.

Inside the faded, brown cover of the file was the record of chemical and mechanical experimentation inflicted upon Charley Orr since 1996. The research began shortly after Charley was declared dead by Gustaf's Medical Examiner, a Dr. Denton Croft. The records indicated that Charley was put on a six-month cycle; three months of chemicals followed by three months of rest, probably, Wayne surmised, to allow the chemicals to filter from his body. Each experiment was followed by a written report describing the results of the alleged research. The reports were usually characterized in terms of behavior, and were, more often than not, listed as "*patient slept*," "*patient remained awake*," or *"patient aggressive, restraints required*." A number, indicating hours, followed each entry. Occasionally, there was a brief report of something Charley had said, but patient commentary didn't seem to be of much interest to the researchers.

The drug experimentation involved varying doses of myriad chemicals, some of which Wayne recognized. The familiar ones, Thorazine, Stelazine, Haldol, Mellaril, were being given in inordinately high doses and in combinations Sam knew to be risky. Medication was typically administered in graduated doses until "*unfavorable response at this dosage*" was reached. The drug or the dosage was then altered. All medications were delivered by injection. Occasionally, a margin entry was made indicating: "*for TW by DC*." DC, Sam and Wayne guessed, was Denton Croft. Neither of them could attach the initials TW to anyone they knew but they both assumed it was someone involved in the research and the money that went with it. They looked at another six files. All contained the same basic information set in the same format. The records were a chronology of experimentation conducted on people *after* they had been declared dead in 1996.

Wayne compared Sam's files to those from Ward C's record room and the ones he'd heisted from the medical clinic the previous night. There was some duplication, but Sam's loot possessed much greater detail regarding the research. Combined, the records offered solid evidence of Gustaf's unethical and probably criminal activity. Croft and his coterie had been abusing Ward C's patients for at least ten years. The records indicated that, in the last eight years, the research had focused chemical experimentation on patients diagnosed with autism. At least two patients had died as a result of the foreign substances introduced into their bodies.

Wayne stacked all the files in alphabetical order in his suitcase and crammed the bulging bag under his bed. He then pulled out the file marked "*miscellaneous*" from his daypack and the newly formed partnership continued their study. At a cost of another couple of hours and quite a few brain cells, Wayne discovered a typed report addressed to Croft from "*TW*," presumably the same one listed in Croft's research notes. It was dated, December 19, 2004. It stated that "*TW*" would be using Croft's data in a "*pilot program*" in the state of Oregon in the United States. The program would involve autistic clients recently removed from an institution and "*TW*" was asking Croft to focus his research strictly on that condition.

Sam's and Wayne's eyes were swollen with fatigue but wide with wonderment. How big was this revelation? Who really was "*TW*"? Was he higher up than Croft on the crime ladder? Where exactly in Oregon was this pilot program? The questions were growing in number and intensity, and their amateur investigation was quickly evolving into something bigger than they'd expected. Despite the copious amounts of caffeine, their minds were withering. They agreed to seek their answers after some much needed sleep. Wayne's next question would be posed to his old professor in the States. He'd know about Oregon.

two

Sandra woke up with a start. Today was Leslie's funeral. She located Jon and Iverson scrunched up on the floor a few feet from where her stiffened muscles tried to untangle themselves. Her shoulder throbbed. She managed to right herself and ambulate over to Jon, where his heavy breathing indicated he wasn't yet ready to greet the new day.

"Jon, wake up," she coaxed. Her efforts were met with resistant groans.

"Jon, please…, it's Sandra. We have to leave."

He slowly turned and looked at her through hazy eyes.

"It's early."

"It's not early, Jon. It's ten-o'clock and we have to get out of here."

Jon shot up, recalling the killings at the cabin. He surveyed the room, saw no threat and took a deep breath.

"What's wrong, Sandra?" he questioned.

"Leslie's funeral is in two hours and I'm not going to miss saying goodbye. And we have to find out when Neil and Deb's funerals are."

Jon wanted this conversation to be part of a bad dream but knew better.

"You're right, Sandra," he replied reluctantly. "I guess I was hoping if I ignored it, it wouldn't be true." Jon flashed back to his mother and his decision to forego her funeral as a means to deny her death—a decision that still pained him.

"I'd like to do that, too, Jon, but I'm afraid we can't."

"I know, Sandra. Believe me, I know. It's painful, but necessary."

The discussion woke Iverson. He rubbed the fog from his eyes and joined the conversation.

"Okay, people," he groused. "Why are we up?"

"Sandra informs me that it's time to go, Sarge."

Iverson gently massaged his aching head and sat up.

"Really? Would someone please share the reason for this part of the schedule?"

"We have some funerals to attend, Sergeant," Jon answered. With a glance toward Sandra, he added, "We really have to go."

Iverson looked at Sandra whose expression declared that the decision wasn't up for debate.

"I don't have to tell you that I disapprove."

"No, Sergeant," replied Sandra, "you don't. And I don't have to tell you that I don't care if you do. I'm going to Leslie's funeral and, hopefully, Jon is going with me." She looked at Jon and received an affirmative nod. "The only question that remains, Sergeant Iverson, is whether you take us there, or if we have to start walking back to town..., wherever the hell it is."

Iverson smiled and slowly stood up. "No, Ms. McKinney, you won't have to walk. I'd be more than happy to take you and Mr. Farrell back to town. That is, if Mr. Farrell manages to get up and walk."

Jon accepted the challenge and stumbled to a bipedal position. He announced he'd be ready momentarily, but quietly questioned his ability to fulfill the commitment.

Iverson stepped outside the old schoolhouse and into the crisp Oregon morning. He deposited a stream of recycled alcohol on the ground beneath him and replayed the prior day's events in his head. He gulped a lung full of cool, fresh air to help clear the haze in his head and returned to Jon and Sandra.

"It's going to be an interesting day, folks," he announced confidently.

"What's your definition of interesting, Sergeant?" asked Sandra.

"Oh…, I'd say some intrigue, an occasional conflict, and maybe a few earth-shattering revelations. You know, the stuff that seems to have become routine for you guys."

"I'd rather have my friends and my boring life back," said Sandra solemnly. "Are you going to the funeral with us, Sergeant?"

"No, I don't think so, Sandra," answered Iverson. "I have a few things to attend to while you two are putting your lives at risk."

Sandra shot Iverson a look of impatience. "I *have* to go to the funeral, Sergeant, and that's that. I'd hoped you would understand."

"I do understand, Ms. McKinney, but I also don't want to add to the funeral list. You've seen enough to know that your life is in danger. Whoever wanted you dead most likely still wants you dead and they'll probably show up at Ms. Covington's funeral hoping for another opportunity."

"I know it's a risk, Sarge, but it's a risk I'll…, we'll have to take."

"I agree with both of you," interrupted Jon. "The risk is certainly there but two elements of that risk now lie dead in that old cabin. And if there are more killers out there, I'm hoping they have an aversion to killing in front of a hundred witnesses. They waited for us to be isolated before."

"That depends on how desperate they've become," countered Iverson.

"You can't protect us forever, Sarge," Jon offered realistically.

"True enough, Mr. Farrell. And if I remember yesterday correctly, I haven't done that great of a job thus far. Hopefully, you're right and they won't risk it. But I want you to wait for me at the cemetery …, preferably with a whole bunch of people hanging around. I'll take care of what business I have and head over there in plenty of time to catch up with you."

"We won't be at the cemetery, Sarge," said Sandra. "Leslie's parents are having her shipped home for burial. Today is a simple service at the funeral home for the benefit of her friends in Ashton. It'll only last a couple of hours."

"That's even better. I'll pick you up at the funeral home at two-o'clock," said Iverson. "Don't leave unless it's with me, agreed?"

"Agreed," said Sandra. Jon contributed a discreet nod of his head. "I'd sure like to clean up and put on some fresh clothes," Sandra added. "But that would mean a stop by my house and I suppose that's out of the question."

Iverson's look indicated his response. He knew Sandra's house was probably being watched and they didn't need to make it that easy for the killers.

"We've got a little time, don't we?" asked Jon. "Maybe we can stop someplace and buy some clothes."

Iverson grudgingly acquiesced to Jon's plan and they left the schoolhouse, headed back to Ashton. They stopped at a department store on the city's western boundary and Iverson watched vigilantly and impatiently while Jon and Sandra purchased clothes suitable for a funeral. When they parted company at the funeral home, Iverson repeated his caution to stay attached to large groups and to not leave until he returned. They agreed on a pick-up spot and the Sergeant watched them walk up the cobblestone path to pay their last respects to Leslie Covington. He hoped he would see them alive again.

three

Iverson decided to risk an appearance at the station. He wanted to contact a couple of detectives he'd met while tasting the fermented beverages of a small town in Germany. The burg sat at the foot of an intimidating mountain whose name he couldn't pronounce, much less remember. The beerfest was the only worthwhile memory of a trip his ex-wife had insisted they take in hopes of reinvigorating their relationship. Their divorce was evidence of her miscalculation. Iverson seldom took time off from his job. He had never been one for travel or for social leisure of any kind. If he did deviate from his life as a detective, it was usually at Beth's insistence. She'd been a good wife, Iverson thought, and that their marriage ended in disaster was probably his fault. If only she hadn't punished him with infidelity. His pride wouldn't allow him to forgive her personal betrayal.

Iverson pulled into the station's parking lot and was relieved to see Captain Denny's Lexus missing from its customary place of honor. He entered the squad room, scanned and assessed the activity within it, and headed to his cluttered desk. His eyes caught those of Bill Firnett and they exchanged contemptible glares but no words. Their relationship had descended to frigid tolerance … an arrangement Iverson could live with and actually preferred. He broke off visual contact with Firnett, sat down, and searched through his desk for the phone book that had collected its share of names over the past twenty-seven years. He found it among the remnants of myriad case files and slowly thumbed through the book's frayed pages. He found the names he sought under E, presumably for Europeans. He paused momentarily, thought of the two detectives he'd gotten drunk with a long time ago, and wondered if they even remembered the occasion.

Iverson glanced at his watch and calculated a time difference of eight or nine hours between his present location and the destination of his call. "What the hell," he said aloud, "if they're good cops, they'll be on the job." He talked first with an operator in charge of international calls and minutes later was listening to a lusty, feminine voice speaking broken English through a thick German accent. After a lengthy and strained dialog, the phone rang through to the police station where Lieutenants Petr Stasky and Ed Medvenov were employed. Iverson asked for Stasky and was put on hold until he was located. While waiting, Iverson again explored his feelings toward Beth. Could their marriage have been saved? Could he have been different? Could he *be* different?

Petr Stasky remembered his drinking buddy and Iverson was both relieved and pleased that he did. They talked about families, politics and the benefits of good and plentiful beer. Twenty minutes later, Iverson got around to the reason for his call. He wanted information on Kirkenes, the city the three professors seemed to consider the ideal vacation stop. Stasky knew it was high up along the Norwegian border with Russia, but had no specific information on the small Scandinavian city. The German detective, however, had connections with most of the major police departments in Europe and was sure he could dig up additional information. He offered to share his findings only if Iverson promised to make another trip to the beer gardens with him. With surprising sincerity, the Sergeant agreed. The call ended with Iverson's feeble effort at a German toast and Stasky's subsequent critique of his linguistic abilities.

Iverson glanced at his watch and decided it was time to leave the station. Denny's power lunch would be running out of energy soon. He was almost through the door when he heard the Captain's nasal screech.

"Iverson! In my office. Now!" Denny commanded.

"Sure, Captain," came the Iverson's sarcastic reply. "I was just going out to look for you."

He followed Denny into his office and slouched down in a chair—a calculated pose of defiant indifference.

"What can I do for you, Captain?"

"You can hand me your shield and your gun, Sergeant. I'm suspending you until further notice pending an IAD review of your involvement in three deaths out on the old river road yesterday."

Iverson's pulse quickened and his face flushed slightly. He swallowed hard and took a deep breath. Hold your cards, he told himself.

"What deaths?"

"Decided to play dumb, huh?" Denny asked cynically. "I figured you might. Well, guess whose finger prints are all over that place, Sergeant?"

"Yours, Captain?" baited Iverson.

Denny shot him a piercing glance of hatred.

"You fucking wish, Iverson. The prints belong to you and two people I believe you're acquainted with. Care to guess who they might be?"

"I can't imagine, Captain, and I don't suppose you're going to give me any clues, are you?"

"You suppose fucking right, Sergeant. You're scheduled for an IAD hearing in two days to tell your side of the story. I'd suggest you bring a lawyer along, if you can find one that's stupid enough to defend you." Denny paused, and then smiled. "I've got you this time, Iverson. It's taken me a while, but I've got your sorry ass. You thought you were too smart for me, didn't you? Well, you're finished as a cop because you refused to play by the rules."

"And whose rules are you talking about, Captain?"

Denny glared but offered no answer. His face displayed a brighter shade of red than Iverson's.

"Thursday, one-o'clock, Sergeant. Be here and be ready to be indicted. We'll see how goddamned smart you are then. Surrender your shield and your gun and get the fuck out of my office."

Iverson rose slowly and methodically, keeping his infamous temper surprisingly under control. He lifted his weapon from its shoulder holster and carefully placed it on the Captain's desk, intentionally pointing the barrel of the weapon directly at Denny. He then removed his badge from the inside pocket of his jacket and laid it next to the revolver. He opened the door to leave, but turned before stepping outside the Captain's chamber.

"Captain Denny," he calmly stated, "it's been a pleasure working with such a fine officer." He saluted Denny with the middle finger of his right hand, turned and slowly walked out of the station.

The confrontation was one Iverson knew to be inevitable and he also knew it would be his last with Denny. One of them would soon be gone and Iverson pretty much figured it would be him. Iverson loved being a cop. Being a cop was who he was. Things were going to be different now but there was still work to do with or without his department issued .38 special and gilded badge. People still needed him and he wasn't about to let them down.

four

Jon and Sandra mingled with mourners burdened with saddened faces and stooped postures. A non-denominational minister made a valiant attempt to portray Leslie Covington's death as somehow explainable. The large number of attendees spoke to the great cadre of friends Leslie had accumulated in her short time in Ashton. Leslie's parents tried their best to be courageous, but toward the end of the service withered into inconsolable grief. Despite her own deep sorrow, Sandra consoled them with heartfelt words and warm embraces. Jon offered Sandra the same remedy. When the ritual ended, he gave Sandra some private time with Leslie's family and made a couple of phone calls he'd wanted to make. The first one was to Neil's family and the conversation was predictably difficult. Neil's body had already been sent home to Ohio and his funeral was scheduled for Saturday. Jon said he would try to make it. The next call was to his old office.

"Futures," said the familiar voice on the other end of the line. "This is Jackie. Can I help you?"

The sound of Jackie's voice brought mixed feelings.

"Hi, Jackie. It's Jon."

"Jon!" exclaimed Jackie. "I've been worried sick. All of us here have. What on earth is going on?"

"It's a long story, Jackie, and still without an ending. When time allows I'll give you all the details, but first things first. Has Gant made any attempt to explain my absence?"

"He called a meeting of the management staff on Monday and told us you'd left Futures due to personal problems."

Jon's jaws clenched and his faced flushed with anger.

"Personal problems? Jackie, if there are personal reasons for my being fired…"

"Fired?" Jackie blurted.

"Jackie, I think you know I wouldn't have quit Futures without telling you about it. Gant called me into my own office on Sunday and fired me. He told me to pack up then and there and not come back."

"I don't understand. Why would he fire you?"

"I've become a threat to him and just why, I'm still trying to figure out. One thing for sure though, Jackie, I'm learning more than I ever wanted to know about pedigreed bottom feeders."

"Has this got something to do with the papers that disappeared?" asked Jackie.

"That's definitely part of the picture," Jon replied. "I don't suppose those papers have surfaced anywhere?"

"Sorry, but no, they haven't. Gant was in your office yesterday for a couple of hours, but I don't know what he was doing in there." Jackie finished her sentence and Jon sensed her tears.

"Jackie," he said with empathy, "I'm really sorry about what's happened, but this isn't over yet. I'm happy to say Gant has underestimated me. Right now you and the staff need to take care of Futures. You can't let all the hard work go for nothing."

"I know," Jackie managed.

"I may not be back for a while … if at all," Jon continued, "certainly not if Gant's in control. He, Walk and

Trenholm are involved in something pretty sleazy and I'm trying to learn what it is."

Jackie paused her sniffling. "Can I help, Jon?" she asked sincerely.

"You can keep your ears and eyes open for me. But don't be overly curious. People are being killed and…"

"Killed?"

"Murdered, Jackie," Jon emphasized. "I've lost some close friends in the past couple of days and been targeted myself more than once. Whatever they're involved in, it's serious enough to kill for."

Silence ruled the phone line for a few, long seconds.

"Jon," asked Jackie, "are you going to be all right?"

"I'm okay now and I have every intention of staying that way. I've discovered that I have a survival instinct...that I'm stronger than I thought I was. I've also developed some new relationships that are proving helpful."

Jon noticed Sandra approaching, still visibly wearing her emotions.

"Jackie, I've got to go. I have some things to take care of, but I'll call you in a couple of days, okay?"

"Jon," she cautioned, "whatever's going on can't be worth getting killed for. Please be careful."

"I will," he assured her. "We'll talk soon."

"Okay. Oh…, wait, Jon. Someone's been trying to reach you. He said he was calling from out of the country. I told him that you'd just left the agency and he seemed more intent on speaking to you after he knew that. He says it's very important. Let's see…, I have the name and number here somewhere." Jackie shuffled through her ample pile of notes. "Ah…, here it is." She gave Jon a long and unfamiliar phone number, the name of the person who'd left it and from where the call came. Jon didn't recognize the name but the city and country rang a very loud bell. Kirkenes, Norway!

five

Jon and Sandra found Iverson at the rendezvous spot they'd agreed upon earlier. The Sergeant sped off as soon as they got into his car.

"What's our destination, Sarge?" asked Jon.

"Not sure," Iverson replied. "But I figure we ought to lose the two guys in the car behind us before we go anywhere."

Jon and Sandra jerked their heads around to see two men in a slate blue, late model car following them at a distance.

"Are you sure they're following us?" asked a hopeful Sandra.

"I'm a cop, remember. Those boys were looking more than a little suspicious when I arrived to pick you up so I watched them watching you."

"So who are they, Sarge?" Sandra asked nervously.

"I'd guess they're replacement parts for the decommissioned ones we left at the cabin."

"So, what now?" urged Jon.

Iverson offered a mischievous smile to his passengers.

"I'd suggest you buckle up."

Sandra and Jon complied without hesitation and the car pitched forward, shrieked, and painted the pavement with ribbons of black, smoking rubber. Iverson accelerated and twisted the car around and through a series of tight corners.

Sandra caught a quick glimpse of Iverson in the rear view mirror and saw intense eyes and a devilish grin.

The city flew by in blurred images accompanied by assorted grunts and colorful obscenities. Iverson punished the car down potholed streets and through paint-scraping alleyways. The car shuddered and whined but forged forward under the Sergeant's command. Behind them, sight and sounds of the pursuing vehicle became progressively distant then, nonexistent. Iverson had won the race. He stopped the car on a narrow backstreet in one of Ashton's older neighborhoods, leaned over and took stock of his human baggage. They were ruffled and shaken, but unharmed. "Seat belt laws," he stated stoically. "A good thing, don't you agree?"

Jon and Sandra peered anxiously out the back window. Their pursuers were nowhere in sight.

"Where are they?" asked Sandra with labored optimism.

"It would appear they've gotten lost," hypothesized the Sergeant. "They should have known better than to play hide and seek in my neighborhood. You guys okay?"

Jon and Sandra took a quick inventory of their anatomy and relayed satisfactory findings to Iverson. He acknowledged their good health and put the car back in motion.

"Where to next, Sarge?" asked Sandra.

"The best hotel in town, my dear."

Iverson reasoned that their antagonists had been all too happy with his previous choice of refuge. The cabin had been remote and possessed few obstacles for someone intent on unseen destruction. His new plan would put them in a public building, challenge their adversary's creativity, and hopefully buy them some time.

******

They arrived at the Grand Hotel in downtown Ashton and Iverson parked as close to the front entrance as possible. He waved off a uniformed valet, got out of the car and took a long look at the area surrounding the antiquated brick building. Feeling secure, he waved Jon and Sandra out of the vehicle and together they strode into the main lobby of the hotel. The underdressed threesome paused to absorb their new surroundings.

The majestic old place had been built with creative patience. It focused on pride rather than profit though both had undoubtedly been realized. The floor was marble, carved in octagonal sections and melded in symmetry with strips of patinated copper. Nebulous beings, hand painted on prodigious pillars, groped for what lay beyond the lofty, domed restraints of the edifice. The lobby's walls were crafted of lacquered woods reflecting a spectrum of color cast from perfectly placed beveled glass windows.

Jon and Sandra were awestruck. They both wondered aloud why they'd not been there before. Their answer surfaced when they approached the desk.

"We need rooms," Iverson told the uptight desk clerk.

"All rooms are $325," reported the skeptical clerk.

"We'll take two," Iverson replied without hesitation. "And I want adjoining rooms, fifth floor, at the end of a hallway and next to a stairway."

The clerk eyed them again closely but continued with well-practiced words.

"Will this be on your charge card, sir?"

"No," replied Iverson emphatically. "I'm on official business with the Ashton Police Department and it will be charged to them." He smiled smugly as he envisioned Captain Denny opening the bill.

The clerk eyed the Sergeant closer but Iverson's return glare made him quickly abort the challenge he had in mind. He handed Iverson a form to sign and plunked two envelopes with key cards onto the counter. A bellboy circled the new guests in search of luggage, found none, but offered to guide them to their rooms. They traveled to the fifth floor via a lavishly ornate elevator, made their way down oak-paneled hallways and stopped when they reached doors with numbers matching those on their envelopes. The bellboy watched with interest as Iverson opened each door, entered every room and surveyed their interiors. He was visibly disappointed when the Sergeant made no offer of a tip. Jon extracted a crumpled dollar bill from his pants pocket, offered it to the red-clad employee and the moist money and the vexed bellhop briskly disappeared.

"Jon," joked Iverson, "I'm sure you'd prefer to bunk with me, but I really think one of us ought to keep Ms. McKinney company. I'm told I'm a noisy sleeper so I thought maybe that chore should fall to you."

Jon pushed his hand through his hair and frowned unconvincingly.

"It'll be a tough job, Sarge, but…, ouch!" Sandra's foot landed squarely on Jon's left buttock.

"The couch is over there, buster," she added and pointed at a rose colored sofa in the middle of the room.

Iverson smiled at their playful behavior.

"We've got adjoining rooms, so we have access to each other without having to come out into the hallway. It's still private though, and I promise I'll knock."

Sandra expressed genuine thanks and they entered their rooms after agreeing to meet in an hour for room service food. They'd worked up another large appetite and, after a much-needed shower, a relaxed meal sounded perfect.

The dinner was postponed as the conjoined cleansing of Jon and Sandra took longer than Iverson expected. His patience had not aged well but he hadn't gotten too old to appreciate his neighbor's passions. He wondered if he'd ever find his own again. He quelled his rumbling stomach with a call to room service and an order of cold beer and the hotel's best appetizers. It would pacify him until his neighbors decided to socialize ... with him.

******

An hour and a half after arrival at the Grand Hotel, they sat together in Iverson's room eating Beef Bourguignon, duck in orange sauce and New Orleans shrimp. A generous selection of wines from a local winery accompanied the gastronomic delights.

"What the hell!" exclaimed Iverson when his guests questioned the extravagant spread. "It's the least Captain Denny can do."

With stomachs full and minds tempered by fermented fruit, they found time to relax on the plush furniture scattered about the room.

"So, ladies and gentlemen," said Iverson, looking alternately at Jon and Sandra, "do you have any suggestions for our next move?"

"I don't even remember what the last one was," responded Sandra. "It's been a long, long day."

"And a taxing one," pointed out Iverson, recalling the funeral of Sandra's best friend. "We're all tired. Hopefully these big, spendy beds will help with that. When we're rested, we'll think better."

"It's still early," argued Jon, not yet ready to give up on the day.

"I'm tired, Jon," Iverson countered. "And my thoughts are tired too. I think we'd all be better off with some sleep."

"I'm with the Sarge," voted Sandra. Her shoulder was throbbing after the night on the schoolhouse floor and the funeral had been emotionally draining. She hadn't complained but she knew her limit was closing in. "That big old bed looks like a fine place to spend the remainder of today and a significant portion of tomorrow."

"Okay," Jon relented. "But I have to share one thing first. I have a lead."

Iverson straightened up. Sandra sagged into her chair and closed her eyes.

"A lead?" Iverson asked somewhat skeptically. "What kind of a lead?"

"Just before our uninvited guests crashed our party at the cabin, you were talking about a town in Norway, right? Some place you pegged as a common link to Gant, Walk and Trenholm."

"Yeah," replied Iverson. "Kirkenes. What about it?"

"I called Futures today while Sandra was with Leslie's family. My secretary, Jackie ..."

"How did you make that call," Iverson interrupted sternly.

Jon stopped short, but presented no answer to Iverson's question.

"Cell phone?" Iverson asked.

"Yeah, Sarge," Jon said contritely. "I guess I thought it'd be okay."

"That's how the guys in the blue sedan found you," admonished Iverson.

Jon looked sheepishly at Iverson and Sandra, then at the tips of his shoes.

"I fucked up, didn't I?"

"Yes," replied Iverson and Sandra in unison.

"I'm really sorry, guys. It won't happen again."

Iverson and Sandra conferred by unspoken means before the sergeant responded.

"Cell phones stay off!" he reprimanded. "Am I clear on that this time?"

Jon answered quickly and affirmatively. Sandra nodded her agreement.

"Now, as you eloquently stated a while back, Jon. Let's move on."

Jon was grateful for the reprieve and continued his report.

"When I talked to Jackie, she told me a man has been trying to reach me. This guy claimed it was extremely important that we speak, and when Jackie informed him I was no longer employed at Futures, he was even more adamant that we talk. This person, Sarge, lives in Kirkenes, Norway."

Iverson rose slowly from his chair and paced methodically up and down the thickly carpeted floor. He stopped by the hotel room's large, bay window, stared out over the city and mumbled something quietly to himself.

"Well, Sarge, what do you think?" Jon asked.

"You have this man's phone number?" he finally asked.

"I do. Jackie gave it to me."

Iverson looked at the clock, gauged the time difference between Ashton and Norway, and decided that a call should wait. Ten seconds later, he changed his mind. As Jon dialed the number, Iverson further eroded a path in the rug. Sandra was asleep by the time Jon reached the overseas connection. He conveyed his request to the operator and was put on hold until the final link was made.

"Is it ringing through yet?" asked Iverson impatiently.

"Not yet. Maybe it's not a real number. Wait. It's ringing."

Iverson stopped pacing and hovered above Jon.

"Well…?"

"Still ringing, Sarge."

The phone rang for a long time. Then someone answered.

WEDNESDAY, SEPTEMBER 28

one

Sam Henke arrived at the Gustaf Clinic and went directly to the personnel office. Once inside its barren confines, his nerves began eating at his resolve. He was there to apologize for his strange behavior of the previous night and to ask for his job back. He realized now that he'd made a serious mistake.

The Personnel Director waved him into his office after a ten-minute wait. He was a weasely looking man with a long nose that leaked syrupy fluid. His long, drawn body moved slowly and was assisted by a wooden cane carved in the shape of a harpoon. He stumbled to his desk, managed to sit down behind it with some difficulty, and began reading something from a stack of papers piled in front of him. He did not look at Sam Henke. Minutes passed and each one pressed against Sam like a cold Scandinavian wind. He wanted very badly to get this over with.

"Mr. Henke," the taut man finally said, "it appears that you have some questions to answer."

"Yes, sir," Sam mumbled. "That's why I'm here, sir. I've been doing a lot of thinking in the last twenty-four hours, and I've come to the conclusion that I made a very serious mistake."

"And what is your mistake, Mr. Henke?"

"Quitting my job, sir."

"Wrong, Mr. Henke," was the unexpected response. Sam's mind raced to his act of thievery and his meeting with Wayne. Did they know? He held his breath. "Your mistake is the way you quit. You can't expect me to look favorably on someone who, in the middle of a work shift, decides they don't like getting a paycheck."

Sam exhaled loudly, gathered his wits and replied.

"I expect nothing, sir. I understand my actions were terribly wrong and I offer no excuses, because none would be acceptable. I'm only asking that you take a look at my entire record and consider giving me another chance. I want to work at the Gustaf Clinic."

The discussion lasted for another twenty minutes, Sam holding a contrite posture and speaking only when spoken to. The punitive result was a probationary period of employment. If he proved himself reformed, he could return to his previous status and pay after six months. During his probation, his supervisor would watch him closely and would be making weekly reports to the Personnel Office. Sam left the office pleased to have his job back.

At the same time Sam walked out of the clinic, Wayne Burgess started his shift on Ward C. Nurse Nemesis eyeballed him coldly as he entered the office and, without saying a word, handed him a list of duties. Her displeasure was obvious and Wayne's coworkers waited with eager anticipation for an entertaining confrontation. They were surprised and disappointed when Wayne graciously accepted his task menu and walked cheerfully out the door.

Wayne finished half of his assignments, returned to Ward C, and went in search of Charley Orr. He found him in his usual spot, snuggled closely to the barred door of the courtyard, dutifully controlling the earth's rotational momentum.

"How's the world turning, Charley?" he asked the planetary director.

There was of course, no reply, save a barely discernible change in penile velocity.

"I've been thinking about your value to mankind, Charley," Wayne continued, "and I've concluded that you're overworked and underappreciated. I think it's time the world knew of your contributions. What would you say to a little change in lifestyle?"

Charley Orr again offered no response. He was obviously serious about his job. Wayne moved closer and lowered his voice.

"Charley," he whispered. "I don't know if you understand what I'm saying, but I'm going to give it my best shot. I know where you go every night and what happens when you get there. I want to stop it, Charley, but you're going to have to help me."

No verbal response resulted but Wayne was convinced Charley's axial rotation had slowed considerably. Charley had heard him, but what that meant exactly remained cloaked behind his inscrutable face. Wayne noticed Nurse Nemesis eyeballing his conversation, so he left Charley Orr to his unflagging function, and set out to complete her assigned tasks.

two

Jon Farrell, Sandra McKinney and Sergeant Stan Iverson started their morning with an early, room service breakfast and discussion of a new plan fueled by fresh associations. Jon and Iverson had spent much of the previous night in intense conversation with Mr. Wayne Burgess, sharing common problems and potential solutions. Now, after much deliberation, the newly expanded group would proceed with an attempt to snare their prey.

They finished breakfast and spent the next few hours refining their scheme. It was Wednesday. Leslie Covington's death was five days old …, Neil and Deb's, three. And, though thoughts of them still lingered strongly, the present and the immediate future were what held their attention. The info gathered the previous night had led to a fully vetted decision to split up. The revised plan called for more players in Kirkenes, Norway, and a closer relationship to Wayne Burgess. Iverson, still tied to the Ashton Police Department, decided it was advantageous to remain in Ashton and continue his investigation from that vantage point. Jon and Sandra would fly to Norway and assist Wayne Burgess. Iverson was more than happy to see Jon and Sandra assume new names and put an ocean between them and the killers.

The Sergeant made a phone call to one of the city's underground printmakers to order paperwork critical to the success of their plan. Passports were needed immediately.

Additional documents, which might be needed in Norway, would be produced later and sent along when their configuration and destination had been established. Iverson provided his counterfeiter with fabricated names and sent him copies of Jon and Sandra's driver's license pictures via a hotel room fax. He gave directions to a drop-off location and insisted on an accelerated delivery time of two hours. Iverson next spoke with someone about booking a series of airline flights in the names that would appear on the fake passports and charged the fares to the Ashton Police Department … another fine gift from Captain Denny. His last call was brief and demanded immediate reimbursement for a prior favor.

The three wayfarers removed overt evidence of their overnight stay and Jon and Sandra pocketed the generous stock of complimentary supplies. They took a last, wistful look at their room, and rode the elevator to the lobby. After a stop at the gift shop for fresh clothes and a travel satchel to put them in, they walked out the door and left the Grand Hotel and its magnificent trappings. It was eight o'clock in the morning.

From the hotel, Iverson drove a circuitous route to their destination. Convinced they weren't followed, he turned down a rutted, dirt road lined with towering firs and scattered maples. Lichen clusters hung from branches like patchy fog on a coastal mountain. Iverson carefully navigated the old road and turned one last time into an opening in the woods. There, carved out amongst embroidered, shallow foliage, was a graveled runway and a waiting plane. A lone man nervously awaited their arrival and he approached Iverson immediately.

"This is the last time, Sergeant," he said sharply. "I don't owe you anything after this."

"You'll always owe me, Lenny," responded a hurried Iverson. "Just be happy I only ask for small favors."

"This ain't no …"

"Not now," Iverson commanded. "You can bitch later. The passports get here?"

"They arrived ten minutes ago," he replied. "Wanna tell me where I'm taking these two, or should I just give them a parachute and tell them to jump when they feel like it?"

"To Portland. And you'd better fly that tin can straight and fast. They need to catch a 12:35 plane to Philly."

"Then they'd better get their asses on board, hadn't they?"

"They're ready," Iverson said sternly. "And I can do without the theatrics."

"No baggage?" asked Lenny, scanning the ground and craning to see inside the car.

Sandra exited Iverson's car and walked up to Lenny. "Just this, Mr. Pilot," she countered, and dropped their satchel at Lenny's feet. "Shall we?"

The pilot glared at the woman giving him orders, stomped over to the plane and jerked open its door. Sandra entered the small craft and took a seat behind the pilot's. Jon spoke a few last words to Iverson, gave him his briefcase and its contents for safekeeping, and took the remaining seat on the plane. Lenny secured the door with a demonstrative slam, took his place behind the controls and started the Cessna's single engine. The plane erupted into metallic cacophony and was soon airborne.

Iverson returned to his vehicle and drove the rickety road back to the city. He drove slowly through Ashton's neighborhoods, gazing solemnly at the streets, structures and people he'd lived with for so many years. The city had changed dramatically in the fifty-four years he'd called it his home. He mentally paged through his career and pondered his life if his badge were not returned. Would his life have meaning if he weren't a cop? He didn't have an answer, and didn't much like the question. He shook the thought out of his head and thumped the accelerator. He had work to do.

three

Steven Gant and his partners decided it was time to make a call and check on their future.

"Pat, this is Steven Gant. We need to meet."

"I thought we agreed not to call each other at work," was the irritated reply.

"We did, and I'm sorry to break that agreement, but current events dictate that we talk."

After a tense pause, Pat replied, "Okay, Steve. When and where?"

"As soon as possible. I'm with Allan and Terrance in my office right now. The three of us would like to meet with you."

"Well..., it's about eleven now. I could get away in about half an hour, I suppose. Where?"

"Just a minute," delayed Gant, as he consulted with his fellow academicians. He returned to the phone. "How about Manley Park?"

"Too many people," said Pat emphatically. "There's another park on the old side of town, Grosvenor. You familiar with it?"

"It's not the kind of place I normally frequent, but I know where it is."

"Mostly transients. Should be safe as far as being recognized."

"Fine. I'll see you there in half an hour."

"Steve," interrupted Pat, "just the two of us. Four's a crowd."

"Just a minute," stalled Gant again.

"Pat…," he finally said, "Allan and Terrance both want to be there."

"Then I hope the three of you have a nice time in the park," Pat said firmly.

"Okay, okay. Just the two of us, Pat. But you're sounding pretty paranoid."

"You're the one asking for a meeting, Steve. If I'm sounding paranoid, it's because of this goddamned mess you've gotten me into."

"We can talk about that at the park, Pat."

"Just so you know, I'm getting tired of this shit."

The discussion ended with concerns and suspicions equally distributed. The relationship had been forged by a desire for money and power and, as is the tendency of such unions, blame flowed freely when things didn't go according to plan.

******

The two men met in the fractured parking lot of Grosvenor Park. Thick, gray skies lurked above a landscape littered with homeless people rolled up in tattered blankets on thinning grass. Their anonymous numbers had grown over the years and the park, once a prosperous playground for young and old, had transmuted into a miniature city of lost souls. The despair was almost palpable.

Gant arrived late and parked directly next to his clandestine business partner. They pressed buttons and windows rolled down.

"Afraid you'll catch something if you get out, Steve?"

Gant gave the remark no visible acknowledgment. He shuffled through a briefcase on his car seat and spoke deliberately.

"We've got problems, Pat."

"We?"

"Yes, we," Gant replied tersely. "Your men have botched the job."

Pat made no effort to hide his contempt.

"Let's take this back a little farther, shall we. If I recall, the documents that have caused all this fuss were taken from the university...your university, Professor Gant. I'd also like to point out that Mr. Farrell was supposed to be under your control. My men wouldn't have had a job to botch if you educated types had taken better care of your end of things."

Gant paused. He hated someone else having the upper hand, but his diplomacy surfaced.

"You're right, Pat," he said, shifting nervously. "But that doesn't change the fact that we have a serious problem on our hands…, one that's going to get us all in trouble if we don't solve it, and soon!"

Pat shifted gears with Gant's admitted ownership of the problem.

"So where do we stand, Steve? I've lost contact with Farrell and the girl but I think it's safe to assume they're still with Iverson."

"And," added Gant, "we should assume they still have copies of the documents. I don't understand why this Iverson hasn't turned them over to you."

"What makes you think he'd do that?"

"Well, Captain Denny, you are his boss, aren't you?"

"Sometimes I wonder," answered Pat Denny, more to himself than to Gant.

"What the hell is that supposed to mean?" demanded Gant. "Aren't you in charge down there? We pay you to cover our ass from that seat in your fancy office."

"Not nearly enough, Steve. Nobody talked about murder when I signed on."

Gant considered a rebuttal but decided against it. Now was not the time to lose Denny's protection even if its value was becoming questionable. Gant had met Denny at a fundraising effort for the city's police department. They'd struck up a relationship based, in large part, on their political aspirations. Gant, seeking information regarding the law and how to circumvent it, had used Denny as his resource but Denny quickly figured out what Gant and his cronies were doing and demanded a cut of the take. The professors figured a police captain on the payroll was a wise investment, and his pipeline to criminals had potential value.

"So, what do you suggest?"

Denny sighed deeply and made a quick, cursory scan of the park before answering.

"I have already replaced the two Iverson eliminated at the river. It wasn't easy finding them, but I did, though they didn't come cheap.

"Don't worry about the money," interrupted Gant.

"I won't," replied Denny. "But the debacle at the cabin cost us some time. We also lost track of Iverson and his friends."

"And how do we find them again?"

"Iverson has a disciplinary hearing tomorrow. If I know him, he won't miss the opportunity to make me look bad. And he won't risk his badge. He'll show up, and after he leaves, I'll have him tailed. Hopefully, he'll lead us to the other two."

"Hopefully?"

"Iverson's not stupid, Steve. As much as I hate to admit it, he's a damn good detective. I find myself admiring him as much as I hate him. I will, however, be more than happy when he's eliminated and I don't have to deal with his self-righteous shit any more."

They talked until they were satisfied that they had an agreed-upon plan. Denny would continue his pursuit of Iverson, Farrell and Sandra McKinney. When found, they would be terminated. They knew too much.

Steven Gant left the park and Pat Denny followed him out ten minutes later. They were both watched with keen interest by a man in a car parked behind an overgrowth of blackberry vines. Stan Iverson had come to Grosvenor Park to do some thinking and take delivery of some recently printed documents he'd be sending to Norway. What he acquired was more than he could have possibly imagined. Neither Pat Denny nor Steven Gant had spotted his car when they had arrived. They hadn't expected to need caution. Iverson had watched them carefully with a small pair of binoculars from the moment of their arrival until they left the park and its melancholic inhabitants. Though he didn't recognize Denny's accomplice, Iverson knew this meeting was held for a reason. The Sergeant lit a cigarette, stroked his graying hair, and smiled a perplexed yet gratified smile.

four

Midway through Wayne's shift, Ward C's personality changed. The patients' activity level shifted from calm to frenetic. Altercations became frequent and, most of the time, violent. The conflicts outnumbered the attendants trying to contain them and both staff and patients were getting injured. The normally passive Charley Orr was among the combatants. He approached the office window displaying a bloodied nose and a lacerated upper lip. He moved past the office porthole and banged his head violently against the metal-strapped door that denied him retreat to the outside world. Wayne attempted to inspect Charley's injuries, but the patient swung a clenched fist that connected squarely with the left side of Wayne's face. The blow sent Wayne sprawling across the hard cement floor in front of the office. The pain was physical, emotional, and considerable. Wayne scrambled to his feet in time to see Charley race back into the dayroom and attack another patient with frenzied rage. Other patients quickly joined the unrestrained brawl, and a whirlwind of flailing bodies was accompanied by a cacophony of high-pitched screams. Chairs crashed on the concrete floor and a cylindrical metal ashtray, jettisoned in the direction of the caged television, clattered down the hallway.

Nurse Nemesis ordered the staff into the office and shut the door behind them. She spoke to eager ears.

"It's obvious things are out of control," she stated calmly and resolutely. "I've called for additional help but none is coming. It's up to the four of us to handle this. Everybody understand me so far?"

"Yes, ma'am," replied Wayne. The others nodded nervously and stared intently at the Charge Nurse.

"Here's what I want," she continued. "First, I need sedatives prepared for each patient." She motioned to the attendant standing next to Wayne. "You," she demanded, "draw up fifteen syringes loaded with 500 milligrams of chloral hydrate."

The attendant hesitated.

"Now!" Nurse Nemesis instructed." The attendant jumped to his feet and bolted to the medication room.

"Next," she pointed a stubby finger at Wayne and the fidgety coworker next to him. "The two of you collect our entire supply of soft ties and cuffs and belts. Then start with the most agitated of the group and secure them to the nearest bed you can wrestle them into." She paused for a moment, took a deep breath and scanned the continuing war in the dayroom. She turned back to her staff, opened the office door wide and waved her arm in the direction of the melée.

"Let's move, gentlemen!" she said calmly. "We have work to do."

They darted out and she slammed the door behind them. Wayne glanced back, and saw her pick up the phone and hammer the numbered buttons.

Wayne took quick stock of his coworker and was relieved to see his fear. He wasn't alone. He also noticed his coworker's forehead was swollen and red.

"Forgot to duck, huh?"

The man replied with a simple nod of his head as they hurried down the hall to the supply closet.

"Me too," Wayne said and offered up his reddened face. "My name's Wayne, by the way."

"I…, I'm Jares," stuttered Wayne's ally in combat.

"Have you ever soft-tied anyone before, Jares?"

"N…, no."

"Neither have I," said Wayne. "I guess we'll have to wing it, won't we?"

"I didn't expect the violence."

"You're obviously newer here than I am."

"I started yesterday."

Wayne realized the situation was untenable but decided to make the best of it. "We'll get through this," he said confidently. "Try and stay away from flailing appendages and remember to duck."

They arrived at the storeroom and searched for the items needed for their human roundup. Wayne grabbed the long, cloth soft ties and handed them to Jares. The cuffs and belts appeared to involve locks and keys. Wayne decided to leave them in the closet. He didn't figure they'd have the time to use them.

"I've seen soft ties used before," reassured Wayne. "The hard part will be getting the patients in a position to apply them. It's going to take teamwork, Jares."

"Just tell me what to do." Jares was nervous but willing.

"More than anything, hold on tight. Once you have a hold, don't let go. Okay?"

"Okay."

They gathered up the soft ties and returned to the frenzied dayroom.

"Pick one," said Wayne.

Jares declined. Wayne looked into the human imbroglio and chose Charley Orr. He wanted to get him safely away from the fray.

"Him," stated Wayne firmly, pointing at Charley.

"Okay," responded Jares with shaky resolve. "I guess I'm ready."

"Let me free up my hands, and we'll get to it."

Wayne left the dayroom and deposited the restraints on the nearest bed inside the long, dark dormitory where Ward

C's patients slept. As he passed the office, he saw Nurse Nemesis still on the phone, her face crimson red, her angry voice audible behind the thick Plexiglas barrier. Wayne hoped she was making a good argument for reinforcements.

He returned to where Jares anxiously waited and they approached Charley Orr, slowly and tactically. Charley had broken from the pack but still had a wild look in his eyes. Wayne and Jares spoke alternately to each other and then to the highly agitated patient. Suddenly, they grabbed Charley, one by each arm, and attempted to control his violent efforts to break free. Charley struck out with every part of his body. His chemically blackened teeth snapped, trying to grasp and rip the flesh of his captors. He spit at them and tried to claw their arms and faces with jagged fingernails. Jares quickly lost his grip, and Wayne's partner was cast aside with strength that both awed and astonished Wayne. Wayne paid the price for Charley's single-limbed freedom with another solid blow to his jaw, this one drawing blood from where teeth met flesh. Jares returned to the fray and latched on to the whirling appendage with a tighter grip.

Wayne knew they were hurting Charley but also knew they had little choice. They managed enough control to drag Charley into the dorm and onto a bed, but the struggle did not abate. Charley broke free and bolted back toward the dayroom and into the continuing bedlam. They pursued and retrieved him, only to endure a repeat performance. Wayne was about to give up, when help arrived in the person of Nurse Nemesis. She barked instructions and Wayne and Jares obediently complied. They managed to return Charley to the bed and the large nurse sat on Charley's thighs as Wayne applied the soft ties to his ankles and Jares struggled to control his thrashing arms. Twice, Charley landed blows to Wayne's face with kicking feet but Wayne finally managed to secure his legs to the rusted bed frame. The arms were next. Charley continued to struggle as Wayne hurriedly applied the soft ties to his wrists and anchored them to the bed. Nurse Nemesis lifted herself from Charley's torso, tied one more strip of cloth over his arched chest, and affixed it tightly to the bed.

Wayne and Jares sat on the floor, wiping sweat from their foreheads, trying to catch their breath. Wayne wanted to remain with Charley and console his now shackled spirit, but Nurse Nemesis ordered them out to the dayroom to gather another patient. Wayne didn't argue and, together with Jares, reluctantly reentered the battlefield. They passed the third attendant, who hurried by with a syringe filled with thick, flaxen liquid. Wayne looked back and watched as he swiftly pierced the long needle through the soiled fabric of Charley's pants and into his rigid muscles. Wayne winced and moved on.

The campaign lasted for more than three hours; its conclusion seeing nine patients tied down and six others collapsed on Ward C's hard, damp floor. Wayne, Jares, and the other attendant were bruised, battered and totally exhausted from the fray. They sat in the office recovering their emotional stability and tending their wounds. Nurse Nemesis huffed out of the ward after the last patient had been secured, mumbling something under her breath about "those fool doctors."

After a brief rest, Wayne left the office and walked slowly and painfully to the bed where Charley Orr lay bridled. He had crusted blood on his nose and fresh seepage coming from the corners of pursed lips. His eyes still fought a battle within his mind. Wayne pushed his chair forward and gently touched Charley's arm in an attempt to convey some calm. Thirty minutes later, Charley's eyes closed.

Wayne remained at Charley's side for much of the remainder of his shift. He occasionally left him to check on the other patients now calmed with chloral hydrate. Ward C was eerily quiet, almost as disconcerting as the kinetic uproar a few hours before. The hushed ambiance gave Wayne time to evaluate what had happened and he was certain the aggressive behaviors were tied to the chemical experiments. Nurse Nemesis' behavior validated his hypothesis. Who was she on the phone with? Who were the "fool doctors" she mumbled about?

Wayne was more than happy to see the day end. He arrived home and immediately fell into his chair. He did not, however, have much time to relax. Company was on its way.

five

Stan Iverson parked his car three blocks away from his home. He paused briefly and surveyed the paved landscape for vehicles manned by suspicious characters. Seeing no overt evidence of surveillance, he exited his car, and navigated stealthily over and around neighborhood fence lines and through fading gardens. He reached the backside of his house and climbed quietly through a rear window he'd left unlatched. Once inside, he drew his weapon and methodically checked every room for waiting assassins. When assured he was alone, he sat behind drawn curtains and calculated the time of day in Germany. It was late, but he needed to check on Petr Stasky's progress. He dialed the number Stasky had provided and after the required connection delay, heard Stasky's thick, German accent on the other end of the line.

"You'll have to speak English, Petr," said Iverson. "I'm still monolingual."

"Stan!" It was a sleepy but cordial reply. It's good to hear from you. I was going to call you tomorrow."

"Then you have some information for me, Petr?"

"I do, and I hope it's information you'll find useful."

"So do I. What have you got?"

Stasky fumbled for a minute, then shared what he'd found.

"A little background first. Kirkenes is the far northern end of the line for everything that moves in Norway. It's up on the Barents Sea where most people don't care to go. It's a terribly harsh climate…, eight months of a severe winter that starts real soon. If you're planning on visiting Kirkenes, Stan, I'd suggest a summer trip."

"I'm hoping to avoid a personal appearance, Petr. What else?"

"Population is somewhere around twelve thousand with a mixture of Norwegians, Swedes, Lapps and now, after the changes in the Soviet Union, some Russians. The main industries are mining iron ore and shipping what's left of it. From what I'm told, the town never recovered from World War II."

"What happened during the war?"

"It was considered strategically valuable and I'm afraid we Germans, as well as everybody else, bombed the hell out of it. Kirkenes, by the way, like most of Norway, apparently has scant crime. Why are you interested in this place, Stan?"

"Let's just say it's becoming more interesting by the day," Iverson answered, "and there's one particular place I'm interested in as of yesterday. It's a hospital, or clinic, or something like that. It's called Gustaf's Clinic. Heard of it?"

"As a matter of fact, a guy I talked to in Bergen did mention something about an old psychiatric hospital a few miles outside of Kirkenes. Apparently, the place used to be prominent but is now closed down."

"Your source was mistaken, Petr. The case I'm working on leads me straight to that clinic."

"Where's your information coming from?" asked Stasky.

"What I know comes from an American working on some sort of research grant at the clinic."

"Is he legit?"

"I can't be sure, but I think so," replied Iverson. "The information he provided corresponds to facts I've gathered here. I've got people on their way to Norway now to follow up on both him and this clinic."

The detectives spoke for another ten minutes and then returned to their previous activity..., Petr Stasky to sleep, Stan Iverson to restless thought. Tomorrow was Thursday, the day of a disciplinary hearing conducted by the Internal Affairs Division in his honor. He still had to figure out a way to extricate himself from that mess.

Iverson collected the material from Kate Howser and Jon Farrell, and reviewed the information on the three professors. On one of the back pages of Terrance Walk's file was a review of a recent study on autism he'd authored. Iverson had noticed the document before, but hadn't given it more than a passing glance. A more thorough examination compelled him to unfold a long, yellowed newspaper clipping stapled to the article. On one side was a photograph of three men. Two of them, both with solemn expressions plastered on their faces, were not familiar to Iverson. The third one, the one with a plastic smile, Iverson knew. It was the man he'd seen in the park with Captain Denny. Iverson moved his eyes to the caption below the photograph. It identified the smiling man as Steven Gant and the other two as his cohorts in crime, Terrance Walk and Allan Trenholm.

Iverson finished his studies and began to crank out a plan for Captain Denny. He'd remained at his house longer than he'd wanted but had accomplished more than he'd expected. One last phone call and he'd move on.

"Hello, Captain Pat Denny?" he asked, hoping to have woken him up.

"Yes, this is Captain Denny. Who's this?"

"This is Stan Iverson. We have a few things to talk about."

Denny paused, and Iverson declined to fill the vacuum. He wanted the Captain to stew a little on his own.

"I can't talk to you," Denny finally said. "It's against IAD policy to discuss your situation, and you know that as well as I do."

"I'm aware of the policy, Captain, but it's not my hearing I wish to discuss. My interest is in a different policy … the one regarding police Captains being criminals."

Again, a pause…, this one longer than the first.

"I suppose you're going to explain yourself, Sergeant?"

"I'll just start by mentioning one name and I'd like you to fill in the rest."

"I'm not in the mood to play games, Iverson. If you think…"

"The name is Steven Gant," interrupted Iverson. "I believe you're familiar with the professor, aren't you, Captain?"

Still another pause.

"So, what if I am?" Denny finally demanded. Iverson could hear the tension creeping into his voice.

"So…, my dear Captain, the game is up."

Iverson allowed the words to penetrate, then continued.

"I'd suggest you come clean, Captain. Your tag team conspiracy is out of the bag and the DA's office will have the evidence in the next few days. You'll be arraigned by the end of the week and in prison within months."

"I have no idea what you're talking about."

"I think you do, Captain, and I'd suggest you take me seriously. You're in a shitload of trouble and I'd start thinking about plea-bargains if I were you. I'm sure you know that neither the courts nor the prisons treat bad cops well. You might want to plea bargain with the DA and avoid ending up a Bubba bride."

"Fuck you, Iverson. I ought to…"

"Personally," interrupted Iverson again, "I tend to think you have a shot at an insanity plea. I've been hearing of a clinic in Norway that offers cut-rate psyche evaluations."

"You don't know shit, Iverson. And if you did, you couldn't prove it."

"Proof is on the way," Iverson bluffed confidently.

"There's no way anyone will believe you," Denny taunted. "You're the one IAD wants. You're the one that's going to prison."

"I'll test my theory with IAD at one o'clock tomorrow, Captain," countered Iverson. "You can run yours by them whenever you choose. I'll bet they find my story interesting enough to run a few questions by Steven Gant and, of course, they'll have those snapshots from Grosvenor Park." Iverson waited for a response. None came.

"Tell you what," he offered, "I'll give you a little time to think about it and call you back. I'd be more than willing to hear your story before I tell mine to IAD. Who knows, if you help me, I might help you."

Denny slammed the phone down in outrage. Iverson wanted to destroy him and he'd undoubtedly enjoy doing it. More importantly, and despite his disdain for Iverson, he knew he was capable of doing it. Everything he'd worked for, the money, the power and the prestige, would be lost. He would go to prison. He frantically paced the downstairs rooms of his plush home, while his wife of twenty-three years and his two young daughters slept. What would they think when they learned he had subsidized their well-to-do lifestyle with infected money? They would be the laughing stock of Ashton.

Denny walked slowly up the stairs to the bedroom where his children slept and gazed with great pain at their cherubic faces. He moved to his bedroom and lingered, tenderly studying the face of the one person he felt truly loved and understood him. Where had it all gone wrong, he wondered?

Denny quietly selected his dress uniform from his closet and returned downstairs. He slowly and fastidiously donned the perfectly pressed blues that had impressed his wife so many years ago, and walked outside into a drizzling rain. He strode tacitly and slowly across a manicured lawn toward a shadowy row of cedar trees he'd planted in more innocent times. After making silent apologies to his family and friends, Patrick Nathaniel Denny gripped the gun he'd carried for twenty years, inserted the barrel deep into his mouth and blew his life away.

THURSDAY, SEPTEMBER 29

one

Jon Farrell and Sandra McKinney landed in Bergen, Norway, after a long, tiresome series of flights. It was late September and Norway was already cold. Bergen was a large city by Scandinavian standards, holding a little over two hundred thousand people within its natural boundaries of fjords and forests. Just north of sixty degrees of latitude and situated between the Norwegian and North seas, it had become Norway's most beautiful city. All of Norway had been covered with thick ice for tens of thousands of years until the frozen water receded one-hundred-and-forty centuries ago. The original Norwegians crossed towering, snow-laden mountains to get here from Central and Western Europe by way of Denmark, Sweden and Russia. Those inhabitants, most famously the Vikings, had left their social, cultural and political mark on a land populated with stubbornly proud people.

Jon and Sandra had a few legs left on their hop-scotching journey to Kirkenes. They would fly another five hours on smaller planes with stops in places christened Bodo, Trondheim, and Tromso. They checked their schedule, found they had a three-hour wait in Bergen, and decided to do some sightseeing. After exchanging American dollars for Norwegian krones, they found an unoccupied taxi by an airport curb and struck up a conversation with the plump man sitting behind the wheel. Sture's spotty English was filtered through a thick Nordic accent but he managed to describe a nearby site worth seeing and charged a reasonable fare. They hopped into Sture's aging Volvo and drove a short distance south to the town of Halhjem. Sture pulled his taxi to the side of a cobbled road and pointed at a footpath with no discernible destination. He motioned toward a small car lot across the road and told them he'd wait there for 30 minutes.

Jon and Sandra set off on the up-sloping footpath and through a short corridor of old buildings. In minutes, they passed a small sign announcing that Karsfjorden was ahead. They climbed another few minutes, walked through a cluster of stooped trees and were greeted with majestic beauty. In front of them was the fjord the signage had promised. The village of Halhjem was tucked into rolling hills along the coastline, its old buildings and ancient canneries crooked with age but still standing proud. The remains of an elderly harbor testified to more prosperous days.

Jon and Sandra gazed across a panorama of crystal blue water that washed the shorelines of a mazed archipelago. Norway's incomparable coastline, riddled with over one-hundred-and-fifty-thousand islands, was viewed in microcosm from the little hill above Halhjem. Karsfjorden, foreboding and alluring, cut into the horizon. The scene was magnificent, mesmerizing and peaceful. The short-term tourists sat quietly on the chilly ground and soaked in a quiet calm they had not had in what seemed a very long time. Sandra eventually broke the silence.

"How did we get involved in all this, Jon?" she asked.

Jon stared out at the open sea and thought about the question.

"I don't think we had a choice, Sandra," he finally replied. "And I must admit it's probably the only way I could have done what I've done."

Sandra was puzzled.

"I don't think I understand, Jon."

"I'm afraid I've never been big on courage, Sandra."

"You're very courageous, Jon," she whispered softly.

Jon continued his gaze at the incredible beauty in front of them and Sandra saw the tears trickling from his eyes. She felt her own cheeks dampen. Jon Farrell had been compelled to evolve in the past few days with force-fed emotions and hastily welded relationships. The perfect man was still a ways off but he was finally discovering who he was and who he could be. His tears were for joy at self-discovery and sadness at the cost of the journey.

The time drifted quickly and the travelers reluctantly returned to Sture's waiting Volvo. Back in Bergen, they boarded the first of the planes that would take them to Kirkenes and what they hoped would be the final chapter of their saga. Six hours later, Jon and Sandra arrived atop the Arctic Circle and landed at the small Kirkenes Airport. They left the cramped quarters of their noisy, single-engine plane and entered the crisp air of Northern Scandinavia. Forebidding Russia was a short, cold walk away.

Jon stared down the tarmac, searching for Wayne Burgess. They were an hour off their schedule, but he hoped his host would be waiting. They entered a Quonset terminal and were greeted by a smiling face and an extended hand.

"Mr. Farrell and Ms. McKinney, I presume?" asked Wayne Burgess.

"You presume correctly," replied Sandra, caught staring at Wayne's puffy face. "And I'm really hoping you're Mr. Burgess."

"I am indeed, Ms. McKinney, and I'm absolutely thrilled to see you. I'd ask you how your flight was, but having recently done that trip, I'll not request the nerve-wracking details."

"Nerve-wracking and loud," amended Jon. "My eardrums may never recover. But we're on the ground now and happy to be here. Where do we go from here?"

"It depends on your state of mind. We have a lot to do but I'm pretty sure you're looking forward to a shower, some food, and a bed to sleep in."

"And you would be correct, Mr. Burgess," responded Sandra resolutely. "But we also understand that we have work to do."

"Please, call me Wayne. Any luggage?"

"Only this," answered Jon as he plucked their duffel from the floor.

"Great!" responded Wayne and motioned toward the airport's exit. "Let's walk and talk."

The two weary travelers followed in step and Wayne laid out an itinerary for their approval.

"I thought we'd take a drive through Kirkenes and then out to the clinic, just to get you acquainted with the lay of the land."

Jon looked over at Sandra and they nodded their unified acceptance of the plan. They reached the airport's exit doors and Jon stopped at a series of ominous looking signs printed in bold red ink. He read the one in English:

"**Proclamation of Royal Decree**," it announced.

#1 Do not cross into the Russian frontier without prior permission from both the Norwegian and Russian governments.

#2 Do not fire any weapons within two miles of the Norway-Russia border.

#3 Do not attempt to take pictures of the area encompassing the common border of Norway and Russia.

#4 Do not talk to anyone on the other side of the border.

#5 Do not show abusive or offensive behavior on the border directed against Russia or its authorities.

Jon pointed out the sign to Sandra and she logged its inauspicious warning.

"Life on the border," Wayne quipped.

Wayne's vehicle had been secured from a neighbor who'd not heard of either a "Mr. Hertz" or "Mr. Avis." There apparently were few automobiles and no car rental agencies at this latitude. Land transportation consisted mostly of skis, sleds or skates for much of the year. Ferries transported people across waterways when ice floes permitted. Wayne's neighbor had inherited an old Mercedes that he'd last used "a few months back." It took Wayne over two hours to get it started.

They drove in and through Kirkenes in less than twenty minutes. The town still bore residual scars from the devastating avalanche of World War II bombs but, for the most part, appeared to be a quietly beautiful place. To the north and west, large volumes of water flowed from the Naatamojoki River into the Barents Sea. To the south stretched miles upon miles of barren tundra. To the east, and more imposing than any geography, was vast and skulking Russia. Kirkenes wasn't in the middle of nowhere, Jon thought. It *was* nowhere.

Wayne left the city and turned down a semi-paved road displaying a rusted road sign marked E6. He drove south for a mile before turning down a narrow road heading into a cluster of tall pines. Seconds later, he stopped the vehicle, got out, and motioned for his guests to follow. They walked briskly over a small rise and stood, staring, at the Gustaf Clinic.

"So that's where the money's been going," Jon muttered softly.

"That's my conclusion," replied Wayne, "and the evidence seems to support it. By the way, did you bring the documents from the university?"

"No," answered Jon. "I left them with Sergeant Iverson."

"Probably a good decision, but I would like to have compared notes."

"You're right, but their safety was my priority. We're going to need them."

"I'm sure it's the right choice," Wayne reassured, and changed the subject. "One more stop, and we'll head to my place. I'd like you to meet the fourth player on our team."

"Fourth player?" Jon asked, half puzzled, half alarmed.

"It's okay," responded Wayne, sensing Jon's concern. "I've got a good feeling about this guy, and we're going to need him."

Sandra emitted a tired sigh, but quickly regained her momentum as they returned to the car and sped off back toward Kirkenes.

"So, who's number four?" she inquired.

"His name is Sam Henke. He's a Gustaf employee …, sort of. We're meeting in town."

"How'd you hook up with him?"

Wayne relayed the story behind his relationship with Sam Henke and it was obvious they were all embarking on a dangerous game with people they hardly knew. A red flag unfurled in Jon's head but he quickly stowed it away. They didn't have time for his fear.

Wayne stopped the car at a small café in the heart of Kirkenes. The town held a cozy mid-section and scattered clusters of people moved through the chilled air.

"Should we be meeting our co-conspirator in the middle of town?" Sandra queried."

"Sam and I agreed a public meeting posed less risk of creating suspicion. Kirkenes is a small town. People here talk, but Sam told me they talk even more about anything remotely out of the ordinary. Meeting here seemed less likely to offer fuel to the rumor furnace."

Jon nodded his acceptance of Wayne's logic and they continued toward the café entrance. Jon offered polite smiles to passing natives and was acknowledged with inquisitive looks, but nothing more. They entered the café and Wayne led them to a man seated alone at a small table tucked in the rear of the room. He was staring into a cup of steaming coffee. Sandra guessed Sam Henke to be forty years old. His weathered skin and gray hair suggested a rough life in a tough climate.

"Hi, Sam," engaged Wayne. "I hope we aren't too late."

"Just a tad," Sam responded. He stood to greet the new arrivals and handshakes and names were exchanged.

"What the heck happened to your face?" Sam asked Wayne.

"Ward C was a war zone yesterday, "Wayne replied. "I'm not sure what caused the bedlam but it was very, very scary. I'll provide details another time. We have more pressing things to discuss."

The group ordered coffee and sat uncomfortably until Wayne moved the conversation in the direction of their task. He scanned the café for Gustaf's personnel and found no one he recognized. He then shared details of late-night sleuthing, human experimentation and Sam's decision to change his life. He described their current situation, including Sam's role as a recently re-employed inside player. Sam worked in a critical area and would provide some timely anxiety for Gustaf's Director. Wayne ended his update, and Sandra continued the discussion with a question addressed directly at Sam Henke.

"And what of you, Mr. Henke?" she asked bluntly. "You have the most to lose. Are you sure you want to be involved in this?"

Sam sized up the beautiful American and offered an honest answer.

"We all have a lot to lose, Ms. McKinney. Please don't kid yourself. We're playing a dangerous game with dangerous people. The risk is high. We could end up dead. I'm taking the risk because I want to like the guy in my mirror."

"Sam," said Wayne, "that's a terrific ideal, but Sandra has a point. Even if we succeed, you have a lot to lose. If you want out, I'd understand."

Sam didn't reply. Kirkenes, Norway, was his home. Unlike the Americans, he would be buried there regardless of the outcome of their endeavor. He was at risk either way.

"Sam," repeated Wayne, "we really would understand."

"No, Wayne," replied Sam with conviction. "We're doing what needs to be done and I need to be a part of that. I have no doubt about that anymore. I just want us to think this thing through and make damn sure we do all that we can to be successful. If we screw up, there'll be a heavy price to pay … for us and those folks in that dungeon. If I end up dead, I at least want the effort to have been worth it."

"Here, here," applauded Sandra. "I'm with Mr. Henke. It's got to be a good plan, or no plan. And we all have to agree to it before we act."

Sandra's proclamation was toasted with thick coffee.

"So where do we go from here, Wayne?" asked Jon.

"You two go to my house for food and rest. I'm sure Sam could use some sleep as well, since he left work only an hour ago. We'll meet later tonight after my shift at Gustaf's to hash out details."

The Norwegian and the three Americans left the café and headed in different directions. Fatigue and excitement sparred in their heads as they reached their homes. Sam Henke checked his mirror, liked what he saw and collapsed satisfied onto his bed. Wayne Burgess cooked burgers and fries for his guests and added information about himself, Denton Croft and Charley Orr. Jon and Sandra consumed the feast and shared stories of Leslie Covington, Neil Danielski and Deb Sutter.

two

Stan Iverson rolled over on the bed in his motel room. He'd rented a low-cost room in a cheap hotel after leaving his home the same way he'd entered it. He needed the rest but his sleep had been sporadic and fitful. His dreams were filled with vague characters bearing distorted qualities of his ex-wife. They spoke to him about things he didn't understand. His attempt at analysis was unsuccessful and short-lived.

The Sergeant washed the Freudian residue from his brain with a long, hot shower. He scraped off his ample stubble and stared at his face in the mirror, examining the nooks and crannies that had multiplied over the years. "What's your future, old man?" he asked himself out loud. He offered no answer for his question. He didn't have one. He threw on the same clothes he'd been wearing for the past several days and took another look in the mirror. He was due at his hearing in a few hours and decided he didn't much give a damn how he looked. If this was his termination party, he could go as he pleased.

Iverson sat on the bed and peeked out the window through frayed curtains. No one appeared to be watching his room. The old Sergeant was still outfoxing the bad guys. He sat back on the rumpled bed and thought about the plan he'd concocted with Jon and Sandra. They should have reached their Norwegian destination by now and he hoped all had gone according to plan. It was his turn to make a move. He opened the outdated, semi-shredded phone book on the table next to the bed and located the listing for Steven Gant. He punched the numbers on the phone that appeared printed next to the professor's name and waited for someone to answer his 8:00 a.m. call.

"Hello, Dr. Steven Gant here."

"Mr. Gant," began Iverson deliberately. "I'm going to suggest that you pay very close attention to what I'm about to say."

"Who is this?" Gant demanded.

"My name is Stan Iverson, Mr. Gant. Sergeant Stan Iverson of the Ashton Police Department."

After a short pause, Gant answered in softened tones. "Good morning, Sergeant Iverson. How can I help you?"

Iverson played the game.

"It's more about how I can help you, Mr. Gant."

"It's *Doctor* Gant, Sergeant. How is it that you can help me?"

"Well, *Doctor,*" Iverson said with calculated cynicism. "I think I can help you and your friend, Pat Denny, spend less time in prison then you probably should."

The thud made by the thumped down phone was Gant's only audible response. Iverson smiled to himself as he returned his phone gently to its cradle. The doctor has a poor bedside manner, he thought, but he'd gotten the response he hoped for. Steven Gant, it appeared, was not cool under pressure.

******

Steven Gant waited until his family had left for their respective weekday destinations of work and school, and dialed the office phone number of Terrance Walk. Walk's workday always started early, his quest for international stardom more intense than Gant's. His secretary answered the phone and put Gant on hold while she located the professor.

He picked up the phone five minutes later, a long wait for an impatient Steven Gant.

"Where the hell have you been, Terrance?" Gant demanded.

"I'd appreciate a different tone from you, Steven. Unlike some professors at this university, I have classes to prepare for."

Gant viscerally detested Walk. They had competed academically since their college days and Walk had usually won.

"I just received a rather disconcerting phone call from a Sergeant Stan Iverson of the Ashton Police."

"Iverson," Walk thought out loud. "Isn't he the one Denny said was working with Farrell?"

"Unfortunately, yes," replied Gant. "And he seems to have made the connection between Denny and us."

"How?"

"How the hell do I know?"

"What did you tell him, Steve?"

"I hung up on the son-of-a-bitch!"

"I'm not sure that was wise, Steven." Walk was being condescending and Gant was not in the mood for it.

"Well, if he calls again, I'll just give him your number."

"Very funny, Steve. Have you talked to Allan yet?"

"No," shot back Gant. "He's next on my list."

"I guess we need to meet," deduced Walk. "And all of us this time. I'll call Allan if you'll get a hold of Denny? I can meet any time after noon."

"Fine. Call me back after you talk to Allan. I'll be at my office in thirty minutes."

They ended their tense conversation without good-byes. Walk called Trenholm immediately and relayed the bad news. Gant waited until he arrived at his office before trying to contact Pat Denny. His call was met with feeble attempts by the Captain's office to explain his absence. He was eventually connected to someone who informed him that he could leave his name, but Captain Denny would not be returning his call. Captain Denny was dead. Gant rejected the proposal and nervously hung up his phone. His ashen face offered the first sign that he was losing control.

******

Stan Iverson called the station to make sure his IAD hearing was still on schedule. The Desk Sergeant, who had reluctantly told Steven Gant about Denny's death, broke the same news to Iverson. He also told him that Denny's death was self-inflicted. Iverson was shocked. He had imagined Denny capable of many things, but suicide wasn't among them. Iverson despised Pat Denny and everything he stood for, yet he couldn't help but suffer a pang of guilt for his death. The remorse quickly gave way to the urgent need to find the killers Denny had hired. Denny could no longer identify them, and they would still try and do the job they had been paid to do.

Due to Denny's death, Iverson's IAD hearing had been postponed indefinitely and he used the reprieve to develop a new plan … a plan excluding Denny. The pressure he'd wanted to exert on the Captain would have to be redirected. Given the reaction he'd received on an earlier phone call, he had a logical choice.

three

It was evenfall before Jon and Sandra saw Wayne again. After a stop at the Kirkenes postkontor, he'd returned home from his shift at the Gustaf Clinic. His guests were scrounging through his refrigerator in search of food. The burgers had been fully digested and they weren't finding replacement rations.

"Not much in there," said Wayne with serious understatement.

"We noticed," responded Sandra wryly.

"I thought instead of taxing my culinary skills, we'd go back to Kirkenes. When in Norway, eat as Norwegians."

"Sounds good," said Jon, closing the door of the barren refrigerator. "What about Sam?"

The knock on the door coincided with Jon's inquiry. Wayne left the kitchen, and returned with Sam Henke.

"Get enough sleep?" he asked the newest arrivals.

"Plenty, Sam," replied Sandra, noticing a difference in Sam's demeanor. "You look pretty chipper this evening. Erotic dreams, maybe?"

"I wish," replied a blushing Sam Henke. "Truth is, my sleep has been off and on these past few days. But this last attempt was successful and I feel better than I have in a long time. Maybe it's the company I've been keeping."

Sandra smiled her approval of Sam's appraisal. Wayne's quiet nod offered trusted membership in their newly formed club.

"How about some food, folks?" asked Wayne.

"About time," shot Sandra in return. "I'm ready whenever you guys are."

They returned to downtown Kirkenes and the restaurant was chosen by the only native Norwegian. The establishment was comfortable, its patrons cordial. Nobody was looking for fast food. Sam offered menu and order assistance and his plan was approved unanimously. He gave their selections to a blue-eyed waitress, then led a discussion on the history of Kirkenes. Their banquet arrived thirty minutes later.

Sandra tried sylte—a veal and pork combo with something Sam didn't include in his menu description, sizeable pigs' feet. She dug in eagerly, despite the porcine revelation. Jon dined on rullepulse—a spicy lamb and veal brew, "tasty and hot." Wayne went American— "steak, medium well, and a baked potato, fully tricked out." Sam nibbled fiskegrot, chased by dark beer.

As they ate, they talked about both the food and the task in front of them. Their plan would begin in the next few hours starting with Sam's alterations of a few medical records. It was a small but crucial piece of their scheme and why Sam had sought reinstatement at the clinic. They reviewed their roles and responsibilities and Sam mapped out structures, passages and critical Norwegian laws. The next morning, they would shake up Dr. Croft and the Gustaf Clinic.

FRIDAY, SEPTEMBER 30

one

At eight-o'clock sharp, Jon Farrell and Sandra McKinney walked into the administrative offices of the Gustaf Clinic dressed as upper-middle class Americans. They approached the curvaceous secretary and asked to see the clinic's director, but were informed they needed an appointment.

"Fine," Sandra huffed. "We'll return with our lawyers and the American Consulate."

The secretary pointed to empty chairs and rang her superior. Dr. Croft emerged a few minutes later. Croft scrutinized the strangers and gestured rigidly toward his office. He closed the door behind them and took a seat behind his glossy desk. The visitors sat down and the plan was launched.

"My name is Michael Alexander Orr and this is my sister Faye Stanton," Jon began. "We have reached what we hope is the end of a very long and arduous journey, Dr. Croft. We are here to remove our brother from your clinic and take him home to the United States."

"Your brother?" Croft asked, his voice wavering slightly.

"Yes, Dr. Croft," answered Sandra. "We have been searching for our brother for almost ten years now, and we have finally located him here at your clinic. His name is Charles T. Orr."

Croft stood up, his tension becoming apparent.

"Do you have identification that would verify your claim as Mr. Orr's relatives?" he asked.

Sandra opened her handbag and produced a series of documents Stan Iverson had faxed to the Kirkenes post office only hours ago.

"These papers should sufficiently establish us as Charles's family, Dr. Croft. We anticipated your need for documentation and therefore came prepared." Jon gave Sandra a subtle nod. She was magnificent, he thought.

Croft fumbled through the papers and scanned the information they contained. The documents appeared to confirm the Americans' identity and their relationship to Charley Orr.

"Well, uh…," stuttered Croft, "I'll have to check the clinic's records to make sure that Mr. Orr is here, you know."

"Dr. Croft," interrupted Sandra, "There are only a handful of patients at this clinic. You can't possibly be telling me that you don't know if one of them is named Charles Orr, can you?"

Croft pushed his chair away from the desk. He decided to take the offensive.

"Quite frankly, Miss, I'm not sure I have to tell you anything. But I will say that all of Gustaf's patients have been state committed, so if he is here, I couldn't simply release him into your custody." Croft rose from his chair and sat on the edge of the desk with folded arms in a smug attempt to intimidate his unwanted guests.

"We would disagree with you on that assessment, Dr. Croft," asserted Sandra calmly. "Our family records, specifically those dating to before my parent's emigration to America, indicate that Charles entered his first institution in Denmark as a voluntary patient. How he ended up here, we're not sure, but it really doesn't matter. He resides in Norway now, and therefore is governed by Norwegian law."

"And what is that supposed to mean?" demanded Croft.

"The laws of Norway, as you must know Dr. Croft, state that the original commitment, wherever it might have been, remains the legal status unless changed by the individuals who committed him or by a court order. My family made the original voluntary commitment and never altered it. And since we have never located a court commitment order from Denmark, Norway, or any other country, it is our position that our brother remains here voluntarily and can leave whenever he wishes."

Sandra had paid close attention to Sam Henke's legal lesson and to the contents of Wayne's files. She was hitting Croft with his own laws and he had no defense. The plan was going well.

Croft returned to his seat behind the desk. He glared at Sandra before picking up his phone and buzzing his secretary.

"I need the file on Charley Orr," he said, and after an unheard response, "Well, get down there and get it. Now, damn it!"

"So you do remember our brother," Sandra said with noticeable sarcasm.

Jon interrupted and deflected the confrontation.

"Please excuse my sister, Dr. Croft. It's been a long search, and we're both very anxious to see our brother."

"I haven't told you that you could see Mr. Orr. Not yet, anyway. I'm still not sure that he is your brother, and even if he is, I'm not sure I can release him. This is going to take some time to straighten out, you know. We have to consider what's best for the patient."

"We'll decide what's best for this particular patient, Doctor," ruled Sandra. "I have waited a very long time to find my brother and I *will* be taking him home."

Croft again rose from his chair.

"Is that a threat?"

"It's a promise, Dr. Croft," countered Sandra. "It's time my brother came home and you have no legal right to stop that from happening."

Croft had no reply. The secretary entered the office, puffing from her hurried trip to wherever Charley's records had been stored. She set a single folder containing a few pieces of loosely gathered paper in front of Gustaf's director and hastily left the tension-filled room. Croft fingered through the documents quickly, then looked again. He tossed aside everything in the folder except one item marked "Admissions History." Croft silently studied Charley's commitment record and, to his visible dismay, found nothing to invalidate his visitors' claim. Sam Henke's editing skills had made certain he wouldn't.

"Well, Dr. Croft," inquired a poised Sandra, "What have you found in your precious files?"

Croft was defensive.

"I'm sorry, but I can't share that with you, Miss…, what was it?

"Stanton, Doctor. Ms. Faye Stanton."

"Of course …, Ms. Stanton. Patient files are confidential. I'm sure you're aware of that."

Sandra was indeed aware.

"I'm not asking to see the file, Doctor. I'm asking to see my brother."

Croft paused, buying time to find a way out of his predicament.

"If you will give me a phone number where I can reach you, I'll contact you in a few days and give you the clinic's decision regarding your brother."

The plan had hit a moment of uncertainty but Jon filled the void.

"One day would be unacceptable, Dr. Croft, and there'll be no need for phone calls. We'll return at precisely ten-thirty and expect to leave shortly thereafter with our brother."

"I can't promise…"

"Ten-thirty," repeated Sandra firmly. "If Charles is not here in your office at that time, our next communication to you will be through the American Consulate."

They got up and walked quickly out of the office, leaving behind an agitated and stressed Denton Croft. Gustaf's director paced his office floor for ten minutes before buzzing his secretary.

"Get me Steven Gant in the United States," he demanded. "And make it quick."

"It's midnight back there," she advised.

"I don't give a damn what time it is," he shouted back. "Call him at his home and get the son-of-a-bitch out of bed if you have to. I need to talk to him…, now!"

two

Steven Gant, Terrance Walk and Allan Trenholm met and debated the impact of Pat Denny's death. With Denny dead, they'd lost the ability to influence police investigations, and any evidence against them would no longer be filtered through the Captain's office. Reputations and well-rehearsed lies were all they had left to shield them. Trenholm, however, suggested Denny's death was a blessing because it removed a potential witness against them. They had not personally hired the gunmen and no one, other than the dead Captain, could tie them to any of the murders. The professors agreed that if evidence led to indictments, it would be their word against that of a crusty old cop, himself under investigation by the very police department he worked for. They left their meeting secure with their status and with an agreement to talk to no one, particularly Sergeant Stan Iverson.

******

Steven Gant sat in his den, trying to escape his escalating predicament. He'd said little during the family dinner and his wife, sensing his stress, had left him alone. He now rested languidly in his easy chair and stared without interest at the book in his lap. Despite the agreement with his colleagues, he sensed things were far from settled. The call from Stan Iverson had dented his invulnerability. The resonant ringing of the phone interrupted his dilemma.

"This is Dr. Steve Gant," he announced.

"Dr. Gant, this is Dr. Denton Croft in Kirkenes, Norway."

Gant was immediately alarmed. He'd previously only spoken to Croft when visiting Kirkenes. Phone conversations with Croft were supposed to be handled by the researchers, Walk and Trenholm.

"It's late, Croft," Gant complained. "What do you want?"

"We've got a situation here at the clinic I thought you should know about."

"And why are you calling me about it, Croft? We agreed phone calls would be directed to Drs. Walk and Trenholm.

"We agreed I'd contact them with issues regarding research. This is not about research, Dr. Gant. This is political in nature and I believe I was told that that is your bailiwick."

Gant digested Croft's logic and silently agreed with his premise. "What kind of situation?" he asked reluctantly.

"I've had a visit from two Americans claiming to be relatives of one of our patients, and they're demanding that I release him to their custody. If I don't, they're threatening to involve their attorneys and the American Consulate."

"When did this happen, Croft?"

"Within the last hour."

Gant's head ached as he measured the crisis. There had to be a connection with Iverson's phone call.

"Can they do that? Can they actually just take a patient out of there?"

Croft shared his newly acquired knowledge of relevant Norwegian law and relayed his discoveries in Charley Orr's altered records. He also shared his conviction that if Charley Orr was taken to the United States, he would undoubtedly be examined by his new family's medical professionals. It would be only a matter of time before Gustaf's unique brand of research was discovered and Croft was convinced that criminal prosecutions and penalties would follow quickly.

"I will not bear this burden alone, Dr. Gant," he threatened.

"What exactly does that mean?" asked Gant.

"It means what it means."

Gant sloughed off the warnings and gave Croft what amounted to a direct order, something Gant was good at.

"Do not, under any circumstances, allow that patient to be removed from your clinic. Stall these so-called relatives anyway you can. I'm betting they're not related to Orr."

"You sound pretty confident about that. Do you mind explaining how you've come to that conclusion?"

"I am confident and I'll take the time to explain why at a later date. You're just going to have to trust me. For now, get yourself under control, call their bluff, and they'll back off."

Croft accepted the instruction reluctantly and hung up the phone. Gant put on a coat and headed out the door. He needed to think and walking always helped that process. He walked rapidly and forcefully, breaking a sweat in the chill air. Myriad scenarios crisscrossed his mind but none offered the perfect solution he wanted. He was playing the game of his life.

******

Jon and Sandra drove the borrowed Mercedes off clinic grounds to a prearranged meeting place on the outskirts of Kirkenes. Sam informed them that Wayne had started his shift about the same time they had entered Croft's office and that he was ready to perform his role in their drama. They analyzed the meeting with Croft, reviewed the next steps of their plan, and then lingered in anxious quiet until it was time for a return to the Gustaf Clinic to find out if Charles T. Orr would be waiting to see them.

******

Jon and Sandra re-entered the administrative offices of the Gustaf Clinic and informed the secretary that they had returned to see Dr. Croft. She buzzed the clinic's director and nervously announced the return of the two Americans. Croft appeared within minutes and again ushered them into his office, closing the door behind them. He offered chairs. They refused.

"I've considered your position," Croft began, "and I've come to the conclusion that I cannot release Mr. Orr to your custody."

Jon and Sandra wasted no time on conversation. They turned together and began walking toward the door. Croft was shocked by their abrupt, unspoken response.

"Wait," he said plaintively. "Where are you going?"

Sandra turned and responded with controlled anger.

"We've had enough discussion, Doctor. You're hiding something here and we're not about to waste time in meaningless banter while you cover your tracks."

"I have no idea what you're talking about, Ms. Stanton," Croft said nervously.

"And you're a liar, Dr. Croft," Sandra snapped back. "Do you think we're fools? We've done our research. We know what's going on here...what's *really* going on. All we've asked for is our brother's return and you have refused. You leave us no choice but to expose you and Gustaf's torture chambers. You have collected the last of your soul money."

Jon and Sandra turned and abruptly left Croft's office without further discussion. Croft slammed the door behind them, poured a large portion of cognac and collapsed fitfully into his chair.

Jon and Sandra drove away from the clinic and Sam Henke arose from his prone position on the back seat of the car.

"How went Plan A?" he inquired.

"We're on to Plan B," answered Jon with unmasked frustration. "I'm glad we wrote two scripts for this play."

Jon made a call to Ward C and informed Wayne that the burden of success had fallen on his shoulders. Wayne responded with tempered resolve and went immediately in search of Charley Orr. He found him in his usual location, at the portal of planetary control.

"Charley," he said at the patient's command station. "We have to take a walk, but we're not going to the medical clinic."

Compliance was habit for Charley Orr. He returned his instrument of control to its socially acceptable sheath and waited with downcast eyes to be led to his destination. Wayne walked past the office and toward the door leading out of Ward C. His autistic companion shuffled slowly behind him.

"Just where do you think you're going?" asked a raspy voice from inside the office.

"Just thought I'd take Charley out for a little walk, Ma'am," Wayne told the Charge Nurse. His legs were trembling.

"Since when do we take Ward C's patients on pleasure trips, Mr. Burgess?"

"Well," Wayne countered, trying desperately to maintain eye contact, "considering what he's been through recently, I thought it might be good to give Mr. Orr a brief change of scenery."

Nurse Nemesis scrunched her face and placed her hands firmly on her hips. Wayne knew she didn't buy his story and prepared himself for the worst.

"So you want to change the way we do things around here, Mr. Burgess," she began. "I thought I'd made your role on Ward C clear."

The Charge Nurse moved out of the office and into the hallway with Wayne and Charley. She closed the door behind her and stepped away from multiple sets of eager ears. Charley shuffled his feet and stared at the floor while Wayne braced himself for the verbal tirade he was certain would be unleashed. The sizeable nurse said nothing while she measured Wayne with intense, round eyes. She then took Wayne firmly by the arm and navigated him inside the dormitory adjacent to the office. Charley dutifully followed.

"Mr. Burgess," she began in a surprisingly hushed voice, "I'm not sure exactly what you're up to, and I'm not sure that I want to know. I do, however, have one thing to say."

Wayne stiffened, not sure what to expect.

"You'd better be damn careful and damn sure about what you're doing," Nurse Nemesis declared. "A lot of people will be affected by what you're about to do and Charley Orr is foremost among them. You have judged us harshly here at Gustaf's, but we aren't all evil. Most of these patients would have died a long time ago had it not been for this place that you eagerly condemn. So go do your savior thing, but be sure you do it well."

Wayne didn't respond. He had no words to offer. He stood briefly and stared at Nurse Lai, then simply nodded and walked toward the door. Charley started to follow but stopped when passing the still imposing nurse. He stood quietly next to her and stared at the floor. She took hold of his shoulders and turned him toward Wayne.

"Go!" she stated forcefully and pointed at Wayne. She turned her back on both of them as Charley followed her directive.

Charley moved alongside Wayne and they walked through the door together. Wayne took one last glance at the

Charge Nurse before he closed and locked Ward C's door behind them. Small droplets of moisture trickled down her hard, proud face.

******

Dr. Croft instructed his secretary to get Ward C's supervisor on the phone.

"Nurse Lai here."

"This is Dr. Croft, Nurse Lai. I have a special order for you regarding one of the patients on your ward."

"And who would that be, Doctor," she asked, with a pretty good idea of who Croft would identify.

"Charles Orr. He's to be kept under close observation until further notice and he's not to leave Ward C under any circumstances. Is that clear, Nurse Lai?"

"I'm afraid Mr. Orr is not here right now, Doctor."

"Not there!" screamed Croft. "Where the hell is he?"

"He's out on the grounds with one of the staff, Doctor. They should be back in an hour or so."

Croft swiveled in his chair, growing angrier at his intensifying dilemma.

"Which staff?" demanded Croft.

"He's with the American student, sir. I believe his name is Wayne Burgess."

Croft was stunned. He'd been set up by those goddamned Americans.

"I want them found and brought back to Ward C immediately. Do you hear? Immediately!" Croft shouted.

"Is there some problem?" the Charge Nurse asked calmly. "Is Mr. Orr in some kind of danger?"

"That does not concern you, Nurse Lai. Just do as you're told." Croft ended the call and buzzed his secretary again. "Get security, now!" he blurted. "I want all of them in my office in five minutes."

Gustaf's security team consisted of three mercenaries imported from nearby Russia. They had been recruited and employed by Croft for the sole purpose of securing the Gustaf Clinic from the outside world. They would do whatever they were told as long as they were paid the blood money Croft had promised them. They had proven useful in the past when lifeless patients had required disposal.

Croft's instructions to his small gang of thugs were brief and clear. Find Wayne Burgess and Charley Orr and bring them to him. If they resisted, kill them. Croft knew killing an American would be risky, but his choices were clear. He either disposed of the evidence or spent his remaining days in a Norwegian prison. The debate was short-lived.

******

Wayne led Charley toward the compound's perimeter. Charley's pace slowed as they reached the gate and he stopped within feet of his freedom.

"Let's go, Charley," Wayne coaxed. "We have friends waiting."

"Friend," Charley murmured softly.

"Yes. Friends," replied Wayne. "They're waiting for us. But we need to hurry, Charley." Wayne moved forward.

Charley balked.

"Charley's friend," said Charley.

"Yes," Wayne responded. "They're Charley's friends."

"No. Friend there," Charley said and pointed to a dilapidated building with shuttered windows across the compound's courtyard. Wayne didn't know what Charley meant but sensed the urgency of moving through the clinic's gate.

"Charley!" he pleaded. "We need to get moving."

"Take Charley's friend," Charley stated clearly and began walking toward the structure he'd pointed to.

"Charley!" Wayne pleaded. "Please. We need to go through the gate."

No response came from Charley Orr. He continued his course toward the old building. Wayne bolted into Charley's path and Charley stopped.

"What are you doing, Charley?" asked Wayne, trying to control a growing panic.

Charley Orr raised his head and looked deep into Wayne's eyes. He spoke clearly and with purpose.

"Charley won't leave without Charley's friend." His expression declared his resolve and Wayne understood his plan would only succeed if done Charley's way. What that meant, he wasn't sure, but he hoped his partners would be there if and when he needed them. He moved out of Charley's path and followed him to the old building.

The doors were padlocked but the corroded hasps came free when Charley deftly pulled out the screws. He'd done this before, Wayne thought. Once inside, Charley silently led Wayne down a narrow and dimly lit hallway. Water dripped from the ceiling and settled into rust-tinged pools on the floor. Old flakes of paint crunched under Wayne's feet and a moldy stink filled his nostrils. They turned a corner to a series of closed doors, each with a small barred window a third of the way down from the top. Wayne peered into the first one they passed and saw a twisted metal bed supporting a stained and shredded mattress. Beside the bed stood a three-legged table and a shadeless lamp. A thick, black electrical cord lay coiled on the floor next to the table.

Wayne stepped back from the grilled portal and peered anxiously down the hallway from where they'd come. No one was there. "Not yet," he thought, and continued after Charley.

Charley stopped at the fourth door. Wayne caught up to him and looked through the opening. Inside he saw a small, frail child curled up in the corner of the room. "Friend," Charley said clearly.

Wayne didn't respond but visually inventoried the room. It was furnished much like the one behind the first door. Charley grabbed his arm tightly. "Charley's friend go too."

Wayne looked back at Charley. He wanted to know more about the boy but time was rapidly running short. Croft's henchmen would certainly be looking for them by now.

"Charley," he pleaded. "What do you want? We don't have much time."

"Charley's friend go, Charley go," was the quick, firm retort.

Wayne quickly discerned two options. Leave without Charley or free the boy behind the door and bring him along. The choice was obvious.

"Okay, Charley," Wayne said, "How do we get in there?"

Charley offered a partial smile, reached over Wayne's right arm and inserted his hand through a narrow hole in the wall adjacent to the old door. Ten seconds later, after an audible thunk, Charley retrieved his hand from the fissure and pushed open the door. Wayne was stunned. Not at the magical access, but at Charley Orr's sudden lucidity.

"Get friend," Charley stated pragmatically.

Wayne stared at Charley, gathered himself, and then walked over to the young boy. He lay on a filthy bed in frayed pajamas, his boney frame visible under a thin layer of pallid flesh. Expressionless eyes sat in dark, hollow sockets and purplish, cracked lips oozed reddish-brown liquid. He was completely unresponsive and Wayne knew the boy wasn't going to walk on his own. He hoisted the boy's emaciated body over his shoulder, turned, and faced Charley. A door slammed and voices were heard coming from where they'd entered the building.

"Go, now!" Charley commanded.

"Go where?" asked Wayne in an urgent whisper. "There's no way out of here now."

Charley didn't answer. He bolted out of the room and into the hallway. Wayne followed. He could hear heavy boots rapidly pounding the floor behind them. Charley took a right turn and headed down the hall toward a boarded-up doorway. They reached the end of the hall and Charley placed his hand on a fragment of plywood three feet from the floor and pushed. The board swung back and revealed a small crawlspace. Charley ducked in and motioned for Wayne to follow. Wayne gently dropped the boy to the floor, squeezed into the opening and pulled the boy in behind him. Charley swung the plywood gate closed just as two guards turned the corner.

The three fugitives crouched behind the thin barrier as the guards raced toward them. Wayne peered through a slivered opening and watched the men burst into the boy's former cell.

"Fuck!" yelled one of the guards. "The kid's not here. Nobody's here. Croft is gonna have a shit fit."

"They gotta be here someplace," countered the other guard. "Let's make sure we check the whole fucking building. I don't want to give Croft a reason for firing us."

The two men lumbered back into Wayne's view.

"You check that side and I'll check this side," ordered the larger of the two guards. They pulled large keys from their pockets and opened the doors on either side of the hall. As each door bolt clunked open, Wayne's heart throbbed louder. His breathing labored and his legs cramped. "Hang on," he told himself.

The guards completed their inspection of the cells and moved around the corner and out of Wayne's sight. He gulped some air and sat back to relax his leg muscles. The respite didn't last long.

"Go now," whispered Charley and didn't wait for a response. He rolled to his knees, and headed through the damp crawlspace and away from the hallway. Wayne followed suit with the boy draped haphazardly over his shoulders. Charley led a zigzagged path past jagged nails, broken pipes and protruding shards of lumber. The boy's back scraped the rough ceiling. Wayne crouched lower and moved ahead quietly despite the burning in his leg muscles. Charley stopped briefly as a large, black rat clambered over his body and down his left leg to the floor. The rodent moved on and so did Charley. They reached another plywood panel and Charley returned to his haunches, pressing his ear to the wall. Wayne rolled the boy to the floor and joined the surveillance. No sound came from behind the wall and Charley swung the panel upward. He crept out of the crawlspace and into a hallway. Wayne followed, stretched his cramped torso upright and heard Charley Orr's next order.

"Go now!" Charley stated emphatically.

"Go where?" asked Wayne.

"Outside," Charley replied and pointed to a doorway at the end of the hall.

"Where's that lead, Charley?"

"Outside!"

"Where outside?"

"Outside!"

Wayne accepted Charley's limit and gestured for him to show the way. Charley led them to the doorway, stopped, bent over and picked up a thin fragment of wood from the floor. He inserted the splinter between the door and the jamb and yanked upward. Something heavy dropped to the ground behind the door and Charley pushed it open. Wayne recoiled as sunlight struck his eyes. A quick survey of the landscape told Wayne he was at the back of the building, opposite where they had entered. He saw no sign of the guards. They needed to get to the gate and find the other friends.

******

Jon, Sandra and Sam waited anxiously outside the entrance of the Gustaf Clinic.

Sandra was the first to spot two figures walking towards them on the graveled road. Jon and Sam exhaled a unified sigh of relief. Their joy stopped short when they saw two more figures following at a distance.

The two men in front moved clumsily forward and Jon strained to grasp why.

"What the hell?" he exclaimed.

"What's wrong?" demanded Sandra.

"I see Wayne, but there's more than one person with him."

"Are you sure?" asked Sam.

"Two are on foot and I think Wayne's carrying someone on his back."

Sandra and Sam refocused their eyes.

"Damn!" exclaimed Sandra. "You're right. What the hell's going on?"

"I'm not sure, but I don't think we'll have time to ask questions. Those other two are from Croft's private army and I'll bet they're not taking prisoners. Sam, get the car over here and ready to roll."

Sam raced to the car, started the engine and backed it up as close as he could to where Jon and Sandra waited. His foot twitched nervously on the accelerator.

The guards closed in on the fugitives. Jon urged them on with shouts of encouragement and warnings of the pursuit. Wayne glanced over his shoulder and caught his first glimpse of his pursuers—fifty yards away and weapons drawn. Adrenaline pushed him and the weight on his back, but Charley's atrophied muscles knew only one pace. They still had another twenty-five yards to go when he tripped and tumbled heavily to the ground. Wayne's attempts to pull Charley to his feet proved futile and his panicked pleas fell on deaf ears. The guards stopped a hundred feet away and pointed their weapons at the stationary targets.

"Stay down, motherfuckers!" one barked. "Move and you'll be shot."

Wayne ignored the warning and tugged at Charley's arm. A gunshot rang out and a bullet ricocheted off a rock six inches from Wayne. Another bullet whistled by, spawning a panic- induced idea.

"Charley," he shouted. "It's time to *really* control your universe. Right fucking now, Charley!"

Charley shot up off the hard ground and bolted for the gate. Wayne and his passenger followed. They cleared the clinic's boundary and jumped headlong through the open doors of the waiting Mercedes.

Sam floored the accelerator amid a hail of bullets, one of which pierced the rear window and lodged in the dashboard just to the right of Sam's elbow. Another shattered the driver's side mirror while countless others ventilated the trunk of the car. The rest were off-target, their accuracy hampered by the car's trailing dust.

A mile down the road, Sam brought the car to a halt, and they carefully surveyed one another for damage.

"It's…, it's great to be alive, huh, fellas?" Sandra finally stuttered. "What's next?"

"I think I'd like to know who's who," suggested Jon.

Wayne took a deep breath and introduced Jon and Sandra to Charley Orr.

"And your other friend?" queried Sandra.

"That'll have to wait," Sam interrupted suddenly. "We have company." A dust cloud was quickly approaching.

"The guards?" asked Jon.

"That's my guess."

Sam punched the gas pedal again and gravel scattered as they headed to Road E6 and Kirkenes. Gunshots again rang out and another bullet pierced, webbed and finally splintered the rear window. Sandra flashed back to the scene on the river and her body trembled. Maybe this time, they wouldn't make it. Jon reached through the seats and held her arm tightly.

"We're gonna make it, Sandra," he said confidently. He was amazed that he actually believed it.

"Everybody down!" yelled Sam, and heads hugged the cushioned car seats. Wayne pushed Charley and the boy to the floor.

Sam reached the pavement of E6, left smoking rubber on its surface and accelerated toward town. The guards followed and Sam pushed the Mercedes to its limit. They reached Kirkenes and the guards veered off. Sam cautiously weaved the car through city streets while peering warily down alleys and walkways. A few Nordic citizens followed their progress with more than curious interest. Automobiles were unusual here, but one with bullet holes and shattered windows would provide gossip for months.

A piercing blast broke the calm and shattered the windshield. A tempest of glass shards flooded the car and rested in flesh. Sam slammed on the brakes and looked through what remained of the Mercedes' front window. Two guards approached slowly, holding the shotguns they had just discharged.

"Punch it!" Jon said quietly, but firmly.

"W… What?" asked Sam, still staring at the guards.

"Hit the god-damned gas pedal, now!" yelled Jon.

Sam's foot attacked the car's accelerator. The Mercedes lurched forward and collided with both guards. The impact launched one guard into a brick façade, the other onto, then over the hood of the car where his flight path ended on the street behind them. Sam slammed on the brakes, leapt from the car and grabbed the shotguns from the ground. Jon did a quick check on the car's occupants.

"Everybody okay?" he asked.

"Been better," replied Sandra numbly.

"Sam?"

"Never better," Sam replied from outside the Mercedes.

"Wayne?" asked Jon, continuing his inspection.

Wayne was still draped over Charley and the boy. He unfurled his body and cautiously looked around.

"I think we're okay here. A little shaky and a little bloody, but it doesn't appear serious. How about you?"

"Ditto," Jon replied. He looked at the inert guards and took a long, deep breath. He couldn't believe how close he'd come to dying … again. He inventoried his emotions and found there were many, but one that felt particularly good. Pride had surfaced again. He was getting to like that one … a lot.

Jon found a packet of tissues in the glove box and gently dabbed some seeping blood from Sandra's face. "You're my hero," he said to her softly. "Now let's find that plane. I'd like to be at ten thousand feet before Croft knows we're gone."

"Before *you're* gone," corrected Sam. "I'm staying here."

"What?" The question came from multiple sources.

"Someone has to clean up this mess," Sam stated calmly. "The people of Kirkenes are about to face an uncomfortable reality. They'll be forced to remove their blinders and see the truth about the dungeon in their midst. I think there's a better chance folks will accept it if it comes from one of their own."

"What makes you sure anybody will believe you, Sam?" asked Wayne.

"I'm not sure, but it's something I've got to do. This is my home."

"Are you really sure?" probed Jon.

"I'm sure, okay? Enough about me. Let's get you to that plane."

Sam headed for Kirkenes' lone runway and Wayne narrated an abbreviated version of Charley's abduction and how he came to bring the boy. They arrived at the airstrip, located the small private plane secured by Stan Iverson, and parked the distressed Mercedes on the tarmac. Sam extracted two duffels from the bullet-ridden trunk while Wayne readied Charley and the boy for their flight to freedom. After melancholy farewells to Sam Henke, the three Americans, Charley Orr and an unknown boy boarded the plane and left Kirkenes behind. At Bergen, they'd cash in another Iverson favor for flights to New York and then home to Ashton. Their puzzle was coming together.

SATURDAY, OCTOBER 1

one

An anxious Stan Iverson waited for the Nordic travelers at Ashton's "Runway Lounge." His nerves always twitched when he sensed a case nearing its climax and he had that feeling now. Cases become more dangerous when the players get backed into corners. Predictability wanes and volatility intensifies. If Iverson wanted this case to end well, he'd have to stay ahead of the curve.

Iverson had just finished his second beer when a monotone voice announced the arrival of his expected flight. With an audible sigh of relief, he left a generous tip and walked slowly down the airport's large lobby. He stationed himself behind a squared stanchion and closely eyeballed the human traffic. He spotted and branded returning Ashtonites as they came down through the terminal and headed to the luggage carousel. The man in the Levi's, with graying hair and a tube tucked under his arm, was probably a contractor. A cluster of men in cheap suits were most likely salesmen returning from yet another boring conference and the two women with slender briefcases and cell phones attached to their ears were obviously real estate agents. A couple of returnees were greeted with hugs and roses but the bulk of the travelers shuffled wearily and purposefully toward where they hoped their baggage awaited.

The Sergeant glanced up at the board behind the airline's counter. Jon and Sandra had not yet come down the tunnel so he checked the flight number with that written on the now crumpled piece of paper in his pocket. The numbers matched. He scanned the gate area and stopped at the word "terminal." A bad choice of word for air travel, he thought.

Iverson finally spotted his allies. He studied them closely as they slowly walked toward him. Jon and Sandra were followed closely by three others. One, a young boy, was in a wheelchair. Iverson's eyes passed by the boy's gaunt face but returned to it quickly. There was something familiar there but his memory couldn't find it. Iverson scanned the airport lobby before moving from behind his sentry post and toward Jon and Sandra. After a solid handshake from Jon and an unexpected hug from Sandra, Iverson was introduced to Wayne Burgess and Charley Orr.

"And this one?" inquired Iverson, as he walked over to the boy in the wheelchair.

"Well, Sarge," answered Sandra, "We aren't real sure who he is and he doesn't seem able to help us out on that."

"He was at the clinic, Sarge," offered Jon.

Iverson looked at the boy intently, his memory searching for a connection.

"Sarge," asked Jon. "Something wrong?"

Iverson looked up. "Probably just an old man's brain playing tricks on itself. My apologies, folks, you've all had a long journey. Anything you need right away?"

Wayne pointed at the Runway Lounge, and they proceeded slowly and deliberately to the bar Iverson had just vacated.

They ordered food and drinks and Jon delivered a condensed version of their Scandinavian adventure with special details provided by Sandra and Wayne. Iverson informed them of the developments regarding Captain Denny and Steven Gant. The food came quickly, to the delight of Charley Orr who consumed anything in front of or around him. Sandra fed the "soup of the day" to the unnamed boy. Iverson finished his meal, sat back in his seat and took a long look at the gathered, tired ensemble. What they'd accomplished in the past two days was amazing.

"So, where do we go from here?" Jon asked.

"We've got a number of things to do," answered Iverson.

"We're listening," said Sandra.

"We need to get our guests of honor into safe hands," Iverson began, nodding at Charley and the boy, "and we need to have them examined to validate the abuse claims we will present to authorities. Unfortunately, our needs are immediate and my list of doctors is short." Iverson wanted a physician who would examine Charley and the boy, but he also needed someone to vigorously question their pasts. The doctor they chose would have to be willing to testify against other doctors, and the medical profession had a reputation of protecting their own.

"I may have an answer for both problems," Jon said confidently. Iverson approved the positive attitude with a knowing smile sent in Sandra's direction. She winked back her acknowledgment and Jon offered his solution.

"There's a doctor, a radical of sorts, who's donated a lot of her time to treat some of Futures' clients and to train staff. I don't think she'd be averse to taking on either the medical or academic establishments."

"How soon can we find out?" asked Wayne.

Jon looked at his watch.

"I'll make the call right now," he replied. "As to where to house these guys, I have a suggestion that your devious minds might appreciate. I've been thinking about it since we left Norway."

"We're still listening," repeated Sandra.

"One of Futures' homes currently has a few vacant rooms. Now, I realize that I'm no longer employed by Futures, but that house is managed by someone I know very well and he might be agreeable to taking Charley and his friend if I offered him Wayne as their personal staff. Wayne could offer the familiarity that both these guys need right now."

The group liked the idea and sanctioned Jon's pursuit of both the doctor and Charley's potential new home. Iverson, in particular, appreciated the irony of Charley finding refuge in an agency controlled by the people who abused him.

Jon left to make his phone calls and the others picked up the talk of the Norwegian getaway. Charley, oblivious to the conversation going on around him, continued to indulge in the victuals that kept appearing on the table. Jon returned ten minutes later with the results of his inquiries. He had an eager and captivated audience.

"Dr. Matkin has agreed to assist us," he announced gleefully.

"How much did you tell her?" asked Sandra.

"I told her what I could, given the time that she had."

"And how much is that?" asked Iverson.

"I told her that Charley came from a clinic in Norway and that we suspected that he'd been abused."

"Did you mention his medical records?" pressed Wayne.

"Actually, she asked me if I had them, and was delighted when I told her I did. She's quite a lady, old Doc Matkin. She must be in her seventies now, but spunkier than ever."

"Did you tell her about the connection to the university?" asked Sandra.

"I didn't have enough time. She's apparently in the middle of the 'free checkup day' she offers once a month. She's inundated with sick kids."

Iverson pushed himself away from the table and moved the conversation on to the next subject. "And what about a place to stay?"

"It's all set up," replied Jon. "They can arrive any time after three-o'clock. Barry, the manager, was delighted to take them, especially after I told him it would piss off Steven

Gant. He has his own reasons for disliking the professor and they're almost as good as mine."

"You didn't tell him everything, did you?" asked Iverson, somewhat alarmed.

"No, Sarge, I didn't. I only told him that his assistance might cause Steven Gant some grief and that was enough to get him involved."

"Excellent!" said Iverson. "When can we see the doctor?"

"She said to just stop by and she'd fit our guys in when she could."

Iverson looked at his watch. It was 11:30 a.m. He surveyed the faces around the table and saw fatigue in all of them. Iverson stared again at the boy. He knew that face.

"You all need some sleep," the Sergeant said, "but first things first. Wayne and Sandra, you'll find a rental car waiting outside by the curb. Take the guys to Dr. Matkin's office and when you're done there, head to the guys' temporary home. Sandra, after Wayne and the guys are settled, go straight to the Pines Motel on Sixth Street. I've secured rooms there for us to hole up in until this affair concludes."

"Another friend that owes you?" asked Sandra.

"Another of many, my dear," he replied and handed Sandra car and room keys. "Once all this is set, we can begin to finish this thing."

"So, Sarge," inquired Sandra deliberately, "what are you and Jon going to be up to?"

"Jon and I, my dear Sandra, will be contacting the good Dr. Gant in hopes of shaking his nerve endings a bit more."

"I think I'm going to like this part," quipped Jon.

"First, however," Iverson stipulated, "Jon and I will spend some time organizing the documents we've accumulated and getting our stories straight. If we're going to coerce the professor, we need our ducks in a row."

Jon showed Iverson the box of Gustaf's documents they had brought with them. It would be added to Leslie Covington's papers and those obtained from Kate Howser. The party broke up and the two groups headed in different directions hoping to accomplish their separate tasks. It was time to put all the pieces together.

two

Dr. Helen Matkin was born into poverty but also into a wealth of love and compassion. Early on, she knew she was destined for a life of service to others. She doggedly focused on her education and achieved enough notoriety through scholastic achievement to be granted a full scholarship to the Harvard Medical School at the age of eighteen. Her challenge, once there, was to overcome not only the academic rigors of the institution, but to also transcend the traditional prejudice toward female medical students. Despite being an unwanted novelty, she accomplished both with honors.

After a few years of tending the frequently fabricated ailments of New York's wealthy elite, she moved west, hoping to return something to her roots of hardship. She opened a clinic in "Old Town" Seattle that catered to the poor and indigent. It was a labor of love, but the persistent shortage of funds and the mountains of paperwork eventually took their toll. In 1989, she left the clinic in capable hands and dropped out of society seeking a closer relationship with what she was convinced was a seriously ill planet. After many years in a remote cabin in the High Cascades, she reappeared and opened the small clinic she now operated on the outskirts of Ashton. She set her fees low and accepted clients that other physicians refused to take. Jon Farrell had found her a willing colleague in the effort to close the state's archaic mental institution.

"So," she said, scanning the four slumped bodies in her waiting room, "you must be Jon Farrell's wayward friends. Sorry about the wait, but it's been a busy day."

Wayne and Sandra made introductions and offered their gratitude for Dr. Matkin's assistance. The doctor sat down between Charley and the boy, gently stroked their backs and eyeballed them carefully. Charley, much to Wayne's surprise, looked up at his new doctor's face and returned her gentle gaze. She led the group into her exam room and instructed that the boy be laid on the cushioned, brushed vinyl table standing in the center of the room. She rolled an opaque curtain around the table, asked Sandra to stay with the boy and directed Wayne and Charley to nearby chairs.

Wayne and Sandra stayed with their assigned wards and watched in hushed silence as Dr. Matkin first examined one and then the other of her new patients. She wrote copious notes punctuated by deep, audible sighs. Her already wrinkled face creased further as her practiced eyes inspected the patients from the top of their heads to the bottom of their toes. The examinations took a little over two hours. Dr. Matkin then escorted her four visitors back to the waiting area, closed herself in her office and quickly reviewed the records taken from the Gustaf Clinic. When she returned, she wasn't smiling.

"Who's responsible for this?"

"It's a long story, Dr. Matkin," answered Wayne."

"I have the time, young man. My exam indicates nothing short of torture and I can't imagine what the lab results will reveal. It's a wonder they're alive. What can you tell me?"

"We'd be happy to share what we know," offered Sandra.

The doctor settled back in her chair and Wayne and Sandra provided an abridged version of their knowledge of the Gustaf Clinic. An hour passed, and the bulk of the information was bared. Wayne tied in the professors. Helen Matkin was more angry than surprised.

"The damned fools," she stated bluntly. "The damned, arrogant fools."

Wayne flashed to Nurse Nemesis. She had said the same thing.

"Doctor," Sandra probed hopefully, "we might need your help in this."

"You've got it, my dear," the doctor replied without hesitation. "Whoever is responsible needs to pay and I'd be happy to help set the price. But what happens to these guys now?"

Wayne relayed their plan. Dr. Matkin approved, but bluntly inquired, "And after this is all over?"

Neither Wayne nor Sandra had an answer. Wayne again flashed to Nurse Nemesis. "Make damned sure you know what you're doing," she'd said.

Dr. Matkin saw the genuine concern.

"Don't worry about it, folks," she said reassuringly. "If you can't figure out what to do with these guys, just bring them back here and we'll work out something. Guaranteed!"

They left the doctor's office and headed to the Futures' house that Charley and the boy would call home for a while. After introductions and some discussion with Barry Grimelly, the home's manager, Charley and his friend were shown to their room. Wayne laid the boy onto his new bed where he quickly curled into a fetal posture and fell fast asleep. Charley displayed uneasiness but followed suit when Wayne plunked himself into the room's overstuffed chair and announced he wasn't going anywhere.

three

Iverson hung up the phone in room seven at the Pines Motel. He had just finished a short conversation with someone in Kirkenes, Norway. He had a smile on his face.

"Well…," asked Jon anxiously.

"I think this might do it, Jon."

"Then let's get started."

Iverson and Jon had spent close to three hours putting together their plan to incriminate Steven Gant. They were ready. Iverson dialed the professor's home telephone number.

"Dr. Steven Gant here," said the voice on the other end of Iverson's phone.

"Good afternoon, Dr. Gant," greeted Iverson. "This is Sergeant Stan Iverson. I was hoping for another conversation with you, preferably longer than the last one."

Gant was tempted to hang up on Iverson again but decided he couldn't allow himself to be intimidated.

"Good afternoon, Sergeant," he said condescendingly. "What is it that you want?"

"As I stated before, I'd like to help you stay out of prison."

"Just what the hell are you talking about, Sergeant," Gant demanded.

"I'm talking about murder, Doctor Gant," responded Iverson. "There're certainly other things to discuss as well, such as misuse of federal funds, fraud, and solicitation, but the big one, the really important one for you, Doctor, is murder."

"I have no idea what you're talking about, Sergeant," Gant said defensively.

"I think you do, Doctor," rebutted Iverson. "But just in case you've had a recent bout of amnesia, I'd be more than happy to refresh your memory."

Gant was hesitant. He, Walk and Trenholm had agreed upon silence. But he wanted to find out how much Iverson really knew.

"Sure, Sergeant," he finally replied. "Go ahead. Refresh my memory."

Iverson began with information on Gant's personal history, largely gleaned from Kate Howser's contributions. It revealed little that Gant considered worrisome and the professor's arrogance reappeared.

"So what?" Gant joked. "That information is common knowledge and in no way ties me to anything criminal. If that's what you're basing your accusations on, you're a pretty poor excuse for a detective."

"Oh, there's more, Professor," interrupted Iverson. "May I continue?"

"Be my guest," Gant said confidently.

Iverson tied in the fraudulent grant documents with Gant's signatures and made the relationship between those papers and the ones Wayne had provided. The connection was beginning to take shape.

"Shall I continue, Professor?" he asked after a stream of disclosures.

Gant was silent and Iverson could sense his anxious hesitation. He was having an impact and he moved ahead without Gant's sanction.

"Then there's the relationship that you and your two compatriots, Terrance Walk and Allan Trenholm, have with a certain clinic in Kirkenes, Norway. Nice town, Kirkenes, but getting cold this time of year."

"Never heard of it," said Gant quickly.

"It's heard of you, Professor." Iverson waited for the impact of the revelation to hit and then added, "Another colleague of yours, Dr. Denton Croft, initially claimed ignorance and innocence, but he's had a change of heart. As a matter of fact, he's at this very moment working very hard to save his ass." Iverson looked at Jon who pumped a tight fist into the air.

"You can't prove a fucking thing," blurted Gant. "You have no idea who I am."

"I most certainly do, Mr. Gant," responded Iverson while consciously demoting Gant's title. "I know who you are and I know what you've done. However, I can only conjecture the why at this point so I'm offering you an opportunity to help with that."

"What the fuck is that supposed to mean?"

Iverson pulled the last two cards from his hand of deception. The first one matched the bluff that put Pat Denny out of the game.

"People crave power, Mr. Gant, and I have found you to be no exception. You and your secret friend, the late Captain Pat Denny, just wanted more than your fair share."

"Denny?" questioned Gant weakly.

"Yeah, Denny, Mr. Gant. If you need a reminder as to who he is, I can send you a copy of a little picture album I put together of your last consulting session at Grosvenor Park. I think a jury might find your relationship interesting after I've tied Denny to four Ashton murders. When they want to know why, I'm quite certain I'll be able to offer a fairly plausible explanation but I'd like to provide the full story. That's where you come in."

Gant was quiet. Iverson was rolling now and he played his trump card confidently.

"And one last thing, Steve," he offered with newly forged familiarity, "there's the matter of Charley Orr."

"Who the hell is Charley Orr?" demanded Gant.

"Charley Orr is, or should I say was, a patient at the Gustaf Clinic. Mr. Orr now safely resides in the United States. I might add that Charley and his entire medical history are currently being subjected to a large dose of professional scrutiny. The sordid details of his life are about to come out, and you, Mr. Gant, are scheduled to be one of the story's main characters."

Gant was quiet for a long time. Iverson's plan was working. He held some concern that Gant might see the writing on the wall and run, but figured the professor's ego would keep him in the game.

"Why are you telling me all of this?" Gant finally asked. His tone approached conciliatory.

"As I stated before, I can help you. If you cooperate with me, you might avoid spending the rest of your life in prison."

This time, Gant did slam down the phone.

four

Steven Gant waited until midnight to place a call to Norway and the Gustaf Clinic. He didn't share the conversation he'd had with Sergeant Iverson with either Walk or Trenholm. He wanted to hear from Croft first. When he finally reached the clinic, the phone was answered by an agitated voice.

"Hello," Gant said impatiently. "This is Dr. Steven Gant. I'm calling from the United States, and I urgently need to speak to Dr. Croft."

"Dr. Croft is not here," was the reply in broken but discernible English.

"Where is he?" demanded Gant. "I must speak to him immediately."

There was a long pause and Gant wondered if he'd lost his connection.

"Hello!" he yelled. "Is there anyone on this line?"

The silence was broken by the same voice that had deserted him.

"Yes, I'm here," the woman said.

"Where's Dr. Croft? It's imperative that I speak to him."

"Dr. Croft is not here, sir. I don't think he will be."

Gant was confused.

"What the hell does that mean?"

"Dr. Croft has left the clinic, sir."

"Left! What do you mean he left?"

"Dr. Croft has been arrested."

Gant was stunned, but his political savvy kept him going.

"Who's in charge of the clinic?" he asked, trying hard to stay controlled.

"In charge?" was the hesitant reply. "The Kirkenes police are in charge, sir. They've told us not to expect Dr. Croft back."

"Police? Why are the police there?"

No reply came over the phone.

"Hello?" Gant demanded. He needed information. "Are you still there?"

After another pause the woman spoke slowly.

"Dr. Croft, was he a friend of yours, sir?"

"Dr. Croft and I are business acquaintances. I demand to know what's going on there."

"There …, there was a shooting," the woman replied. "One of the clinic's employees was shot. The police apparently think Dr. Croft shot him. They took him to the Kirkenes police station."

Gant had heard enough. He hung up and paced the red oak floor of his den. He thought about his conversation with Iverson and made a typical Steven Gant decision.

SUNDAY, OCTOBER 2

one

Jon and Sandra left their rooms and found Iverson at the small café adjacent to the Pines Motel. The Sergeant had already made two phone calls and was in the middle of another. His disheveled appearance suggested a busy and sleepless night.

"Tough night, Sarge?" inquired Jon.

"A long one, Mr. Farrell," he said drily. "Some of us are still working you know." A sly glance toward Sandra indicated his tone was only playful.

"Any new revelations?" she asked.

"I snuck into my old office last night to check out a hunch … something I needed to know. I found what I wanted to find but don't ask me what it is. I'm not ready to share just yet. It'll be my surprise to everyone."

"Sounds mysterious, Sarge," said Sandra.

"And for now, that's how it'll stay. I think you'll be pleased with the extra ammunition against the professors it has provided."

"I like it already," said Jon. "So what's on our plate this morning?"

"We need to contact Walk and launch what we discussed yesterday."

Jon nodded toward Sandra, and she gave him a look of concern. He had filled her in on their scheme, and she couldn't help but feel apprehensive. They were planning to confront the professors and back them into a corner. Cornered animals, she knew, could be dangerous.

"And me?" asked Sandra.

"We need to stash you someplace safe while we meet with the professors. The less people in that play the better, and I've already scheduled in extras."

"Extras?" queried Jon.

"You'll meet them later," said Iverson dismissively. "We need to get moving. Sandra, I'd prefer you be with people. Any ideas?"

Sandra thought for a moment. "If I can't talk my way into going with the two of you …"

"And you can't, Sandra," stated Iverson emphatically.

"Okay, if that's out, then I'll go back to where Wayne and the guys are. If they're safe there, I should be too." They all nodded their silent agreement.

"Then it's settled. Let's get started," ordered the Sergeant.

two

Terrance Walk's phone rang three times before he picked it up.

"Terrance, this is Jon Farrell." Walk was surprised but gave no audible hint of it.

"Hello, Jon," he responded calmly. "What can I do for you?"

"I've been reviewing my situation with some people, and I've decided I want to meet with Futures' Board of Directors to discuss my rather abrupt and unexplained termination."

"I don't see why that's necessary, Jon."

"Well, Terrance," lied Jon, "my attorney seems to think it advisable."

"Am I to perceive that as a litigious threat?" asked Walk.

"I'm not really concerned with what you perceive, Terrance. I would, however, suggest that if you want to keep this affair civil and out of the papers, you should probably meet with me."

"I'll have to get back to you," said Walk.

"That won't work, Terrance," insisted Jon. "I want the meeting today, 1:00 p.m., in Futures' office."

"It's Sunday, Jon. I don't work on Sundays."

"I'd suggest you make an exception."

"And if I choose not to?"

"Then you'll suffer the consequences." Jon was enjoying his role immensely.

"Are you threatening me, Farrell?"

"Simply stating facts, Terrance. I'll be at Futures at 1:00 p.m. and I strongly recommend that you and your colleagues be there as well." Jon hung up. Terrance Walk called Allan Trenholm.

Trenholm was suspicious but calculated that it might not be a bad idea to meet with Farrell. They might gain some information and he was sure they could see through any scheme Farrell might have hatched. Walk was more cautious. He didn't want to tempt fate by confronting someone they'd tried to have killed. They decided to let the tie-breaking vote be cast by Steven Gant. Walk made the call.

"Steven, this is Terrance. Got a minute?"

"A few," Gant replied.

"I just received a call from Jon Farrell."

"What the hell does he want?"

"He wants a meeting and he wants it this afternoon at one-o'clock at Futures' office."

"What's this all about, Terrance?"

Walk relayed Jon Farrell's not so subtle threat about lawsuits and public exposure regarding his dismissal from Futures, Inc. He also informed Gant that he was the deciding vote as to whether or not they granted Farrell an audience.

"What do you think he really wants?" asked Gant, his suspicions already heightened by his conversation with Sergeant Iverson. "Do you think he knows the truth?"

"I don't know," answered Walk. "I just don't want to dig our hole any deeper."

"What's Allan think?"

"He thinks we ought to meet with him."

"I agree," Gant said. "Let's meet and find out what he's up to. What harm can it do?"

"I'm not sure," replied Walk, "and that's what worries me."

"I didn't think you worried about anything, Terrance," said Gant cynically.

"Futures at one-o'clock," Walk countered. "Try not to be late for a change."

Gant took note of Walk's subtle rebuttal but ignored it. He was tired of their relationship.

three

Jon felt uncommonly comfortable. He was back in Futures' office, his feet on his desk, his gaze firmly locked on the gentle, inexorable surge of the Willamette River. He'd arrived thirty minutes ahead of his scheduled rendezvous with the professors to give his nerves a chance to settle and to practice his part in the play that was about to unfold. He was alone with his thoughts for the first time in a week and the flood of feelings was intense. His life's course had been altered and he'd been forced to change. He'd been functional, but emotional inertia had kept him isolated and fueled his loneliness. The past week had changed all that. He'd been repeatedly challenged to examine who he was and who he wanted to be. He'd dug deep, hung in, and evolved. Jon Farrell had changed and he liked the replacement.

Walk and Trenholm arrived at exactly one-o'clock. Gant, true to form, walked in ten minutes later. The four men sat around the table in the conference room, Jon on one side of the table, the professors closely assembled on the other. Trenholm wore a sport coat over a red sweater vest, Walk a preppy polo shirt, and Gant a university monogrammed sweatshirt with a floppy collar. Behind them on the wall was the black and white montage of Futures' clients that Jon had commissioned as a visual reminder of the work they were doing. The three Board members had never offered any notice or comment on the pictures. Their disinterest was always transparent. Jon spoke to the three men clustered opposite him.

"Thanks for coming, gentlemen."

"We're here, Farrell," interrupted Trenholm. "And we're busy people. So if you don't mind, let's get down to business. What is it that you want?"

Jon was amused with Trenholm's attitude. It was all too familiar, but right now the relationship was different.

"What I want, gentlemen, is a piece of the action."

The three professors looked at each other with taciturn faces. After a thirty-second vacuum, Trenholm spoke again.

"A piece of what action, Farrell?"

"I don't think I need to explain what we all know."

"I have no idea what you're talking about," claimed Walk.

"Let me give you a few hints," offered Jon. "I'll start with grant money, more specifically, U.S. Department of Education grant money. Then there's Kirkenes, Norway, and a place called the Gustaf Clinic." Jon looked smugly at the three men. "After that," he continued, "I'd take the quantum leap to murder…, specifically, four murders and a couple of failed attempts. One of those attempts was directed at me which undoubtedly contributes greatly to my current attitude toward the three of you. Shall I continue, gentlemen?"

Trenholm reacted with typical hostility.

"You're talking rubbish, Farrell. If this is why I came here, then I think I have better ways to spend my time."

"Let's hold on a few minutes, Allan," said Gant. "It appears Jon is under the impression that the three of us are involved in some sort of criminal activity. I'd personally like to know how he has come to that conclusion."

Trenholm folded his arms and thumped back into his chair. Walk fidgeted nervously, and a bead of sweat slowly trickled down his right brow.

"Jon," Gant began, "just what information fuels your vivid imagination?"

Jon looked intently at the academic elite opposite him; three powerful men possessing undeniable and admirable intellect. At some point, and for some reason, they had left their ivory tower and taken a path of crime to fill their insatiable appetites for fame and fortune. His gaze moved from one to the other and he wondered which one had initiated the idea of a career move from educators to criminals. Who had first suggested that deceit, torture and murder were justifiable in the pursuit of self-aggrandizement? How difficult had it been to grant themselves permission to be gods? He looked at them across the table and realized he no longer felt intimidated by them. It was anger he now felt; anger that they'd murdered his friends, and anger at their sanction of the torture of Charley Orr.

"Well…, *Steven*," Jon responded cynically. "It's not imagined. The Gustaf Clinic is real … I've been there. Two boxes of medical records and grant applications are real … I've read every page. And the four murders are *very* real; the bodies will attest to that. I've done my homework, gentlemen, and now I want to get paid for my effort. Your alternative is the disclosure of all that I know, and I'd imagine both the Ashton Police and the university president would find my reports of great interest."

"You have proof of nothing, Farrell," asserted Trenholm.

"By myself, you may be right, Allan. But since I've had this extra time on my hands, I've developed an interesting and informative relationship with a certain police sergeant. This poor, misguided public servant is under the impression that I'm actually working with him. He obviously doesn't interpret Darwin's Law the same way you and I do."

"What's Darwin got to do with this?" Walk asked Trenholm quietly.

Trenholm shot Walk a disgusted glance and turned on Jon again.

"So you have a relationship with a cop," sneered Trenholm. "Is that supposed to intimidate me?"

"Let him finish, Allan," commanded Gant. Trenholm glared, his eyes popping wide and red.

"Just before you boys fired me," Jon continued, "I was contacted by a young woman named Leslie Covington. She'd uncovered evidence regarding government funding fraud and connected it to some professors at the university. Ms. Covington was murdered, but not before she shared that evidence with me. I studied the documents she gave me very carefully and quickly discovered that they could hold my financial future...a potentially very lucrative future. My recent trip to Norway provided proof of your connection to the hell hole called the Gustaf Clinic and your ill-chosen partner in crime, Denton Croft, unwittingly supplied additional evidence. You boys have been busy getting rich and famous at a deadly cost to others. You, however, can keep all the fame. I simply want a share…, a significant share of the riches."

Jon sat back in his chair and waited for a response. Gant offered it.

"I think I've heard enough," he stated calmly. "How about you, gentlemen?"

"Too much," answered Trenholm.

Jon interrupted.

"I think it's only fair to tell you that I'm not a patient man, particularly with the likes of you three." Jon rose from his chair and raised his voice. "Talk it over. I'm going to have a cup of coffee, watch the clock tick down and return in fifteen minutes for your answer. If it's not the one I want, your next conversation will most likely be with the Ashton police."

Jon paused, drew a deep breath and leaned over the table.

"To tell you the truth, it would be a real pleasure to see you fall on your arrogant faces. But I happen to be greedy enough to forego that reward for an earlier retirement." Jon turned, left the conference room and strolled down the hall to his office. His legs wobbled and his heart raced. He'd never felt better.

The conference room now held three somber men. They didn't speak until Gant reminded them of the time limit Jon had imposed.

"Gentlemen," he stated coolly. "We have a decision to make."

"That little son-of-a-bitch," said Trenholm. "Who the fuck does he think he is? Doesn't he understand who he's dealing with?"

"I think he does, Allan," answered Walk.

"And just what the hell do *you* propose we do, Terrance?" His tone reeked of condescension.

Walk shrank back. A palpable pause filled the room.

"Look," asserted Gant, "he obviously knows more than we thought he did. If he really does have proof that we're involved in those killings …

"We didn't kill anybody," intruded Walk, defensively.

"No, we didn't, but we paid for it, didn't we?"

Both Walk and Trenholm glared at Gant.

"Well…, didn't we?" he repeated.

"We did, but …" Walk's words trailed off and Trenholm shot him another look of disgust.

"Yes, we did," said Trenholm firmly.

The door of the conference room burst open and three uniformed policemen rushed in and positioned themselves behind the professors.

"What the fuck is this?" demanded Trenholm as he rose from his chair.

"Shut up and sit down," commanded one of the officers.

"I'm leaving," Trenholm announced and started toward the door.

Sergeant Stan Iverson met him at the doorway holding a videotape in his hand. Jon Farrell stood directly behind him.

"I don't think you are, Professor," Iverson corrected. Trenholm's blood rushed to his face but he didn't respond. He walked slowly back to his chair and sat down. Iverson walked to the head of the conference table and placed the cassette in full view.

"Gentlemen, I wish to thank you for your cooperation," Iverson announced. "And I'd like to express my special thanks to Dr. Gant for assisting us in extracting Mr. Trenholm's last statement for our videotape. Juries love a good movie."

Allan Trenholm was livid.

"Gant, you bastard!" he screamed. He lunged toward him, fists clenched, eyes wide with rage.

Gant lurched back in his chair to avoid Trenholm's fury. The officer standing behind Trenholm manhandled him back into his chair.

"I had no choice, Allan," Gant said calmly. "Our luck ran out, and I had to create a little of my own."

Terrance Walk sat silently in his chair, fidgeting nervously and staring at the floor. "What's happening?" he whimpered.

Iverson heard his question and walked over to him.

"Your research has been canceled, Doc. But look on the bright side. You're going to have plenty of time to catch up on your reading."

Iverson smiled at the professors and nodded to the three men in blue. Steven Gant, Terrance Walk and Allan Trenholm were handcuffed and led ignominiously toward the door. Trenholm continued his profane assault on Gant. Walk shuffled past Jon, stared at him blankly, and began to cry. Jon felt sorry for the man.

The three professors would soon be checked into Ashton's city jail where they would share cramped space with people they'd have considered pawns for their games. Iverson knew their trials would be long, tedious and complicated. He also knew there was a good chance they would somehow circumvent the justice they deserved. Gant would most certainly cut a deal for his cooperation. More killers might still be out there, but that was another task for a different day. The head had been cut from the serpent and this job was done. It was time for a beer.

MONDAY, OCTOBER 3

one

Jon opened a new bottle of Jack Daniels and poured a drink for each of his guests. He gently struck the half-filled tumblers of Stan Iverson, Wayne Burgess and Sandra McKinney and proposed a toast.

"To Neil Danielski, Deb Sutter and Leslie Covington," he said, and they drank in memory of those dearly missed.

"To new friends, including one left behind in Norway," toasted Wayne and they tipped their glasses again.

"To a kinder and gentler future," said Sandra, and they drained what remained in their cups.

Jon refilled the glasses, and they all found a seat in the chaos of his living room.

"So what's next?" asked Sandra.

"Back to work tomorrow," answered Jon. "Jackie told me I've got messages stacked a mile high."

"And you, Wayne?"

"I'm going back to Kirkenes. Thanks to Jon's reinstatement at Futures, Inc., Charley and his friend have a permanent home. Sam's decided to make the rehabilitation of the Gustaf Clinic a personal project and he's gonna need all the help he can get. I think I may have found a calling in Norway."

They all nodded their approval and made a silent toast with raised glasses.

"And you, Sandra?" queried Wayne. "Have you found a calling?"

"What I found was Jon," Sandra replied quickly, "and a new appreciation for life. I want to kick back for awhile and relax. Jon has been kind enough to offer me a place to heal my wounds and rest my mind and I'm taking him up on his offer. One look around here and you can tell Jon needs help." The group toasted their agreement with her assessment.

"And," Wayne continued, "what has Sergeant Stan Iverson found?"

Iverson smiled at the gathering of new friends and emptied his glass of its contents. He pulled a large manila envelope from behind his seat and placed it on the table.

"I've actually found three things," he stated. "One that I'd lost hope of finding, one that I hadn't realized I was looking for, and one I had missed but didn't know it."

"Wow! You've certainly got my attention, Sarge," Sandra said eagerly.

Iverson pulled an eight by ten inch photograph from the envelope.

"I'd like you all to meet Christopher Langham." It was a picture of a young boy they all recognized instantly as the boy they'd rescued from the Gustaf Clinic. The picture showed a younger, healthier boy, but it was undeniably Charley Orr's best friend.

But …," started Sandra.

"When I saw the boy at the airport, I knew I'd seen him before...had seen those eyes before. Those eyes have haunted me for two years. When I went back to my office, I went through my records and found Christopher's file and this picture. The eyes matched."

"So who is Christopher Langham, Sarge," asked Jon.

"He's an autistic boy who disappeared from Ashton two years ago. The department, as well as much of the city, searched high and low for him before his case was closed. He was technically listed as missing but everyone felt he'd been kidnapped, killed and dumped somewhere. It now appears he was abducted and sent away to Norway to be used in Gustaf's research. If we can find some hard evidence for that, it would really strengthen the case against the professors."

"That's incredible, Sarge," said Sandra.

"You have no idea, Sandra. Finding this boy has filled a hole in my soul and returned joy to the hearts of two parents who'd also thought him forever lost. For me, it's the perfect ending to our story."

"So Christopher will be reunited with his parents," Jon thought aloud. "I wonder how Charley will feel about that."

"The Langhams told me they're thinking about moving back to Ashton. If they do, Charley and Christopher should get plenty of time together, especially with Jon back running Futures."

Jon and Wayne nodded their approval.

"Okay Sarge," Sandra said softly while wiping away a few tears. "But you said three things."

"Yes, I did. The second thing I discovered was that I no longer wish to be *Sergeant* Iverson. I'm retiring from the Ashton Police Department."

Surprised looks filled the room.

"Why, Sarge?" asked a concerned Jon.

"The time is right," explained Iverson.

"But you love what you do and you're damn good at it," countered Jon. "How do you replace that?"

"Gumshoeing," Iverson responded with a measured smile. "I've been buried in bureaucracy for a long time and have become increasingly stifled by rules I don't comprehend. It's time to cut that cord. Thanks to all of you, a light bulb has gone on. I don't know how many more years I'll be doing this work, but I know now that I'll do it on my own terms."

"Gumshoeing?" Sandra asked, genuinely puzzled.

"Sarge is going to be a private detective," explained Jon. "I think that's terrific. You'll be the best ever."

"Will you be opening an office in Norway?" Wayne asked only half-jokingly.

"You should probably wait until you see my fee chart," responded Iverson with equal humor. "Truth is, I've renewed some acquaintances across the pond and it might be a possibility."

"What's number three, Sarge?" asked Sandra, not one to lose count and eager for more.

"It's probably the most difficult," he replied.

"Let's hear it, Sarge," insisted Sandra.

"I've found I miss my ex. I don't know if we can mend the whole fence, but I think it's time to explore the possibilities."

Oohs and aahs filled the room and Jon distributed more of Mr. Daniels.

"And what about you?" Iverson asked Jon. "Surely you have discovered something of interest during this extraordinary chapter in your life."

Jon offered his glass up for a collective toast.

"Indeed I have, Sarge," he declared confidently. "I have discovered Jon Farrell."